River,
Cross My Heart

River, Cross My Heart

BREENA CLARKE

Little, Brown and Company
Boston New York London

Copyright © 1999 by Breena Clarke

All rights reserved. No part of this book may be reproduced in any form or by any electronic or mechanical means, including information storage and retrieval systems, without permission in writing from the publisher, except by a reviewer who may quote brief passages in a review.

FIRST EDITION

LIBRARY OF CONGRESS CATALOGING-IN-PUBLICATION DATA
Clarke, Breena.
  River, cross my heart : a novel / Breena Clarke. — 1st ed.
    p.   cm.
  ISBN 0-316-89999-2
  1. Afro-Americans—Washington (D.C.)—Fiction.   I. Title.
  PS3553.L298R58   1999
  813'.54—dc21   99-12672

10 9 8 7 6 5 4 3 2

MV-NY

Book design by Melodie Wertelet

Printed in the United States of America

To my parents,
Edna Higgins Payne Clarke
and James Sheridan Clarke,
*who have twice given me
a place to begin*

Author's Note

This is a work of fiction. Many of the characters are composites of people whom I first heard about in the many stories my parents told me about growing up in the Georgetown neighborhood of Washington, D.C. Blacks have lived in and been an integral part of Georgetown from its beginnings in the 1700s. They established several local churches, most notably the Mount Zion United Methodist Church in 1816 and the Epiphany Catholic Church in 1923, which was founded by black Catholics who no longer wished to attend the segregated Holy Trinity Church. Black Georgetowners owned and operated businesses, formed civic and social organizations, owned property, and were served by black doctors, dentists, morticians, and other professionals. Many of the District of Columbia public school system's most outstanding black educators were residents of Georgetown. After the passage of the Old Georgetown Act in 1950, an ordinance that sought to preserve the community's historic architecture, a great many black Georgetowners moved away from the neighborhood. The spirit of the community lives on, however, in several annual events sponsored by the Black Georgetown Reunion Committee.

I am grateful to the following individuals who have shared their recollections of Georgetown with me: Mr. Carter Bowman, archivist of the Mount Zion United Methodist Church; Mr. James S. Clarke; Mrs. Edna Higgins Payne Clarke; Mr. Maurice Clarke; Mrs. Eva Calloway; and Mrs. Luise Jeter. Special thanks to my husband, Helmar Augustus Cooper, for loving support and to my agent, Cynthia Cannell, for much encouragement.

*River,
Cross My Heart*

1

Dangerous ideas come to life and spread like sparks on dry twigs. It could have been Lula who thought of it first. Or it could have been Tiny or possibly Johnnie Mae. Somebody said, "Let's walk on down past there. It's cooler there." The small troupe—Mabel, Lula, Hannah, Tiny, Sarey, and the sisters Johnnie Mae and Clara—never actually decided to walk to the Three Sisters. It began as an idea that one or the other had and became accomplished fact without planning. The afternoon was hot and the advancing dusk brought no relief. Heat clung to the low-hanging branches of trees and permitted no breeze to stir them. The girls' raucous laughter was not muted by the shrubbery that lined the C&O canal towpath, and the seven pairs of bare feet simply walked westward toward the Three Sisters.

Higgins Hole is a spot on the C&O canal where colored children used to gather daily in summer and clamber over debris in order to swim. Water still sluices southward through the abandoned locks of the old canal, no longer used for mule-drawn barge transportation from Cumberland, Maryland, through Great Falls and Little Falls, under Chain Bridge, and down through Georgetown below M Street alongside the Potomac River.

Gnats and wildflowers are thick on the towpath beside the canal. Some fishers after carp and catfish drop lines from footbridges over the canal or from spots nestled in the shadow of the Francis Scott Key Bridge. Water-loving trees lock boughs far above the heads of strollers on the path.

In the late afternoon on hot days, Johnnie Mae, her baby sister, Clara, and their playmates collected at Higgins Hole with their swimming suits on under cotton shifts. Other groups of boys and girls, older and younger, gathered there too. Some of the girls came just to stand around, but Johnnie Mae always stripped off her shift immediately, pulled on her swimming cap, and plunged into the water, stroking, cavorting, and sponging up coolness.

Since they opened the public swimming pool for white folks only on Volta Place, right across the street from her aunt Ina's house, the pleasures of Higgins Hole were diminished for Johnnie Mae. In that public pool the water was so clear! Clara said it must be ice water. Clara said they must get big blocks of ice from the ice man on Potomac Street and put them in there. She was certain of this because the white boys and girls they saw through the fence and bushes surrounding the pool were always shivering.

The water at Higgins Hole, though not brackish, was not transparent like the water in the swimming pool on Volta Place. The canal carried the husky bouquet of decaying organic matter rather than the scent of chlorine. There were things growing in the canal that clouded the surface and entangled the ankles of swimmers. There were fish, and sometimes dead fish floated on the water's surface. Higgins Hole had begun to feel like a secondhand pair of shoes to Johnnie Mae. It was useful as a place to swim, but it was no longer special.

Below M Street, below Higgins Hole on the canal, the Potomac River looks calm and quiet on its surface but roils behind its hand. The Potomac River, brood sow for spots, rock, carp, and herring, is also a foam-bedecked doxy lounging against verdant banks, carving out sitting places and lying places and sleeping places all the way from Sharpsburg, Maryland, to the Chesapeake Bay. The Potomac River jumps massive rocks and roars downstream at Great Falls. Its spray shoots toward the clouds before falling quiet and running headlong toward Georgetown and Washington and then proceeding past them.

This river is not one thing or another. It is both. The Potomac River has a face no one should trust. It is as duplicitous as a two-dollar whore. It welcomes company but abuses its guests by pitching them silly on small boats.

Legends abound that the Potomac River is a widowmaker, a childtaker, and a woman-swallower. According to the most famous tale, the river has already swallowed three sisters — three Catholic nuns. Yet it did not swallow them, only drowned them and belched them back up in the form of three small rock islands. They lie halfway between one shore and the other, each with a wimple made of seabirds' wings.

The Three Sisters is a landmark. When you say "the Three Sisters," people know you're going to tell about something that happened on the river to cause grief. And it isn't really clear whether it's the boulders or the river at that spot that causes the grief. Nobody in his right mind goes swimming near the Three Sisters. The river has hands for sure at this spot. Maybe even the three nuns themselves, beneath the water's surface, are grabbing ankles to pull down some company.

The girls were not supposed to go in the river. Parents regularly warned their children not to swim there. Alice and Willie Bynum, knowing Johnnie Mae's fondness for swimming, had warned her off the banks of the Potomac. Nobody trusts the Potomac River. It's not benign like the aqua-glass swimming pool for the white children up on Volta Place. It is not plodding and dirty like the canal. It is treacherous. It is beguiling. Just walking along the riverbank can be dangerous if you've got a worry spot or a grief stone or an anger or resentment that you can't quite name.

At first the girls stood there. Then they sat among the tall weedy grasses of the littered bank. Much of what gets discarded in Georgetown ends up here, twisted and tangled among black-eyed Susans and Queen Anne's lace. Splintered planks with nails sticking out hide in the shin-high grasses. "Watch where you steppin'! Look out there!" Lula suddenly adopted a big-mama voice and broke the hypnotic silence that had brought them wordlessly to this spot. "Clara, look where you walkin', girl! You hear me?" Johnnie Mae's voice was an echo of Lula's—a reflex exhortation—a pit-of-the-stomach reminder that they had no business here and were tempting fate just by stepping, just by breathing. The earth closest to the river edge was mud. In twos and threes—Hannah and Tiny, Mabel and Lula and Clara, Johnnie Mae and Sarey—the girls sat at the river's edge and dangled their feet in the muddy, gunmetal green water. A rotting, downed tree branch covered with terraces of toadstools jutted out from the bank diagonally into the water and provided a place to sit. Rows of ants marched back and forth along its length. Clara sat cautiously on the low end while Mabel and Lula scooted along the log until they were several feet from the bank, swinging their legs out over the water. Hannah and Tiny climbed aboard the log between Clara and the girls on the outer end. Johnnie Mae and Sarey leaned against the log with their ankles mired in cool mud. Johnnie Mae thought about the glistening girls in the swimming pool on Volta Place. Those girls sat on the sides of their pool and only dangled their ankles in the water. The slimy, cool earth banked her anger.

Mabel's sudden shrieking as she belly flopped into the river jerked Johnnie Mae back from her thoughts. Lula followed Mabel into the river and the log shifted and bucked as she springboarded into the water. Johnnie Mae bounded onto the log and ran its length, maintaining her balance as perfectly as an aerialist. She swooped past Hannah and Tiny, nearly knocking them off as she launched herself as far out into the river as possible. The water was of uncertain depth here, but Johnnie Mae was not at all concerned with depth, just breadth. It was her foolish thought that the far bank of the Potomac was within reach of her strokes. And the water was cool, blessedly cool.

Clara sat quietly, watching Johnnie Mae and the other girls. Her quiet allowed them to ignore her. She was a constant appendage to her sister and seemed content to be so. None of the other girls noticed Clara moving along the log to the high end that jutted out over the water. Hannah and Tiny slid off the log into the water, causing it to shift.

Clara maneuvered herself along the log to get a better view

of the other girls. They swam together in groups, weaving in and out of each other's arms. They dunked each other's heads and cannonaded each other by slapping the water's surface. Mabel, the oldest, pulled her wet swimming suit away from her chest to show the others her nipples, tight and wrinkled with excitement and cold. The girls giggled, they laughed uproariously, they didn't notice Clara.

Johnnie Mae was obliged to remember Clara. It had been her responsibility to watch Clara ever since Clara was a baby. But Johnnie Mae's mind was elsewhere. She was, right then, considering swimming straight across the river to Roslyn on the opposite bank. It didn't look too far. It looked like something she might be able to do.

Johnnie Mae did not hear Clara splash into the river when the rotted log collapsed. Johnnie Mae ducked her head under the surface of the river, her shoulders following, then her back and hips. Her flapping ankles churned the water's surface. She arched her back and pulled up to the surface with long, graceful arms. The splashing sound, she thought, was her own body slicing the water.

But it was Clara's body that slid beneath the water. The fingers of the undertow swooped her. The others did not see her go down. They looked at the place on the bank where Clara and the log had been, and now Clara and the log were gone. It was as though the log were a hobbyhorse and Clara was riding it. The canopy of leaves draping the bank seemed unmoved by Clara's sudden absence. The effect was of viewing a scene through a stereopticon: The first image contained Clara and the log, and the second did not.

Johnnie Mae dove twenty times before the others realized what had happened. Johnnie Mae rose to the surface, tread water, and screamed wildly. She filled her lungs with air and she dove again. The other girls grabbed her after it became clear that she would continue to plunge. The girls grasped arms around the struggling, screaming, exhausted Johnnie Mae and drew in close around her, like petals on a daisy. Johnnie Mae thrashed against them at first, then collapsed. They swam in tandem to the bank. A white ribbon off Clara's plait floated on the surface of the river.

2

That morning it was hot as soon as the sun got up. Johnnie Mae rose just after. Heat entered the house uninvited — in fact, had never left from the night before. July in Washington is simply hot.

Alice Bynum's crisp, precise movements were creating the only breeze. Johnnie Mae slid out of bed and hurried downstairs to the kitchen to gather up under the tall, graceful woman whose mobile hips fanned the kitchen between sink and stove. Her mama heard her footsteps on the stairs and called out, "You're up, Johnnie Mae? Good morning. Empty the slop jar and then see about the milk." Her voice was busy but affectionate.

"Yes, ma'am," Johnnie Mae answered. She went back upstairs to the room she shared with her younger sister and scooted under the bed with the still-sleeping Clara in it. She retrieved the slop jar and walked with it gingerly down the stairs, through the kitchen, and out the back screen door to the outdoor toilet. "That Clara can't hold her bladder ten minutes, much less through the night! And then again she sleeps late. Turning over after everybody else is up and stirring!" Johnnie Mae muttered under her breath, mindful that Mama Alice did not approve of carping and complaining.

"Just go on about your business and hoe the row that God has given you," Alice Bynum would say briskly on her way from one task to another. "If looking after your sister is your obligation in life, then be thankful you have a sister."

Johnnie Mae perched a moment on the toilet seat, let her early morning urine patter down into the abyss, and thought about her mother's endless string of obligations. Obliged to rise up out of bed before husband and daughters to straighten up the neat but rickety little frame house; obliged to stay up long past dark to knit socks, sweaters, and scarves; obliged to think up excuses for the landlord and grocer when accounts were past due; obliged to wear a whalebone corset under a fussy dress on Sunday and sit there all day fanning and singing; obliged to make the biggest and sweetest three-layer chocolate cake ever known for the church bake sale and for anybody's and everybody's birthday. And obliged to clean from top to bottom and over again the house of the woman she worked for. "Doesn't she ever do something she wants to do?" Instinctively Johnnie Mae knew that if the answer to this question was no, then it didn't bode well for a life of ease for her. For everybody always said, "She's the spitting image of her mama. That girl is just like Alice!" The toilet gave a satisfactory *whoosh* as Johnnie Mae rose from the seat.

"Morning, Daddy," Johnnie Mae called to her father, who was bent over his tomato plants, as she expressed water from the hydrant to wash out the chamber pot.

"Morning, Maezie," Willie answered without turning toward her, continuing to stake his beefsteaks. His attention was riveted on the backyard crops, especially in the nervous growing season of Washington. "It's hard to know what kind of weather we're bound to have in this town" was his favorite lament. That explained the great many vegetable failures. "Too damn hot when it ought to be cool, too damn cool when it ought to be hot! This a backwards town, I tell you! Not like Carolina. No, sir, not like Carolina!"

For Willie Bynum and others of the migrating Carolinians rumbling into Washington, D.C., the city was best described as "not like Carolina." But ever since the family moved to the lopsided two-story house on O Street, with the big yard out back, Willie had, in spring and summer, spent his spare hours tending tomatoes, pole beans, cucumbers, lettuce, squash, corn, and greens. Willie's garden provided a modest boost to family finances and reminded him of Carolina. "Looks like we'll have a bumper crop this year, Maezie," he said now, straightening up over the last staked plant and spitting a ball of mucus and tobacco juice between his feet.

"Johnnie Mae, what about the milk, girl?" Mama called out. Her sharp, authoritative voice pulled Johnnie Mae's eyes away from the pale yellow maggots crawling over and under one another in the uncovered garbage pail.

"Yes, ma'am," she answered respectfully and blew a tiny black ant from the back of her hand.

The screen door banged as Johnnie Mae reentered the house. "Don't slam that door, girl! What'd I tell you about that!" her mother scolded.

Johnnie Mae hadn't meant to slam the door; nonetheless she hoped the noise had awakened Clara. "Old lazybones, crybaby, silly little rat," Johnnie Mae grumbled to herself. Mama always said that Clara was delicate and needed her sleep and couldn't be ripping and running around. But Johnnie Mae didn't believe there was really anything wrong with Clara. It was all just an act that Clara put on for the folks. She liked being thought of as shy and sickly so she could get out of doing her share of the work.

Johnnie Mae was the red-brown one, with hair that was half straight, half nappy and that would stay plaited all day if it was brushed and oiled. Mama said it was good hair. Clara was the pecan-colored one with nappy hair worn in two small braids that crept loose all day. Mama never said that Clara had bad hair, but she said that Clara's hair wasn't "good."

From the time Clara was born, she had seemed like a doll baby to Johnnie Mae, who loved to comb and brush and plait and replait her sister's hair. Johnnie Mae liked to stand behind Clara's chair in the kitchen and section the hair, rubbing in a fragrant pomade, looping and twisting the sections over and under with deft fingers. Johnnie Mae was tall for twelve years old. She stood straight. Her athletic body was always primed for movement. Clara was six, slightly plump, and easily winded.

"Come get your coffee, Willie! Come and get a bite. It's 'bout time you were gittin' down there, isn't it?" Mama called out. She skimmed cream off the bottle of milk, then poured a glass of milk for Johnnie Mae and one for Clara, who just then sidled into the kitchen rubbing her eyes. Mama poured a few drops of cream and two big spoons of sugar into her coffee. Sugar was the only real extravagance Alice Bynum allowed herself. Papa, Johnnie Mae, and Clara helped themselves to biscuits and bacon, and Mama slid fried eggs onto the sides of their plates.

"You picking up clothes for Miss Ann-Martha today? Watch out you don't get heatstroke running up and down. It's going to be a hot one today." Mama slurped down the dregs of her coffee. She put her work shoes in a paper bag and patted her hair down. "Go by Aunt Ina's and set awhile."

Johnnie Mae fought to keep her face respectfully immobile. It took effort not to indicate how tired she was of hearing the same instructions each morning as her mother got ready to leave for work. She knew full well all the watching out for heatstroke was her responsibility. In wintertime it was watching out for chills and uncovered ears, feet, and head. In Mama's lexicon, every season had its dangers, and Johnnie Mae was her mother's lieutenant in charge of "watching out." At the door Mama turned, as usual, to issue a final directive. "Clean up the kitchen before you leave this house, hear me?"

Papa added nothing to Mama's list of orders. He put bacon inside the last two biscuits and stuffed them in his pocket for later. He followed her out the front door.

Clara sat at the kitchen table, twirling a slice of bacon. With both parents out of earshot, Johnnie Mae turned her displeasure toward her "obligation." "Finish up that milk and help me wipe this place up!"

∽

Ann-Martha Pendel was the freckled, laughing, meriny woman who did washing for white people. In summer, her laundry room was the overgrown, weed-choked yard behind her house at 32nd and P streets. Drying sheets hung on rope lines that extended from the porch roof to several tall but measly trees at the rear boundary of the yard. As they fanned out over the yard, the sheets created a labyrinth. Ann-Martha was to be found somewhere in their midst, arms pumping up and down on a wooden scrub board.

Miss Ann-Martha, with no husband or children, was considered a colored woman of independent means and uncertain morals. Alice Bynum, resigned to the expediency of her daughters' work as Ann-Martha's runners, had warned them—especially the maturing Johnnie Mae—against engaging in idle talk with the woman. "No need to sit about jawin' with Ann-Martha Pendel. Just make the runs and collect the money, hear me?" Of course, Johnnie Mae knew you didn't have to sit around jawing to catch the tenor of Miss Ann-Martha's moral behavior. The careless way her breasts flopped underneath her shift and the slackness of her lips when she spoke out of the side of her mouth were unmistakably the signs of low moral character. Even a child could see that.

Johnnie Mae didn't particularly like the musky smell of the woman and usually tried to stand as far from her as was practical. Yet Ann-Martha managed to whisper conspiratorially, out of Clara's earshot. "A yella gal can rule the mens if she's smart, especially colored mens. A brown gal got to work a bit harder. A blue-black gal is got no chance. You remember that!"

The full import of this foolishness would be lost on Johnnie Mae even if she could understand all the broken-up shards of words Ann-Martha used in her chuckling conversation. What'd she mean by that? Best to ignore her talk and tend to the laundry only.

Johnnie Mae and Clara loaded the clean bundles for delivery to Miss Ann-Martha's customers and pulled the wagon back through the maze of hanging clothes. As usual, Clara couldn't resist hurling herself face first and giggling into the ballooning sheets at the back of the yard, beyond Miss Ann-Martha's line of vision. Johnnie Mae fussed at Clara. "Come on, girl, we got no time for foolishness!"

Grown folks often noticed Johnnie Mae Bynum's industriousness and commented on it. "That girl is just like her mama—always busy," they said. White folks, too, took note of the brusquely respectful little colored girl who collected and delivered laundry. Her back was always arrow straight as she approached the back doors of Miss Ann-Martha's customers. Mama's advice rang in her ears. "Don't have too much to say to them. Just yes-ma'am 'em and no-ma'am 'em and go about your business. And don't be grinning like a Cheshire cat if they offer you a cookie." Waiting solemnly while they inspected the clean clothes and handed over the dirty bundles, Johnnie Mae gravely counted the nickels and accepted a cookie or a bun with glancing but polite acknowledgment and a slip of a smile.

A scowling, down-on-her-luck white woman on Dumbarton Avenue was the first customer on the route. She resented a proud demeanor in a nigger. It just didn't suit her to see a colored child presenting herself so uppity, so businesslike.

"They say a Chinaman's opened up a laundry shop down on Water Street." Her nasal twang was razorlike. "He'll run Ann-Martha out of business for sure."

Standing straight, Johnnie Mae made no reply. Mama's words reverberated in her head: "Keep your mind on what you want, not on what they say." Clara, beside the wagon at the bottom of the steps, shifted from one foot to the other. Her bottom lip quivered. She was ready to run.

The woman went back into the house for the fifteen cents due, placed the coins on the porch rail, and held open the screen door for Johnnie Mae to carry in the three clean bundles and put them on the kitchen table. The woman bent down, whisked up the dirty bundle, and pushed it into Johnnie Mae's arms.

At the porch rail, Johnnie Mae heaved the bundle down the stairs into the wagon. Snatching up the money, she took the steps two and three at a time as she descended. At the bottom, grateful for a signal to move, Clara punched the laundry down into the wagon.

"You be careful of my laundry. Tell Ann-Martha I don't want no cat's paws on those shirts. If I see any, I'll take my business to the Chinaman," the small, raw woman hollered after Johnnie Mae, who jumped off the last step, picked up the wagon handle, and left the woman's yard as quickly as the rickety conveyance could be pulled over uneven ground.

Hanging on to the tail of the wagon and breathing out of her mouth as she struggled to keep up with her sister, Clara asked, "What's a Chinaman, Johnnie?"

Without turning around, Johnnie Mae answered in a flat, authoritative voice, "A yellow man with a pigtail."

"Oh. Yellow like Miss Ann-Martha?"

"No. Yellow with a long pigtail and funny eyes."

It was noon when Johnnie Mae and Clara turned down 30th Street toward Miss Ann-Martha's to drop off the dirty loads and collect their twenty cents. Mr. Pud Allen's street-cleaning wagon, drawn by a swaybacked horse, moseyed along ahead of them. When the horse deposited a stinking pile at the corner of 30th and N streets, Clara giggled and pinched her nose. Johnnie Mae laughed too and wondered what was the use of Mr. Pud Allen washing the street if his old nasty horse was letting loose every other block. At this rate, Mr. Pud Allen and his horse would always have a job of work.

Johnnie Mae handed Clara three pennies and pocketed seven cents. The rest, one dime, was for Mama's housekeeping. Alice Bynum allowed her girls to keep some of the money they earned hauling clothes for Miss Ann-Martha. In this, the Bynums were different from many of the other colored families in Georgetown. Most of the recent southern migrants kept all the money earned by their sons and daughters and pooled it with the rest of the household's earnings. There were no idle children among the colored families of Georgetown, except those too feeble or too young. And every child old enough to stand was old enough to work. If they worked for pay, they turned it over to their folks. The bigger girls had younger siblings to tend while their mamas cleaned, cooked, did laundry, or took care of the white people's children. Many of these girls also cooked and kept the house if their mama "lived in" and came home only one day of the week.

The clay brick sidewalk was as hot as a griddle when Johnnie Mae and Clara returned home to put away the wagon and then head up to Aunt Ina's. On the morning laundry rounds, Johnnie Mae had been thinking about the fragrant coolness of Volta Place and the quiet dark of Aunt Ina's parlor. The spreading, rounded crowns of ailanthus, white mulberry, eastern cottonwood, and red oak canopied Volta Place as it wandered west from the Wisconsin Avenue thoroughfare. The trees blocked sunlight and protected the large, rich folks' houses, the narrow carriage houses, and the alley dwellings of poor folks. Rosebushes—every variety—stood beside doorways and trailed along trellises. The smell of Volta Place was sweet—rose, lavender, lilac, sweet grass, and onion grass.

The smells wafting out of 3304 Volta Place were of chicken and cornbread fried in the early morning. Johnnie

Mae and Clara were expected to eat at Aunt Ina's on summer afternoons. Clara especially was supposed to eat and "set awhile" out of the heat of high noon. Aunt Ina, once she had finished her early morning cooking, would position herself at the small window in her parlor. From there she would peep through the branches of the box elder as she sewed collars, buttonholes, buttons, and socks, looking to catch sight of Johnnie Mae and Clara rounding the corner from the avenue. Ina Carson was one of the few colored women in Georgetown with a sit-down job.

Aunt Ina's sewing was so neat, her stitches so small and even, that the seams of her garments seemed to be joined by a wish. Her filet crochet adorned the bosoms of some of the wealthiest ladies in Georgetown. Ina's own arms, bosom, and bottom were fleshy and soft, yet her fingers were lean and muscular. Her face, too, was round and soft, and the total effect reminded Johnnie Mae of one of the red tomato pincushions in Aunt Ina's sewing basket. Completing the picture were the neat rows of threaded needles stuck in the bodice of Aunt Ina's housedress, which made it prudent not to hug her but instead to peck her cheeks at arm's length.

After eating, Johnnie Mae and Clara sat on the cloth-covered hassocks at Aunt Ina's feet and practiced sewing tiny skirts and blouses for the dolls they'd made out of Aunt Ina's empty spools. The girls threaded needles, sorted buttons, and peeped out the window at folks meandering down Volta Place. Occasionally they ran out to the curb to fetch something for Aunt Ina from a passing huckster wagon.

Some afternoons Johnnie Mae and Clara ran errands for Aunt Ina over to Kate Murray's, a store for notions and fabrics on Wisconsin Avenue. The girls would buy buttons, elastic, or ribbon for Aunt Ina's special customers. The young women clerks at Kate Murray's, a haughty bunch not much older than Johnnie Mae, were dressed up to look matronly in high starched collars and long, black serge skirts. Though Johnnie Mae and Clara enjoyed staring down into the store's glass cases at spools of thread and knitting wool, Johnnie Mae knew the snippy clerks in Kate Murray's liked nothing better than to speak sharply to colored children and shoo them out of the store for breathing on the glass countertops. She sometimes scolded Clara before one of the clerks could fix her mouth to. "Don't lean on the glass, Clara, stand up!" But Johnnie Mae was secretly happy that Clara's breath created a circular cloud of condensation on the glass above the spools of red and orange thread.

The police precinct was located on Volta Place, too, and proximity to it gave Ina Carson unquestioned authority on the moral turpitude of most of black Georgetown. On Saturdays, foot traffic on Volta Place usually included bowlegged, listing, colored drunks prodded by nightsticks up toward the Number 7 precinct. And the late night quiet was often punctuated by the thumping and thwacking of billies upside colored heads, male and female.

The goings-on in Bell's Court, an alley settlement of "dirtpoor Negroes" situated in the middle of that block of Volta Place and extending back to P Street, frequently gave Ina reason to shake her head and purse her lips and were often the subject of conversation with her cousin Alice. Aunt Ina strictly forbade Johnnie Mae and Clara to venture down the alleyway that intersected Volta Place in the middle of the block. The noisy, card-playing folks packed in practically on top of each other in wooden shacks in Bell's Court were, in

Ina's opinion, an embarrassment to the colored race. Most were "just this minute" up from the Deep South and hadn't had schooling and didn't know the first thing about city living. You could hear them hoo-rawing after their half-naked children and cursing each other any time of the day.

Across from Bell's Court, on the north side of the street, stretching northward a full block, was a playground surrounded by a vine-covered metal fence. Nestled within the fence, guarded by ailanthus, were swings, a sliding board, a sandpile, and a swimming pool. The pool's shimmering aqua water promised cool-as-a-cucumber refreshment to anyone who was allowed in. Colored children were not allowed in. Johnnie Mae, Clara, and their edible playmates—gingerbread Mabel, caramel Lula, black-coffee Hannah, Sarey the banana, and Tiny, the tall, slim girl colored the same as the skin of an eggplant—were kept to the periphery of this paradise.

Johnnie Mae overheard Aunt Ina tell her mama that some of the children of Miss Helen Pear had gone in there. The Pears were colored, but had been allowed in the pool because the white people hadn't known they were colored. Aunt Ina had witnessed the folderol when the truth became known and the Pears were marched off the premises in their swimming suits and taken into Number 7 for a strong reprimand. Aunt Ina said that Mr. William Pear had been made to pay a big fine.

With no errand to run that afternoon and lulled by food and quiet talk, Clara fell asleep. Her head rested on the windowsill and a string of saliva slid onto the hand propping her cheek. Aunt Ina's chin fell to her bosom and her hands were still except when a fly alighted on her face. Swatting and snoring lightly, the two rested in the husky late afternoon air.

Johnnie Mae slipped out of the house and left Aunt Ina and Clara dozing in the front window. She crossed the street and stood at the fence outside the whites-only playground. Honeysuckle blossoms twined in and out of the crisscrossed rods of the fence that ran the length of the playground. The vine's blossoms hosted hundreds of yellow jackets that might easily be mistaken for buds. Johnnie Mae brooded that the honeysuckle had surely been trained to the fence to draw the yellow jackets so they would sting colored children and discourage them from peeping through the fence.

Johnnie Mae found a spot under a large tree where she was concealed from the view of those in the pool but could still see inside. She lay with the tree's roots running under her stomach, her hands linked behind her head. Johnnie Mae stared at the swimmers. Some floated, some dove from the board and swam the pool's length, and some stood around giggling and showing off. A redheaded boy pounded his chest, strutted along the edge of the pool, and teased a group of girls nearby. Johnnie Mae seethed at the profligacy of the pale girls who lined the edges of the pool bobbing only their feet in the water. They wasted the pool's exquisite coolness on giggling and wiggling. Why didn't those girls cut through the water and let it rinse all the sticky sweat off them? Why didn't they want to show up that redheaded boy?

"I'd show that redheaded boy some stuff," Johnnie Mae muttered to the girl in her soul who bristled with angry pride and only grudgingly accepted the injustices that grown folks wouldn't talk about. "I can swim better than any of 'em! If they let me in there, I wouldn't just sit on the side!"

"How come we can't go in that pool and swim?" Johnnie Mae had repeatedly asked Aunt Ina since the beginning of summer. The girl's moaning and moping about swimming in the "white people's" pool had begun to test Ina's patience. Johnnie Mae was Ina's heart and she'd always been able to see straight down to the nut of the girl. She knew that Johnnie Mae understood full well how things were for colored folks—even here in Georgetown, where things were a bit better.

"You don't need to be over there anyway," Aunt Ina had answered time and again. "Those people ought to know better. They built that children's playground on top of an old graveyard. That's hallowed ground. They had no business disturbing the dead by building a children's playground over their heads. Be glad you're not in there. I recall they found many a false tooth and finger ring in there when they turned over the ground. That's no place for children to be playing. The dead want to rest." All Aunt Ina was doing was trying to thwart the child's questioning. She knew well enough that this reasoning didn't cut any mustard with Johnnie Mae.

And exactly who, Johnnie Mae wondered, were "they," anyway? Was President Coolidge the one? Was he the head white person who said colored couldn't swim in the pool? Did the white people get together in secret meetings and decide that colored people ought to step to the back door and couldn't go into the restaurants and sit down to eat? Were all the white people in on the plot?

Last night, stretched out for sleep on pallets on the second-floor porch, hoping to catch what cool breezes might come along, Johnnie Mae and Clara had listened as the voices of their parents wafted up from the kitchen. Willie and Alice turned over the question that Johnnie Mae had been peppering them with as well: "How come they won't let colored children swim in the pool on Volta Place?"

Willie shook his head downward toward his shoes. "That girl's got a worry, Alice. She don't understand this thing, and she's not gonna let go of it easy."

Alice flared to her daughter's defense. "Nor should she! What reason they got to keep them out of that playground, or the school, for that matter? We pay our rent money the same as these others around here. Some of the colored own their own homes here. Still they say our children can't play in the playground."

Willie was afraid of his wife's passion. He was a man who plowed under any strong emotion. Coming up on a tenant farm, Willie had been raised by people who reached the end of the day too tired to talk about their tiredness. Bereft of parents, then grandmother, then sister, Willie had grown up taciturn, though easygoing. But his Alice was a geyser—a hot spring—boiling up with the sense of injustice. And she knew full well the price colored folks paid for such anger.

"We've not been here long enough to spout off about what is and isn't right," Willie said.

"What you talking about, man? How long've we got to be in a place before we spout off? You saying this place is no better than Carolina? What we leave Carolina for?"

Not wanting to hear the answer to her own question, Alice rose quickly to scoop their two coffee cups from the table. She extinguished the coal oil lamp that stood on the table between them. She didn't want to see Willie's face now. She didn't want to see his face and recall how frightened he'd looked when she had first started talking about leaving Marabel and coming to Georgetown. Sometimes that look still flitted across his face. Alice knew that sometimes he was still frightened that they'd come so far from their home.

It had been Alice's idea to leave North Carolina for Washington. She'd caught wind of better times in Washington from folks who'd moved and come back to carry the tale. The smell of the city's promise stayed in her nostrils until she'd been able to convince Willie. He hadn't wanted to chance it. But he'd been fearful that she would find a way to go without him and he didn't want—couldn't stand the thought—that the soft and pretty, dimpled Alice would leave him.

Alice had wanted to come and here they were. It would always be between them that she had wanted to and so they had come. The white people here seemed the same to Willie as the white folks in Marabel. A different style of coat, but cut from the same cloth. He knew the realization of this bothered Alice. So he thought he'd spare her pride by denying it. "'Tain't quite as bad. These white folks aren't quite as mean as Carolina," he said softly. Lightning bugs chased each other in through the wide-open kitchen windows and back out into the pitch dark.

In truth, Washington, especially Georgetown, was quite a bit different from the rural town in North Carolina they'd come from. There was work here—plenty of it—for folks who wanted to work at something besides farming. Here a man or woman could latch on to something other than the rear end of a mule or a cow's titties. There was better schooling for Johnnie Mae and Clara and no stepping off the sidewalks to let a white person pass. Still, the white people ruled the roost here. That was no surprise. But there were also many well-off colored people here: doctors, dentists, schoolteachers. And there was more quiet in the night here. No riders breaking up the calm with hooves and ropes and fire.

Listening to her parents, hearing the angry resignation in their voices, did not help Johnnie Mae understand who the "they" were who circumscribed their lives. It didn't help her know whom to blame for being locked out of the magical coolness of the Volta Place swimming pool. This pool, so small in reality, but so much a symbol of the line drawn around her life by prejudice, had become an obsession. Throughout the stagnant July days, a clear but fanciful image of herself stroking lap after lap the length of the pool dominated Johnnie Mae's thoughts. She imagined the pale girls of the periphery gaping in surprise, not at the audacity of this colored girl using their playground and their pool, but at her absolute, consummate skill. The boys would fall back in wonderment too. In this picture Johnnie Mae mounted the diving board, threw back her head, brought her arms around and above her head, and sailed off the edge of the board. She was so fluent and graceful that she was able to glide under the blue-green water without causing even a ripple on its surface.

3

It got caught on debris along the riverbank, still white, still tied in a bow. Before the onlookers came, before divers for the city came, before the dredging equipment was lowered into the water, Press Parker, a workhorse of a man with short muscular legs, dove in near where the white ribbon was caught on a piece of driftwood. Parker, who had been whitewashing a bungalow on M Street, was the first man on the scene after the five girls started hoo-rawing that Clara had been swallowed by the river. He didn't put down his paintbrush before he started running toward the commotion so there was a trail of white down M Street leading straight to the spot where he dove into the river. His paint-speckled cap flew off his head and landed in a tangle of weeds.

Mabel, Lula, Hannah, Tiny, and Sarey had pulled Johnnie Mae to the bank and let her slip to the grass. Her chest rose and fell spasmodically. Her head thrashed about, and ropes of green water and mucus ran out of her nose. For a few moments the girls had simply run circles around one another, screaming. Hannah and Mabel had recovered first and scrambled up the hill, calling out for help.

Word of the tragedy traveled in relay fashion up the street toward the St. Pierre house, where Alice Bynum was working that day. The coal-black boy whom people called Snow, whose name was really Clarence Simpson, had been wading with the girls earlier at Higgins Hole. He saw Mabel and Hannah come barreling over the rise to M Street. They called out that Clara was missing in the water. A moment later, Press Parker raced past him like a bullet. Snow took off down M Street bellowing, "That little girl done drownt! That little girl done drownt!"

He shouted into the faces of passersby, setting off a tizzy of panic in each one. At the corner of Wisconsin Avenue and M Street, Snow stopped and told all he knew to a knot of people. Miz Belle Dockery, as soon as she got the scant facts, headed toward the riverbank with no regard for four-wheeled conveyances. The traffic cop in his narrow booth at the middle of the intersection blew his whistle at her back as Miz Belle Dockery careened in front of a car. She didn't stop, and the cop abandoned his post to follow her.

Overhearing the talk, Lexter Gorson, who shined shoes in front of the Farmers' and Mechanics' Bank, puffed north on Wisconsin Avenue. Eventually he grabbed a passing boy and held him in a viselike grip until the boy swore he'd go nowhere but up to the St. Pierres' house on Dumbarton Avenue and tell Miz Alice Bynum that one of her girls—this much they knew—had fallen into the Potomac at the Three Sisters.

Alice felt a spreading panic in her stomach as soon as she saw the boy's bulging eyes. She put down the bowl of cake batter she had been stirring, knocked the boy against the screen door, and ran out the back gate, setting the blood-red rosebush bucking and snapping. She swooped her skirt and apron up and held them against her chest.

As the news spread, colored people rained down Wisconsin Avenue, the seventy-five steps from Prospect Avenue to M Street, and every other north-south artery in Georgetown, then turned west toward the Three Sisters. At the corner of P Street and Wisconsin Avenue, Mahmoud Hadad, a Syrian cobbler, stood in the doorway of his shop and attempted to piece together the crisis. He caught at words and snatches of words uttered by the people hurtling themselves toward the river. By the time Alice Bynum reached his store, he had summoned his youngest boy, Omar, and instructed him to unhitch the horse and cart tied to a post at the curb. "Boy, drive this cart!" he yelled. Hadad grabbed Alice around the waist as she was passing his doorway, and he swooped her into the back of the cart with him. "Drive down to the river, boy!" Alice fell back against Mr. Hadad, quickly righted herself, and gripped the sides of the cart. As they overtook people running in the street, the tassels and bells on the horse's bridle flew. Mr. Hadad yelled, "Move, ya! Move, ya!"

A thin line of white paint led to a spot on the bank just a bit downstream of the three boulders. The surface of the river appeared closed, grim and unemotional. When Alice Bynum reached the crowded riverbank in the lap of Mr. Hadad's cart, she screamed sharply three times, then fell silent. It was not until this moment that she fully realized it was Clara who'd fallen in the river. Press Parker had plucked Clara's white ribbon, still knotted, from some jagged driftwood and held it in his hand like a flower.

~

Ella Bromsen, partially hidden by the box elder tree that stood between her house and Ina's, watched the procession that brought Johnnie Mae to Ina Carson's house on Volta Place. The women escorting Johnnie Mae walked close together. The head of the semiconscious girl lolled back and forth. The women walked smoothly and evenly and allowed little space between them. Their hips brushed lightly against Johnnie Mae and they spoke quietly, encouragingly. "Come on, baby. Just a little ways more, sugar."

It had been decided that Ina Carson would go ahead and ready the bed for her niece. Johnnie Mae would stay with her aunt Ina until someone could figure out what to do next. Ina huffed her short, plump body ahead of the other women as they walked from the riverbank, struggling to reach her house before them. Every now and then she paused to catch breath and turned back to look at Johnnie Mae's slumped-over body.

At midnight, the sky was still bright. The full moon was a yellow dime — perfectly round, with no mottling. Willie Bynum stood as still as a flagpole. He had remained in one spot the whole time they were dredging the river. Alice had allowed Willie to say it seemed best for the womenfolk and children to go home and wait for word. She let the menfolk suggest that whatever happened next, the women need not be there to see it. Bertha Howard, Elva Bemis, and Eva Copsey took Alice home. She was too wrung and twisted by this time to resist them. All her stalwart neighbor Eva had to do was gently touch her elbow and say, "Come on, let's go back to the house. Let the menfolk handle it from here." The women turned from the riverbank and walked homeward along the canal road, a line of children trailing them like solemn ducklings.

Willie had stayed, occasionally sipping coffee pushed into

his hands by the men who waited on the riverbank. Despite the heat, the men built a bonfire, which threw up bright flame and giant shadow and provided light for those working the river. One of the men broke driftwood with his foot and stoked the fire. Great ropes of sweat poured down the faces of the men facing the fire. Willie stood stock-still and cried and sweated.

They did not pull the body from the river for twelve hours. Press Parker waded into the water when the dredging chains raised something to the surface. He grabbed hold of the chain to keep the body from swinging. There was little talk — only moans and "Lord have mercy"s from the bystanders. A cry went up from the group when the ropes and chains pulled Clara's body out onto the bank. It had been buffeted by the currents and by the dredging equipment so that it looked like badly bruised fruit.

The policeman in charge, Sergeant Michael Cronin, didn't waste compassion on Willie when he ordered him to look under the tarpaulin that covered Clara's body. "Yes, sir," Willie said, then pulled a rumpled white handkerchief from his back pocket to wipe his eyes.

Lexter Gorson, the shoe-shine man, spoke in a husky whiskey voice. "Here, man," he said and passed a flask to Willie. After Willie took a swallow, the bottle was passed around the circle of men. Even the white policemen standing around kicking dirt with their toes each took a swallow. Michael Cronin gladly drank some when the flask was passed to him.

The police wanted to take Clara's body to the morgue for an autopsy, for reasons that they could not clearly convey to the men standing by to transport her small body to the

B. Jenkins Funeral Home. Reverend Buford Jenkins, black Georgetown's leading churchman and mortician, who was accustomed to dealing directly with white people in a way most of the other men were not, spoke up. "Sergeant Cronin, this is a baby. Her people couldn't hardly stand to have her cut up down at the morgue. Now you know this was an accident. Let me put her to rest like she is." Although Sergeant Cronin resented a colored man speaking up to white people, he agreed that it didn't make much sense to draw this matter out. He decided it was all right for Reverend Jenkins, Willie, and several of the other men to carry Clara up Wisconsin Avenue to the funeral parlor.

The party that left the bank of the Potomac carrying Clara on a wooden pallet covered by a dull green blanket looked like a marching stand of trees. Their ranks were closed, their heads were bowed, they made no sound.

Reverend Jenkins tossed Teaspoon Tyler a penny and sent him off to tell Miz Jenkins to go around to the funeral parlor, open things up, and ready his equipment. By the time the procession got to the corner of Wisconsin Avenue and M Street, Viola Jenkins was waiting there with a long, sanctified cloth of embroidered white silk. She lofted the cloth and it settled over Clara's body. The men did not lose step as they proceeded to the funeral parlor.

—

Ina was surprised to see her next-door neighbor Ella Bromsen at her door around dusk of the next evening. Most everyone in Georgetown was over at the Bynums' house on O Street with Alice and Willie. Ina did not know that Ella had been standing out behind the tree, looking in now and again—biding her time before knocking. Ella carried a large mason jar containing an amber liquid and some stalks. She carried the jar reverently, and Ina stiffened a little, wondering what unholy mess was being toted up to her door. Hospitality won out over suspicion, and Ina opened her screen door and invited Ella into her parlor.

Ella Bromsen wore a red trainman's bandanna tied around her head. Her arms were folded over her chest, guarding the large breasts on her narrow, muscular frame. Ella's was a slow face. Her eyes never darted. Her nose, cheek muscles, and eyebrows moved at the speed of molasses.

Most of Georgetown was inclined to think of Ella Bromsen as a conjure woman of the dangerous sort. A few women were sure that she was the one who had put a hex on their man and run him off. But Ella made her primary living by making and selling brooms. She kept the tools of her trade—bundles of straw, driftwood, fresh-milled broom handles, and spools of cord—stacked about her house, outside and in. Ella Bromsen's uncurtained kitchen windows were lined with mason jars filled with decoctions in shades of green, pink, and amber and with satchels of seed and roots. With these, Ella supplemented her broom-making business by catering to folk who wanted a backwoods remedy for croup, constipation, insomnia, rheumatism, lack of vigor, or female troubles.

"I won't stay, Miss Ina," Ella said, standing just inside Ina's front door. "Here is something for the girl. This is a potion—a decoction for tea—for the girl. This one will help her. Give it to her as a tea in morning and at night. This one will help her to sleep real deep and heal herself way down." Ella said all she had to say on one breath and handed the jar to Ina. Then she turned and left.

Ina called after her, "Thank you. I say thank you. I give it to her when, you say?"

Halfway between the two houses, Ella turned around. "A cup in the morning. A cup in the evening. Start this evening."

"Thank you. Thank you," Ina called out.

Many another person would have been reluctant to give much credence to the power of a potion as sickly looking as the liquid Ella gave Ina. But Ina had a feeling that Ella knew something about herbs and teas and such and that this brew might help to drive away the demons pulling at the fragile stalk of what was left of Johnnie Mae. The girl had thrashed about on the bed the previous night—in fact, ever since she'd been brought to the house. Her eyes, under the tightly shut lids, seemed to be fluttering backward up into her skull. She had not opened her mouth to let in food or drink. Ina was puzzled as to how she'd be able to get Ella's brew down the girl's throat.

After Ina warmed a bit of the brew in a cup and tested it on her own lips, she put Johnnie Mae's head in the nest of her elbow and slid small teaspoonfuls between her teeth. The first two spoonfuls dribbled down her chin, then the girl's lips parted slightly. After several spoonfuls, Johnnie Mae's mouth opened more. Ina poured the rest of the decoction down the girl's throat. Johnnie Mae shuddered and her breathing became soundless. Her body sank into the doughy mattress.

A Clara came into the room. A Clara whose head was swollen to twice the size of what had been her normal size, a swollen-headed Clara with large prune-colored eyes. The face was a face of eyes only. The large face had no mouth or nose, but it made a laughing, snorting sound that infected the room. The face played a game and laughed at its own game—a game of dancing over cobblestones. Johnnie Mae struggled to see the feet of the figure but she could not. She heard the feet clearly and her eyes ached in their sockets with the effort of trying to locate the source of the sound. She heard the feet strike cobblestones like horse's hooves. *Clip-clop, clip-clop.* The huge head—the face full of eyes, Clara's eyes—laughed at the *clip-clop* sound the feet were making and seemed to laugh also at the great effort Johnnie Mae was making to locate the feet. The face laughed uproariously, pulling Johnnie Mae's body off the mattress with its manic energy, drawing Johnnie Mae into the game. "Step on a crack, break your mother's back."

After sitting with Johnnie Mae for eight straight hours, in which time the girl did not move a muscle, Ina became worried. She jumped up, ran next door, and banged on Ella Bromsen's back door. Ella made her way to the kitchen suspiciously and opened the door a crack. Ina's voice was a fluttery whisper. "She's sleeping so deep I think she's going to slip away."

"That tea is s'posed to take the river water out of her blood. She needs to sleep deep until this is over with," Ella said. Ina looked at Ella's face and was startled to see amber flecks in eyes that she remembered as coal black. Ella's eyes appeared like a brackish stream—full of organic matter, and slowly moving.

Ina said nothing more, and Ella closed the door on her. Walking back across the yard, Ina fussed at herself for being gullible, for not having the doctor come look at the girl, for not being patient enough to let God work his will.

When Ina returned to the bedroom, the smell of urine was strong. The bedclothes under Johnnie Mae were soaking wet. Ina undressed her, undressed the bed, changed the sheets, washed the girl. She washed her gently all over, and Johnnie Mae did not flutter an eyelid all the while. Her muscles were completely limp, her face as smooth and unworried as a baby's. Ina massaged petrolatum on the girl's arms and legs and belly, and put a cool cloth on her head. She sat on a chair between the bed and the highboy and twined her fingers together but would not peak them. The rest of the night she slept in the chair and left it only to make her water. Periodically Johnnie Mae sucked a sharp breath through partly opened lips and the breath rattled at the back of her throat, escaping as a small gasp. Ina plumped and straightened the bedcovers and patted her head but observed no change in the girl's condition.

Sculling the surface of her dream state, Johnnie Mae's thoughts rose to a penumbral sphere one rung below full consciousness every so often throughout the night and day and night that she lay in Ina's bed. Her eyes remained firmly closed, but Ina's whispered words occasionally broke through. Johnnie Mae smelled salves, soaps, bleaches, and coffee. She felt soft things brush her skin.

4

When Johnnie Mae looked up and saw the house on O Street her legs locked. Burning urine threatened to flow down her legs and soil her white ankle socks. She stood stock-still, squeezing her thighs together, staring at the black funeral bunting hanging on the door to her house. Aunt Ina, holding her firmly against the right side of her body, crushed Johnnie Mae's face underneath her breasts. A stale-sweet powder fragrance permeated the fabric of Aunt Ina's dress.

Aunt Ina brought Johnnie Mae back to the family's house dressed in a black wool dress that she had altered to the girl's size but that had the appearance of an older woman's dress. Johnnie Mae's willowy, athletic body seemed to have shrunk since Clara's drowning—as if some essential part of her had drained off. Walking along the street, she appeared to be sinking down into her dress as she progressed toward the house. Once or twice Aunt Ina had to urge Johnnie Mae to pick up her feet.

Aunt Ina gasped, "Lord, have mercy, Jesus!" when her urgings failed to move Johnnie Mae up the steps to the front door. The girl just stood on the sidewalk and looked at the door. She was perfectly still except that her lips trembled. Ina feared that she'd not be able to get Johnnie Mae into the house.

Press Parker, whose big old paws scooping under the water hadn't been able to bring Clara back to the surface, came up behind Johnnie Mae and Ina. He lifted the girl into his arms and carried her up the steps. He placed her on the threshold and smoothed the wrinkles he had made in her dress.

Press Parker built coffins for B. Jenkins Funeral Home. He had hiccuped uncontrollably the night before while hammering the short planks of pine for Clara's little box. The pine was young and unfinished-looking. Several long pulls on a bottle of corn whiskey eased Parker's hiccups. He drew out a pair of ornate brass handles wrapped in chamois from a metal chest in his work shed. They were a keepsake he'd never breathed a word about. Foraging through the underbrush behind the Mount Zion cemetery looking for dead wood and what-all-else, he'd seen the handles sticking up out of the ground. The shifting and settling swampy earth had probably loosened them from the coffin of a rich man buried when the cemetery had been part of the old Methodist burying ground. Parker had been saving the brass handles this long while for the oak casket he planned to build for himself. But he felt like he ought to add something special to Clara's box, since he'd been the first to get to the river and had not been able to save her. The handles added heft to Clara's coffin and made him feel better about her. His hiccups stopped and the whiskey did its best work around dawn, when Parker lay his head against Clara's box.

The round black-and-yellow faces of oxeye daisies looked

out from every corner of the front room. Here and there red columbine, their bell-like flowers drooped over as if in prayer, broke up the monotony of so many daisies. Early that morning, Ella Bromsen had gone on a long rambling tramp through the field behind Georgetown University to collect flowers for the Bynums' parlor. She'd left her house just before dawn and made it up to Holy Hill as the sun rose. She'd skirted behind the buildings and crossed the campus's open fields awash with trash flowers. She'd carried the wildflowers, still damp, wrapped in the fullness of her skirt.

Both of Johnnie Mae's parents were seated in the front room when she and Aunt Ina came in through the screen door. As they entered, Willie stood up abruptly and crossed the room. He cried out sour, mewling sobs and grabbed Johnnie Mae to him. His arms, grasping her around her rib cage, forced a low grunt from her. Alice looked up at the sound of Willie's crying and Johnnie Mae's gasp. When she broke free of her father's embrace, Johnnie Mae crossed to her mother.

Johnnie Mae had not seen her mother or father — certainly did not remember seeing them — since the drowning. She had not spoken to them. How would their voices sound? How might her own sound? Her throat and mouth felt like plaster. Could they understand how quickly things had happened? Would she be able to tell them what had happened? Would they know that she had tried to save Clara? Johnnie Mae dove and dove and tried to save her sister. But Clara had ridden a whorl of water to the bottom of the Potomac.

Every muscle in Johnnie Mae's body hardened against what her parents' questions must be. What had they meant by swimming there? How many times had she been told not to swim in the Potomac? How could she have let Clara fall into the river? Why had she taken her eyes off Clara even for a second?

But they did not ask anything. They seemed to know all the details or were satisfied with what they'd been told by others. They did not seem to blame Johnnie Mae. But who could they blame but her? And blame seemed necessary. Their eyes were soft, pitying—not angry. There was a slightly perplexed expression, the same in both pairs of eyes, as if a question were there but not the courage to ask it.

Reverend Buford Jenkins, the mortician who was pastor of Mount Zion Church, approached the Bynum house and his quarrelsome stomach started talking back. "I do wish I had some soda," he muttered as acid churned around in his gut and the inside of his mouth became dry. The condition of Clara's remains had disturbed him and challenged his abilities to cosmeticize. A child ought to look like a sleeping angel resting on a bed of satin and flowers. But in the hours before they pulled Clara's body free of the water, before the river let them take it back, her small body had slammed against submerged rocks. It was snagged on a forked branch that was caught on pilings beneath the water's surface and had not actually been far from the place where the girl went under. There was no way to make a sleeping angel. Clara looked dead—and bruised. For the sake of sensibilities and to preserve the reputation of his business, Reverend Jenkins intended to convince the Bynums not to have an open casket.

Jenkins came into the house belching quietly and settling his clothes. The Bynums' parlor was stifling with sympathy. Neighbors ringed the grieving parents like a necklace. Some neglected their own families to cook, wash, look after callers, and comfort Willie and Alice. Each woman put her hand to a special dish: candied sweets, corn pudding, collards, fried chicken, fried fish, meat loaf, mashed potatoes, cake or pie. Each tried to outdo the other in cooking and ministering to the grieving parents. They and most of the recent migrants from Carolina subscribed to the trusted country wisdom: Starve the fever and feed the cold, hungry, sorrowful, lonely, and confused.

Alice Bynum had not eaten anything in the days since Clara's drowning. It was a plate of Bertha Howard's fried chicken and candied sweets that finally woke her palate. When this first helping of food got down to her stomach her bowels rumbled and sweat coursed out of her pores. A sense of what had happened began to return with her appetite.

Alice slumped into her chair at the sight of Reverend Jenkins. "Sister Bynum, I'll need to know your particular wishes," he said. "It's my feeling that we shouldn't have a viewing of the body, Sister Bynum."

Alice looked blankly toward a worn spot on the rug. The women on either side of her, who had gasped at the reverend's words, patted Alice's hands. Her lips parted slightly as if she were going to speak and Eva Copsey put a glass of water to her mouth. "Have a bit of water, honey, please," she said.

Alice didn't speak. She didn't drink the water either. Her mind wanted to scream out some reply, she wanted to push the glass of water away, but she felt her tongue drop to the floor of her mouth and lie motionless, and her lips closed firmly. Instead of speaking, she removed an embroidered handkerchief from her pocket and put it over the rug's bare spot. The women exchanged compassionate looks. A strangled sound came from Ina Carson.

Reverend Jenkins, practiced in handling the grief-stricken, stood with his hat in his hand and let his words settle on the women. "Sisters," he said finally, sweeping his eyes along all the women's faces. "May I please have a glass of soda for my stomach? I have a particular need for it."

The men walked back and forth between the rooms and in and out of the doors, back and front. They took turns at seats around the kitchen table where Willie Bynum had settled. He sat bent over at the waist with his head between his knees. Now and then, Willie brought his head up and leaned back against his chair. The men brewed strong coffee and put shots of whiskey in the cups. Someone fiddled with the stove.

Willie held his coffee cup as if he were holding his own skull, massaging it between his fingers. Someone filled the cup each time it became nearly empty. The men had been in the kitchen like this—heads bowed, keeping the fire lit despite the season, pouring the coffee—since coming back from the river with Clara's body. Several shivered as if chilled to the bone, yet sweat ran down their faces.

Reverend Jenkins came out to the kitchen on the heels of Ina Carson. She was the one who jumped up to get the reverend a glass of bicarbonate of soda, and she had slyly crooked her finger at him to pull him along behind her. When she had him trapped with his back to the kitchen sink she started to question him.

"Her mama and papa and you yourself can see her," Reverend Jenkins said, because he knew very well why Ina had him cornered at the sink. "But all and everybody shouldn't look on the baby like she is now. I can't do anything else with her."

After he downed the glass of soda, Jenkins asked five or six of the men collected in the room to come with him to bring the coffin to the house. Willie rose to join them.

"Brother Bynum," Jenkins said, placing his open palm gently on Willie's chest.

Willie blew breath out of his nostrils like a dray horse. Lexter Gorson, who'd sat most of the day in a corner of the kitchen, caught Willie's arm and sat him back down. "Brother Bynum, this one row you don't need to hoe."

Johnnie Mae sat on a hard chair near the radio in the front room, drawing herself in and away from the constantly moving mourners. When she closed her eyes she could identify the gender of each by the fragrances wafting past. The men smelled of tobacco, starch, wisps of whiskey, and perspiration. The women smelled of talcum, toilet water, butter, and baby urine. Johnnie Mae folded her arms over her chest and clamped her two knees together rigidly. If no limb were hanging loose, she thought, then no one could pat or grasp or stroke her. Each of the women in the room came over to her corner, bent down to look into her face, extended a soft, moist hand toward her. Johnnie Mae sank back into the chair.

There was a parade of baking powder biscuits through the Bynums' house in the days after Clara's death. Every woman who paid a call brought a pan of biscuits. And there were some women who made good baking powder biscuits, some who made heavenly ones, some who made rubbery ones, and some whose biscuits were as hard as rocks. If Saint Peter paid a nickel for each time a woman said in reply to a compliment that her mother's or her grandmother's biscuits were the finest, the lightest, the fluffiest, the most delicately browned she had ever tasted, there would be nickels under every pillow in town.

"My mama was a boss baker. She showed me. I do it just the way she did. She didn't have a recipe. She didn't need one." There was pride in their voices when they accepted compliments on their biscuits. And following the custom of female modesty, they were required to give credit to someone other than themselves for their mastery of the craft.

And while a biscuit can be made with no more than some flour, some baking powder, some salt, some milk if you have it, some water if you don't, and a wish, it is in the firm but gentle touch that the excellent biscuit is created.

As president of the Ladies of Olives burial society, Miz Elva Bemis had brought the requisite pan of biscuits. Everyone who tasted them agreed that Miz Elva Bemis's biscuits were fluffy enough to rise by themselves on Judgment Day.

Miz Elva had come expressly to press on the Bynums the money for Clara's dressing, laying-out, and plot at Mount Zion. Both Alice and Ina had joined the Ladies of Olives soon after they'd got settled in Georgetown and had faithfully paid their dues each week. Neither had thought that she would be the one who would need help. But the Ladies of Olives had helped Ina with Cap, and now they were helping to put baby Clara to rest. "Lord, Lord, Lord" was all Miz Elva said when she handed Alice the bundle of bills wrapped in newspaper.

Miz Elva, legs unsteadied by arthritis and leaning on a cane, crossed the room to Johnnie Mae and pressed three striped peppermint balls into her hand and pushed one against the girl's lips until she opened her mouth. Miz Elva smiled and shook her head encouragingly when Johnnie Mae sucked the candy. Holding her cane in her left hand, eyes closed, and face turned toward the ceiling, she said in a tinny voice that rose above the mourning hum, "Don't forget the little sweetness of life. Do, Jesus! Don't forget now!"

Reverend Jenkins had just come in from the kitchen. He grasped Miz Elva Bemis's hands and Johnnie Mae thought he meant to do the patty cake with her. He, too, closed his eyes and answered, "Yes, Lord. Thank you, Sister Bemis." Several "Amens" reverberated through the room. Miz Elva Bemis crossed to Alice and put three peppermint balls in her lap.

"I've got something to say to you, Sister Alice," Elva Bemis continued. Alice raised her gaze from her lap in response to the gentle authority of the old woman's voice. Miz Elva's lips and the soft, crinkled skin around them opened and closed like a drawstring purse over her snaggled, protruding teeth.

"Sister Alice, you all have not been in Georgetown very long. You came to us a short while ago. We don't know all of you all's people, but we know you are Christian people. And we know you are good working people. You all are members of the church here. Your little girl will rest in hallowed ground here. She'll rest with the saints. Sister Alice, you already got a kin person up there. Brother Cap Carson, Sister Ina's husband, is up there. My baby, Sally, is up there. My husband and four of my boys are up there. Miz Nan Dockery and others of the Dockerys are up there. The Harrises, the Chaneys have got people up there. Why, Pearl Stewart that was a Nevins lies up there with her husband, Mr. Arthur Stewart."

Belle Dockery, who credited her grandma Belle Peatly with the invention of sweet potato biscuits, came and sat in the front room with a pan of string beans to snap. "My grandma Belle Peatly is up there in Mount Zion," she said.

Miz Elva kept on in her trembly voice. "All of these people that've been here in Georgetown awhile have people up there. We'll put this baby up there too." Her voice rose on the refrain of "up there," and scattered voices about the room answered "Amen." A spell got working in the parlor and the men came in from the kitchen to join it. The men and women — some standing, some sitting — bowed their heads and murmured "Amen." Folks slapped two palms together and continued the refrain. Miz Elva Bemis got truly happy and her tongue danced along the roof of her mouth, vibrating at the back of her throat. Her voice left spoken word and ululated, "Up there! Up there!"

―――

Wearing a simple long black skirt, a black blouse with small cloth-covered buttons at the neck, and a black kerchief on her head, Ella Bromsen looked as demure as a postulant as she entered the church leading her blind father, Mr. Butter Bromsen. Most everyone among the colored of Georgetown came to the funeral. Lexter Gorson recovered himself from drunkenness, plastered his hair down with carbolated petroleum jelly, wiped off a threadbare suit with too-short pants and a moth-eaten coat, and entered the church quietly. Mahmoud Hadad removed his shapeless hat at the church door, hitched his pants, and sat at the back with his four black-haired sons. The Bemis family, the Copseys, and the Howards came with their numerous children, all wearing white shirts and blouses with black arm bands. Belle Dockery's ten streamed in after her. Mabel, her oldest, fell against her mother's broad back as the procession filed past the flower-shrouded bier.

Ina Carson, whose right arm was twined around Johnnie Mae's back to keep her walking upright, drew herself to a height and marched into the church. The Epworth League marched two parallel lines of solemnly dressed young people down the center aisle just before Alice Bynum was escorted in, surrounded by white-clad members of the Women's Society of Christian Service. Willie followed them in a black-crow suit of clothes.

After all the others filed in, Ann-Martha Pendel slipped onto the bench next to Lexter Gorson with a series of grunts and huffings. She appeared uncomfortable in a black dress with coarse lisle stockings rolled below her knees. After a moment on the bench she pulled herself up and stood near the door.

Reverend Jenkins's voice, like a huge, calloused hand struggling to be soft, caressed his audience.

"The Lord giveth . . . and the Lord taketh away."

The listeners moaned and shivered. "Amen." Cardboard fans slapped and shushed, pushing hot air through the nave.

"When the old folks pass we're mostly happy. We're sorry to see them go, but happy for them that this hard, hard life is done. They gonna get their reward."

"Amen, uh-huh."

"Papa, you rest from plowing now, the furrows are straight. You've seen the end of the row. Mother, sit down now. Just bake a cake for baby Jesus now. No more scrubbin' to be done."

"Amen."

"But when a baby dies—well, we don't know. There's no sense of finish. The candle didn't burn down after glowing all the night. A cold wind came through and it blew out long before the dawn."

"Yes, Jesus!"

"The cold wind! The cold wind!"

"Amen."

"The people we love, we only borrowing them. They don't belong to us. They belong to the Lord. Mother, you've lost the fruit of your womb. It's going to take some hard grieving to recover yourself. Father, you've lost the fruit of your loins. Gird yourself, the seas are going to be rough before you see dry land. Brother Bynum, Sister Bynum, you have lost the precious fruit from the topmost branch—a branch that, Lord willing, was going to extend down the ages carrying your hopes and aspirations. That fruit was dashed to the ground through Jesus's divine hand. We do not understand this. Our hearts are torn asunder with grief. We do not understand, Lord. But Lord, we do not question your divine wisdom."

"Amen."

"Lord Jesus, we do not see your plan. The taking of one so young and innocent. A baby, Lord. A baby child so young in the world that she couldn't have done a sinful thing—'cause she just wasn't here long enough. She wasn't here long enough to cause anybody real injury. She wasn't here long enough to speak ill of her neighbors. She wasn't here long enough to break her word—to take her neighbor's husband—to abuse the sanctity of her woman's body—to take her neighbor's hard-earned goods. She just wasn't here long enough! This was a baby, Lord. She comes to you, sweet Jesus, without a sin on her soul. And since you called her, Lord, O Lord, take her to your bosom. Give that comfort to her grieving parents, Lord. Let them know that in your tender mercy and complete wisdom, you hold their precious baby to your bosom even this very day. Let them feel the certainty of your divine covenant. Fill their grieving hearts with the sure knowledge that even as your son died for our sins upon the cross, Lord, he died so that each and every one of us—including this baby girl who has gone before her parents—will rest in your kingdom after their weary travail here on earth."

"Amen."

"And, baby Clara, look down on us with mercy for our sins. Because we know that all is visible to the great God and those whose spirits rest in his bosom. Look down upon your mother and father and your sister, Johnnie Mae, and all your peoples. Look down and comfort their grief and guide their steps.

"Sister Alice Bynum, Brother Willie Bynum, and young Johnnie Mae, you have lost your beloved. Amen."

"Amen!"

"But you have not lost everything. You have not lost the love of God. And the love of God will see you through."

Reverend Jenkins cleared his throat and was answered by several other throats. He turned away from the assemblage to hide his profound confusion. In reality, he couldn't see the Lord's plan in taking this little one, but he would not show this doubt to the congregation. He cleared his throat again and was again answered by other throats.

The organist began with a whisper of chords, and Jenny

Throckmorton's gently sweet voice rose urgently from a bosom so womanly it belied the youth and chastity of her soprano.

> *In bright mansions above*
> *In bright mansions above*
> *Lord, I want to live up yonder*
> *In bright mansions above.*
>
> *My father's gone to glory*
> *I want to go there, too*
> *Lord, I want to live up yonder*
> *In bright mansions above.*

5

"Only a teaspoon of self-pity, girl. Every day give yourself a teaspoonful, but only a teaspoonful. Fill it up full, but only once! Don't let yourself have more. You can't live off it. But just a bit of it is like a tonic." Ina's voice was firm but compassionate as the two women sat at the Bynums' kitchen table when the neighbors had gone after the funeral. What with "this one, that one, and the other one" in Alice's house and patting on her, Ina had felt a little like a stepchild. She and Alice were as close as sisters. In the last few days, though, all the years and all the giggling secrets had felt distant. Ina hadn't had the chance to sit with Alice alone and talk. Did Alice think that she'd failed to take care of Clara? That maybe there was something she should have done? But there hadn't been any way to know this was going to happen. There wasn't any sign or omen.

The two women sat in silence for a long stretch until Ina became nervous at the quiet and broke in on Alice's sorrowful musings.

"When Cap died, I didn't honestly think I'd ever crack

my face to smile again. I didn't want to smile. It wasn't even that I was sad all of the time. I just didn't want to give anybody the satisfaction of making me enjoy anything again. Cap made me so happy. Everything about him was a gift. Every hair on his head was like a special gift tied up in a bow on Christmas morning. You loved him. Everybody loved him. Even my papa, who didn't like anybody, liked Cap. Even your papa liked him. Everybody liked him. And everybody pitied me when Cap died—including me. I fed on that self-pity, I got fat on it. I craved self-pity more than Cap after a while. I just didn't want happiness again. Not at all. That kept on until I realized that I was losing the very part of Cap I wanted to keep—the joyful part."

A carpetbag of threads, needles, and scraps sat on the floor at Ina's feet as she worked cross-stitch on a pillowcase. "I sit up in the house some of these days while I'm sewing and I talk to Cap. We laugh a bit and talk and I tell him all about everything. I've told him about your babies. He knows them. He knows what's happened to baby Clara. He knows. Sugar, Cap'll look after her."

"How do you know it's Cap you're talking to?" Alice asked. "How do you know it isn't somebody else or maybe just yourself you're talking to?" She allowed a small smile to play over her lips. It tickled, the way Ina always made God seem like a kind old man who lived next door.

"I know who I'm talking to when I talk out and Cap talks back to me. I know it's him. I know my Cap. He said to me one time, 'Don't pass up happiness, Ina Mae. You've got to have some joy.' I take a little bit of Cap—a little bit—a little sweetening—a little bit of all these feelings. That keeps a life going. One teaspoonful of these feelings: this sorrow, this joy, this and that worry and disappointment, and this and that of what the old people used to call fire in the loins. A teaspoonful of each of these things is what makes a good life. You've had your luck, in a way. You've had the attention of two decent men and you still got a healthy firstborn child. That's more luck than some women get in a whole lifetime."

It was Cap Carson who had started the chain of events that brought them all to Washington. It was Cap who had peppercorns in his shoes and who couldn't be content in one place too long after he came back from the war. His first idea was to move to Tulsa, Oklahoma. Tales had circulated and the colored papers were full of stories about the limitless opportunities in Oklahoma.

Going to Tulsa, though, would mean that the men would have to go first and start some money-making venture and send for the women to join them when the living was assured. Willie didn't like this plan, but he had been ashamed to tell Cap. He was worried that Alice wouldn't remember that she belonged to him if he wasn't there to remind her. Alice wasn't a tramp, but she had been bold enough to go against her father in the matter of the Indian, Sam Logan. She might strike up a new plan that didn't include Willie. It would be better for all of them if they moved together.

Alice was itching to leave Marabel, itching to get away from her papa. Pleasant and easygoing as long as she bent to his wishes, Old Man Walker had become a wild, mad bull since Alice had brazenly defied him with Sam Logan. Her sisters, too, had her in a web of soft but constricting tangles. Bessie had tried to convince her to get rid of the baby. Lula talked against that and begged her not to run off with Sam Logan. After Sam Logan had gone, it was her sisters who encouraged the romance between her and Willie.

The decision to move to Georgetown was a fallback from the grander plan of moving out west. When the news reached Marabel that white folks had burned the colored part of Tulsa, that sealed it. They would go to Washington—to Georgetown.

Of course, Washington, D.C., was not without its worries and uncertainties. Mrs. Adelaide Circe's son Leon had been in the war and was in Washington in '19 when they were burning and shooting colored. He told it around that he and many of the other colored had acquitted themselves well in the rioting. But Leon Circe further maintained that when the war was over he decided to be through with fighting. And he came back home to Marabel and married Mabel Reliford.

Cap and Ina came to Washington first when Cap got wind of jobs to be had on the waterfront at the navy yard. He fancied himself a stevedore after his work in the Great War. But he couldn't get hired as a stevedore. They shut colored out of that trade. He managed instead to get on a construction crew working on the Key Bridge. Cap kept working on the bridge until he and the other colored got rowdied out of their jobs by the Irish.

Ina did baby nursing for some women that lived in for the first several months after she and Cap arrived. Then she got herself a live-in job with a good family. After a while, though, Ina felt this work arrangement was leaving poor Cap without a hot meal at the end of the day. And living apart wasn't the proper thing, in her mind, for a married woman. When she confided her intention to quit the live-in job to Miz Beulah Gibson, the live-out laundrywoman who worked for her family, Miz Gibson put her on to a colored woman who did piecework. This woman had more sewing work than she could handle from her regular customers and was happy to take on an assistant. From this, Ina worked around and started to build her own list of customers. Ina's needlework was so neat and so quickly done that she was very soon established as one of the best colored seamstresses in Georgetown.

Willie and Alice and the two girls followed Cap and Ina to Georgetown after the harvest in the fall of '24. When the canning was done and people could no longer throw up reasons for them to stay in Marabel, they left. Alice's sisters campaigned to keep Johnnie Mae and Clara while Willie and Alice got established in Washington. But Alice insisted that they would come to Washington all together as a family: Willie, her, Johnnie Mae, and baby Clara.

By the age of five, Johnnie Mae had already learned her letters and could count reliably on her ten fingers. Her counting ability came naturally from her mama. It was Mama who was always figuring up and weighing — bags of flour left; spoons of sugar; dozens of eggs needed; rows of stitches remaining; how many miles to the city; how many different trains to catch; how many days the nest egg would stretch; how much a pound, a bunch, a yard, a piece, a week.

Johnnie Mae was the tiny doll within the larger doll her mother was that day in November when they arrived at Union Station, Washington, D.C. Clara was the still smaller doll. Willie left the three of them in the station waiting room while he went looking for Cap and Ina. He looked back at Alice and Clara and Johnnie Mae and wanted to cry. They were so like three small brown chicks. They looked frightened, and he worried that he'd be unable to allay their fears.

Was he going to be able to take care of them all? Alice had been so hot to come here, but did she know what they'd be facing? She'd pumped him up, saying, "You'll be sure to get something. Cap says there's plenty of work. Cap's got a good job. You'll get something good, too." Willie wasn't so sure about that.

Though Alice was frightened of the hubbub of Washington that first day, it was the City. She knew completely that day that she was a woman for the city, a city like Washington, D.C. She was here to be tried and tested. This city had a feeling of things being possible. Action would have true consequences here. Hard work would pay off; education would pay off; dreaming would pay off.

Johnnie Mae, standing next to her mother in the train station, felt only her parents' excitement at the newness and the possibilities of the city. Their trepidation did not reach down to her. It stayed up in their chests and on their foreheads, well above her line of perception.

The network of customers and acquaintances that Ina Carson had established would serve Alice well. While live-in jobs were plentiful for young colored women who came up from the South, Alice wouldn't consider being away from her children and husband for six days at a time. Most of the women who did live-in work and had children found somebody else to care for the children or left them to care for themselves. This was a change from what they were used to. Back home, when a colored woman took care of a white woman's children and cooked and cleaned her house, she brought her own babies with her to play in the yard while she was working and to help her out when they got up a size to. Here in Washington, the white woman didn't want no little chickens pecking around in her yard and associating with her children. It was much stricter here about how you worked and how you dressed and how you conducted yourself while you were working. And the white folks here were scared about spreading sickness among the children. They would hardly let a colored woman enter their house if they suspected her children were at home with the croup.

Some women who were well established told Alice she was being foolish to pass up live-in work. They said the good families would only want a colored woman who was willing to live in and wear a uniform. You could expect a good pay and tips and holidays from these families. But you had to live on premises. The "best" families expected it. They wanted it. They required it.

Some lucky women worked and lived in a place where their man worked too. The luckiest ones, it looked to Ina and Alice, were the ones who worked out and came home to their children at night. But days work could be hard to get at times and often not regular enough. The pay was lower too. Oftentimes the families that couldn't afford a complete live-in staff, the ones that used day workers, were the ones who lived above their true means and might come up short on payday. But Alice and Ina decided that they would risk it in order to come home to their own place at night.

Alexis St. Pierre considered Alice attractive, for a colored woman. She was not thick or plain or blue-black. Alexis, Mrs. Douglas St. Pierre, preferred a yellow or medium-brown colored woman to work in her house because she thought dark-black colored people were difficult to communicate with. It was sometimes difficult to discern their reaction to one's words; their very dark faces appeared so dense. The slightly brown or yellow maids seemed more amenable. Alexis especially liked Alice because she was not fat, only pleasantly round and filled out.

Alice had never wanted to work solely for one woman. But Alexis St. Pierre had been gentle and persistent in her request. She'd said she would fix a good weekly rate and Alice would never be obliged to stay late. She'd said she would hire out for parties. Taking care of children would be unnecessary because she and Douglas were never going to have children. Alexis had told Alice that she would have half a day off on Saturday and all day Sunday because Douglas was Catholic and believed that no one should work on Sunday. She'd said airily that Alice should take the silk kimono Douglas had given her for her last birthday because it was the wrong color for her but would be just right for Alice. This gift had sealed the bargain. Alice would come to work for Alexis and Douglas and work for them only.

Alice's sudden, tragic loss was confusing to Alexis. It was hard to know how to respond. Alexis had known the child. She had seen both of Alice's girls briefly. She recalled them perched on the top step of the back porch. The day she saw them, they had been chattering like magpies and had started when she opened the screen door and walked onto the porch. She had been surprised by them too. She was, perhaps, more surprised by them than they were by her. Oddly, they hadn't looked like they could be Alice's children and Alexis had had to question herself as to what she had expected. They sat that day on the top step like two small brown birds — Alice's two.

When Alexis looked into Alice's face the first morning she returned to work after Clara's death, Alexis knew that it was ridiculous to suppose that this tragedy would roll off her easily. She was ashamed that she'd caught herself thinking like some old Virginia planter about how "nigger women whelp like dogs and care no more about their pups than a bitch." The tale was told on Alice's face—in her eyes. This woman had been to the other side of grief and might not be back to stay—not yet.

"I can work some. I'll work some, then go home." Alice looked levelly at Alexis St. Pierre and spoke without polite preamble or dissembling. Alice did general straightening and dusting. She faltered only once—pausing to swipe tears from her face as she removed, dusted, and replaced the framed photographs of Douglas's and Alexis's families. Before leaving at midday, Alice plucked a chicken and washed up the dishes. Alexis assured Alice that she could put the chicken on to cook herself. As Alice left, she paused with her hand on the knob of the screen door and turned back toward Alexis. She let her eyes and cheeks suggest a smile.

~

Leaving her own house the next day, Alice said, "Willie, walk up past Miz St. Pierre's. Tell her I'm not coming today. I can't come today. I'll catch up tomorrow."

She walked out of the house with nothing in her hands. Her arms, unaccustomed to idleness, weren't content to hang at her sides but looped and twisted behind her back. She would have looked like someone out only to stroll if one could imagine that a woman like her had time to stroll. Her face was placid and she walked as if she had no destination. But her mind was on the spot—her mind was on the Three Sisters. There was a breeze that morning and the wind billowed her dress intermittently.

The scent of the air changed where the road sloped down to the river. The air was gauzy, absorbent. The moisture held on to every fragrance. The odors were strong on the path that ran alongside the river. They were odors unknown to Alice. She could not pick out specific things causing the aromas. She felt as though she were wading through their thickness.

The Potomac was a sullen battleship gray. And it was still, leaden. The surface appeared impenetrable. It would not be possible to swim through this mass—not even for a swimmer.

Alice walked along the path her daughters had taken on that day. She felt drawn along to complete a task of mothering by putting her feet into the same spots they had taken the day Clara died. She wanted to complete the picture so she could put it alongside what else she knew about the events of that day. She would review the pictures of what she was seeing and what had been described to her and then she'd know more of what had happened.

She imagined the day. She put aside the thoughts of how the mother would wish to see her two girls and saw them as the children they must have been. They would have been naively misbehaving, following the unexamined, unconscious urges of children. Knowing so little about fear and danger, they would have been simply walking.

Johnnie Mae had taken to water like a tadpole. The sizable stream a quarter mile behind Old Man Walker's place, near Marabel, North Carolina, was enough of a waterway to float a raft. Rafting had been the way he brought his crops to market in the older days. Alice's papa had a habit of swimming the width of his stream for pleasure and his constitutional. Before Johnnie Mae learned to walk, Old Man Walker swam the stream with her tucked under one arm. He'd stroke with his free arm and grunt and spit water in front of him. Johnnie Mae had floated along, skimming the surface of the water, held up by her grandpa. Instinctively she kept her eyes wide open and her little arms and legs stroking. She and Grandpa would dog-paddle out to the center of the stream. Johnnie Mae believed for all the world that she was towing Grandpa. Old Man Walker laughed out loud and wide. "The squaw's baby can swim. She's a natural swimmer." The water was thrilling to her. Her baby heart pumped like forty—pumped as if the force that propelled her through the water was of her own devising.

Alice had always been a slight bit afraid of water, had not taken to it like Papa and the boys. She and her sisters had never followed the urge to swim in their papa's stream. The boys and Papa took a lusty thrill in the water and had made a particularly masculine exercise of it. Alice had no particular reason to fear the water. She'd never come close to drowning because she'd never even tried to swim. Fear depends on a certain knowledge, however incomplete, of the dread consequences of an action. Children are unafraid of the fishhook until they have once snagged their hand. Forever after they've got some reaction to it: wariness, caution, distaste, some something that keeps them from getting snagged again. Alice had never been afraid of water because she'd never put herself at the mercy of it. But she was leery of it. Johnnie Mae—was she scared of water? Had she ever been? Didn't even Clara's drowning make her frightened?

Clara's footsteps would have been smaller, softer than

Johnnie Mae's or the other girls'. The branches that slapped at Alice's rib cage as she passed by would have slapped at Clara's cheeks. The branches would have stung her face and she would have stifled her discomfort so as not to be left behind by the others. Threading through brambles at the bank, Alice was surprised at how difficult it was to find and keep to the path.

She avoided the edge of the river. She was frightened of the Potomac. She felt the need to be protective of her own life. If she'd been there the day Clara drowned, would she have leapt into the water to save her? If it had been only the two of them? If there had been no one else near who could have swum to Clara, would she have gone into the water? Frightened and unable to swim? Would she have gone with Clara rather than stood on the shore? Would she have told herself, in the split seconds she would have had to decide, that she had another daughter to live for—a husband, too—and others?

Alice shivered and her shoulders rose to touch her earlobes. In truth, Johnnie Mae had done—the other girls who were there told it—what she, Clara's mother, could not. Johnnie Mae had dived and dived and tried to save Clara. That, with all her fears and foibles, Alice could never have done.

6

Always says "Clara" now when she talks about her. She says "Clara" now. She doesn't dare call her "Rat," even in her mind. She doesn't dare whisper "Rat." Her mama would tan her blue and boil her in oil if she heard her say "Rat" now. She wishes she could get her jaws to say it. She wishes she could hear herself say "Rat" out loud. She doesn't even sound like herself when she says "Clara" sometimes. It feels like she's talking about somebody else, or that somebody other than herself is doing the talking.

"I think I've forgot her. But if you remember that you forgot somebody—or come real close—then you've caught yourself in time."

Rat was the perfect name for her. Clara was too big a name anyway. Rat is what you get from Clara if you turn it around on the page when you write the letters. Mouse was more like what she acted like, but you can't get that from turning the letters around and dropping some and adding a tail. You get Rat and that's her—Clara the rat, Clara the tattletale, Clara that couldn't keep her mouth closed when you wanted her to and couldn't open her mouth to say anything when she was supposed to.

Johnnie Mae saw Clara Bow in the pictures at the Blue Mouse Theater, and Clara Bow had skin as white as snowflakes. Clara, when she was a little baby, was tiny and pecan brown. But Mama had called the baby Clara, and the sound blended with her sweet skin smell and her little baby cuteness.

Rat was the name Johnnie Mae gave her. Her mama hated that name because she hated rats. Mama hated them because she was scared of them. Some of the houses they'd rented in Georgetown had rats. Mama wasn't used to them. She said that in the country all they had were field mice plus a whole lot of other creatures. In the country they had wild game like possums, snakes, woodchucks, snapping turtles, but not these city rats. The city rats came up to the house bold and dirty and low to the ground. And the city rats weren't afraid of people either.

One evening at dusk Mama was cleaning fish Papa had brought from a fishing trip he had gone on with Mr. Birdaxe and Mr. Pud Allen and some two or three other men he called "the boys." They had gone up by the conduit to drop lines. Mama was gutting the catch on the back porch steps of the house they'd lived in on Grace Street. Everything about that house was rickety and it kept a smell of mildew.

Johnnie Mae handed fish out of the bucket to Mama and put the cleaned ones in another pan. The pail Mama was dropping the guts and heads into was sitting one step below the step she was sitting on. Mama chopped off the heads with the same hatchet she used to chop off the heads of wrung chickens. She lay the fish flat on the step, whacked off the head in one clean motion, and pushed the head off the step into the basin with the flat of the hatchet. After a while the blood-and-guts odor got thick in the air and a big, wide rat swaggered up through the yard toward them. He walked out in the open, slowly. He wasn't one bit afraid of anyone. He walked toward where Mama was sitting, stopped about four feet away, and locked eyes with her. There was absolutely no fear in the rat. Somebody's poison had made him cocky. Mama was as stiff in the back as the porch rail. She was scared. Anybody who knew her would know it by the way she held her bottom lip, as if she needed to clamp down to keep from screaming out. She told Johnnie Mae to get up slowly and walk back into the house and close the screen door. Then she rose from the step and sat in the chair the girl had been sitting in. She placed the hatchet in her lap and sat completely still in the chair. She waited for the rat to move. He didn't. He stared at her. After a long wait, the expression in his eyes changed from pure aggression to desperation. The rat's nose twitched in the direction of the fish heads floating in the pail. Mama said later that she knew he was rabid or had just gotten some poison because of the way he eyed that pail. He was mad with thirst and would likely attack anyone between him and the pail. Mama crossed her hands over the hatchet without moving her arms. She slowed her breathing and must have lulled the rat into thinking she was frozen in fear. When he lunged straight for the fish heads, she raised the hatchet up and brought it down on the rat's outstretched neck. The hatchet split him open and got stuck in the step. Mama sat back in the chair and stared at the split-open rat and the fish guts dripping down the porch steps. "Lord have mercy," she said. After a little while she got a bucket of water, washed down the steps, and cleaned off the hatchet. Then she finished cleaning the rest of the catch.

Later that night Mama told Papa they'd have to move—would have to find a house on higher ground because Grace Street was too close to the river. The rats just came up out of the river.

The Potomac River disgorges a fair number of rats every night into the streets of Georgetown. They skulk along Water Street and exploit swampy, subterranean tunnels to get into basements all through the town. Aunt Ina whispered to Mama and Papa in the kitchen one night that rats had shunned the Potomac for three days after Clara drowned. From a perch at the top of the steps, Johnnie Mae listened to the adults' conversation after they'd sent her off to sleep. Aunt Ina said, in a hushed voice punctuated with "umph, umph," that folks said after Clara's body was drawn out of the river, hundreds of rats—later, thousands of rats it was—had climbed out and stood staring back at the water. Aunt Ina said that someone said—once she said Press Parker, once she said it was Miz Dottie Sham—that it was as if those rats blamed the river and were ashamed to swim in it. Those nasty rats that will skim garbage off the surface of the water, with greasy sludge covering their backs, were thick along the riverbank for three nights after Clara drowned! Aunt Ina told it as absolute fact though it was only hearsay.

Clara the rat hightailed it down Dumbarton Avenue, running scared one day. One day! Every other day, just about. Old fraidy cat! It didn't take much to get Clara wailing and hightailing it down the street. Of course, she was a little girl and her feelings got hurt real easy.

Her feelings got hurt pretty bad one day by the big old

rawboned girl called Bessie Daley. Bessie was a lobster-red white girl whose mother and father got drunk every Saturday at dusk and stayed pie-eyed and belligerent until Monday morning. Bessie's father was a general laborer who mostly cleaned furnaces at the white churches and up at Georgetown University. Most of the time you saw him, his lobster-red face was half covered with soot. Bessie's mother spent most of her day lounging on a sofa in her front room. She was a daylong drinker, and neither her clothes, her hair, nor her home was ever quite clean.

This was what got Johnnie Mae mad—this betrayal. She charged down O Street in a rage of indignation with Clara following behind, still bawling. Who did that big, old dumb-looking gal think she was, calling Clara out of her name? Bessie, who pretended to be a friend to everybody, called Clara a dirty little nigger in front of her cousins from out of town. She had always petted Clara and talked silly to her and had given her penny candy from time to time. She had made a point of seeking out the Bynum girls for friendship because she wasn't too popular among her own. This fact wasn't lost on the girls, especially on Johnnie Mae. And Johnnie Mae wanted to shake Clara and set her head bobbing because she couldn't stand up for herself or stop herself from crying. But she knew what her duty was. It was plain: She'd have to whip the daylights out of Bessie Daley.

Johnnie Mae landed a solid punch up beside Bessie Daley's broad nose and knocked her on her tailbone before two words had passed between them. In fact, the punch was prefaced by only two words, delivered with a big voice full of threat and vow: "Bessie Daley!" The punch caused Bessie to wail and carry on and started a stream of blood and mucus coursing out of her nose. Bessie and any others who had it in mind to pick on Clara learned a lesson that day. Johnnie Mae could take care of herself and Clara, too.

The first day Johnnie Mae came back around to Ann-Martha's to deliver bundles of laundry after Clara died, the woman looked her in the eyes with the plain, unequivocal look of a bull. "You push her? Did you?" Ann-Martha asked.

This was the question that nobody else had asked. Not even Johnnie Mae's parents had asked her this. But Ann-Martha came right out with it and in so doing gave Johnnie Mae the first chance to say out loud, "No! No, Miss Ann-Martha, I didn't push her."

Johnnie Mae was going to go on and say that she really loved Clara despite how she may have treated her sometimes. But Ann-Martha raised her hand sharply like a traffic cop and said, "That's all I want to know. That's all." They fell into their work and didn't speak about Clara again.

Four large galvanized tin tubs were arranged in a row on Ann-Martha's kitchen floor. There was a tub for soaking clothes, a tub for clothes being scrubbed, a tub for rinsing, and a tub of soaking baby diapers. Ann-Martha did three, sometimes four separate washes a day and insisted that delicates and coarse goods, bedding and colored items could not be washed or rinsed together. Baby diapers also received a special handling. Ann-Martha was particular about how the washes were done, a fact that was belied by the slovenly look about her person and her house.

The wood stove roared under several large pots of boiling

water. A dwindling pile of wood was near the back door next to an empty bin for coal and a half-filled one for newspapers. Outside of the effort she put into actually washing clothes, Ann-Martha had to expend considerable in keeping her stove alive, too.

Little for food preparation was visible in her kitchen. There were only two coffee cups, one spoon, a tin of sugar, a tin of Luzianne coffee, and a coffeepot. An opened box of Argo starch was on the kitchen table, and flecks of white clung to the side of Ann-Martha's face.

Ann-Martha worked quickly, pinching open her clothespins and arranging sheets neatly on the lines, overlapping their corners. The effort caused her to huff and snort like a locomotive. Oddly, Ann-Martha was always anxious about the clothespins she carried in a large pocket in her apron. From this pocket, which created an additional layer to her wide midriff, she transferred each clothespin to her mouth and then to her fingers. Each one reversed this track back to her apron when clothes were removed from the lines. She hardly ever left one on the table or anywhere about the premises.

Johnnie Mae stood and waited for Ann-Martha to finish assembling clean bundles. She placed herself near the end of the table closest to the door and rested her fingers against its edge. She knew better than to drum her fingers on Ann-Martha's table, and she knew better than to sit down in the woman's presence unless invited to. Johnnie Mae had been taught that it was not proper for a girl to show impatience or to be too womanish.

All the washing was Ann-Martha's province. She had made that plain from early on in their relationship. As she spat snuff juice into a tin can near her feet, Ann-Martha had let slide from under her lips, "I know what dirts to look for. A young girl like you won't know what-all to be looking for. You had your monthly yet?"

Johnnie Mae had felt warmth creep into her face and looked down at her feet. "No, ma'am," she said. Not wanting to be thought a mere child and wanting credit for everything she did know, even allowing that she had much to learn, she said, "I know about that thing. I know what to look for."

Ann-Martha had chuckled, recognizing the girl's pluck. "Once you've had your first monthly you have to be careful of the mens. Don't let them come up on you or you'll get a belly. And for God's sake, don't let 'em come behind you. Don't let them in there or you'll get a big butt. Where you think all these big-butt women got theirs? Steer clear of mens. Keep your back to the wall." Ann-Martha roared with laughter at the end of this "talk," and Johnnie Mae narrowed her eyes at the woman to make it clear she didn't believe a word of this but was too well brought up to answer back. She knew a girl was officially considered a woman after she'd had her first monthly. And she knew you could get "in trouble" if you let a man have at you after this point. But everybody knew that the surest way to get a big butt was to have a fondness for buttered biscuits and jam.

On Wednesdays, the delivery route started at the Alban Towers Hotel up on Wisconsin Avenue. The wagon was loaded down with a large pile of sheets for the hotel and starched shirts for Mr. Wainwright and Mr. Percy, bachelor men who lived at Alban Towers. Johnnie Mae had to be careful not to tip over the wagon under the top-heavy load. If the hotel's sheets arrived soiled, the hawk-faced woman who was the head housekeeper wouldn't take them and wouldn't pay.

Mr. Wainwright was always courtly. He bowed as he took his bundle of shirts and bowed again as he handed her his knot of dirty shirts and his payment. Mr. Percy scowled at Johnnie Mae's intrusion and pushed his soiled shirts toward her with his foot. It was Mr. Percy's habit to place his payment on the edge of the carpet in the hallway and quickly close his door before Johnnie Mae had bent to pick up the coins.

The hotel's sheets returning to Ann-Martha were a large, smelly bundle that took up most of the wagon. Care had to be taken with the dirty bundles, too. Ann-Martha would be salty if they arrived with extra dirt from the street.

On the second trip, neatly folded, sweet-smelling baby diapers were delivered to five households on Dumbarton Avenue. Ann-Martha had drilled Johnnie Mae to deliver the clean diapers as she headed west along Dumbarton and to pick up the dirty ones as she came back east toward Wisconsin Avenue. That way, clean diapers would not ride next to the soiled ones returning to be boiled and stirred.

The fragrance of the returning pile was ripe. As Johnnie Mae wound her way back to Ann-Martha's, she thought about Clara's reaction to the stink of the sheets and diapers in the summer. Johnnie Mae giggled. Clara had often made faces and threatened to puke as they pulled the stinking piles back to Ann-Martha's.

There was respect between Johnnie Mae and Ann-Martha as concerned the money. The girl had enough moxie to ask for the payments from customers and was smart and honest enough to bring it all back. From what Ann-Martha could see, there wasn't much foolishness about the girl, and her shoe-button eyes were level when the time came for getting paid. She would not be shorted by accident or design.

Ann-Martha counted out Johnnie Mae's pay and grunted, "Tomorrow," to end their commerce. Johnnie Mae knew it was her place then to say, "Yes, ma'am," and leave.

The streets of Georgetown were the prettiest streets of any in Washington city, maybe the prettiest streets anywhere! Johnnie Mae was convinced of this though she had nothing to compare them to. All she remembered of her hometown in North Carolina was all that there was to it: a collection of ramshackle buildings connected by a dirt track. But Georgetown—pretty trees, pretty houses! These must be the loveliest, most graceful thoroughfares of any place in the world. And loveliest of all being when the Fontarellis made their rounds lighting all of Georgetown's gas street lamps.

Clara used to say that she thought the Fontarellis had the responsibility for all the lights in the world. But what they actually had was the concession for Georgetown. The beefy, dark-haired sons and grandsons of Angelo Fontarelli turned on the streetlights at dusk and turned them off at dawn throughout Georgetown. The Fontarellis hired a few colored boys to work for them in Bell's Court and Poplar Alley, but they jealously guarded the rest of their concession. Street by street, lamp by lamp, the big-thighed Fontarellis hooked the pull chains on the gas lamps with long poles. When a pilot was out, they shimmied up like monkeys onto the narrow platforms on the lamps and relit the pilots with a match. Lamplighting time was the signal for the small children to go inside from play, and groups of children on every block would dance along ahead of the Fontarellis to steal a few more minutes outside.

The occupants of the big fancy houses with elegant gas porch lamps on their porticoes would call to one of the roving colored boys at dusk and toss him a penny to light their lamps.

Johnnie Mae had seen Washington's streets and they were nowhere near as pretty as Georgetown's. Maybe it was the people. The people of Georgetown were a prettier-looking bunch, she thought. On her way home from Ann-Martha's, Johnnie Mae stopped in front of a large picture window on R Street to gaze at a woman playing a grand piano. She watched and listened. The music floated out the window and filled the street. The woman's body seemed to rise out of the piano bench like a sapling.

Johnnie Mae stepped forward to get a closer look at the woman's hands. She had once chuckled conspiratorially with Papa as he teased Mama about her hands. "You got hands like a white woman, Alice, all soft and smallish. You must don't do any kind of work. You must be sittin' down on your biscuits rockin' and fannin' all day."

Mama laughed. "You ought to take a look at my feet. You'll lose ten years off your life at the sight of them. As little sitting as I do between work and home, my biscuits never touch a seat."

Papa's look shifted when she said this. His eyes rolled away from Johnnie Mae and the conspiracy shifted. Mama's eyes likewise rolled backward over her left shoulder. Johnnie Mae saw these looks pass and dropped her gaze to the floor. "I got feathers for you," Papa said in a quiet voice.

What did a white woman's hands look like? Sorting through grown people's conversation and pulling together nuance, innuendo, and gossip, a picture emerged in Johnnie Mae's mind of something to put yourself up against, something small, white, and lissome. From where she stood on the sidewalk, the skin on the woman's hands looked like the small porcelain bisque figurines on Alexis St. Pierre's mantel.

7

Folks always say, "You come in this world alone, and you must leave it alone." They ought to know better. Because it isn't so. It's not that way at all. The child comes to life very much attached and stays attached and is mired all its life in a soup of relations. This child struggles to be born. It comes out pushing and pulling with the cord attached and still holding on way up. The child has to pull and push and make a place for itself in and among all the people that are already here.

When they pulled Clara's body out of the Potomac it didn't look at all like the corpses Willie had seen, except that it was unmoving. The skin was mottled, not smooth and sweet like Little Mama's or even shrunken away and sagging like Big Mama's.

Willie's pet name for Clara was Little Mama, denoting a thing in her nature that was small, birdlike, and vulnerable. Clara was Willie's second Little Mama. His first Little Mama had raised Willie. She was his sister, Merle, two years older than him, who died of cholera in the year of the big epidemic.

From the beginning, Willie had felt a quality of awe in Clara's presence because she was so much like Merle. Well before she'd got of an age to favor anyone, he knew she was Merle come again. There was a quality to her breath, a scent he'd smelled the first time he held her, that was like Merle's. He seldom talked of these feelings with Alice, who was so protective of the child. Once he had said, "She's so like Little Mama, like Merle, like my sister." Alice had nodded and said, "Do you think so?"

Early in the marriage, Alice had been concerned about Willie's feelings for Merle. Someone told Alice the story of how Willie had been found the morning after Merle died with his head resting on her breast. Merle's white shift was crushed in his fist. Folks say it's not good for a person to rest their head on a dead person's chest. If you do you can never be free of them. They'll carry a bit of your spirit away with them. Of course, some folks so love their people that they want to be carried away with them and just as surely they put their head onto the dead's chest and pray to go along. That's what Willie had done. So devastated to be left again, he'd begged Merle to take him too. He got so mad with her still body that he punched her and twisted her shift in his hands. But Merle didn't move a muscle. Willie lay his head on her chest and fell to sleep. Drifting off, he was sure she stroked his brow and said, "Willie, Willie, Willie, Bab Bruh."

Neighbors came by in the morning and pried him loose from her. Mal Packing finally had to break Merle's arm at the elbow to free Willie's head. Ma Tibo, an old crone who had a reputation for conjuring, said Willie would be tormented forever. She said he'd always be dreaming of Merle because she'd died with her hands wrapped around him.

In Clara's first winter she had been so sick—the croup was bad that year—that Alice and Willie despaired of keeping her. The night of their worst fear for the child's life, Alice had stood up from the bedside with a look and said, "Now is the time—now. If you've got a prayer in you, it's time to pray." Willie had knelt by Clara's bed with one knee down and the other up—not wanting to crouch below the side of the bed, not wanting to leave the sight of Clara's small brown face in so much billowing white covers. She looked for all the world like the photograph of Merle they'd taken at her laying-out in Big Mama's shack.

Willie had only that one photograph of Merle. Her face was perfectly composed, as in sleep. Maybe there was a jinx on his seed that made his womenfolk weak and slippery and liable to slip away? He'd come to think of women like little chicks, soft and fragile, not able to stand much handling. Big as Big Mama had once been, she had shrunk to a chick and finally slipped away. Then Little Mama lay down one day, saying, "It's just a little sickenin'." She never got up. She shrunk to a chick and slipped away like Big Mama.

With Clara gone, Willie's heart had become a barn with several stalls: Big Mama, Little Mama, and now little Clara. Thoughts about any one of them gave him a pinging feeling in the chest. There was a sore place there you could practically put your finger on.

∽

Bringing Clara had been easy for Alice compared to bringing Johnnie Mae. With Johnnie Mae it had been painful and frightening. All the bossy women had been around her. The midwife and her stepmother, Flora and Bessie and Lula—all of them had talked shrilly and harshly. Only Lula spoke soothingly, and she had stopped when she got scared at the sight of all the blood. And when the big pain came and had built up and broke over her like a torrent, it made her tremble all through. Her whole body quivered and she had pushed Johnnie Mae nearly all the way out on the one big push. She had felt blood gush from between her legs and the smell and sound and feeling of it sickened her. Compared to that, Clara had slid out.

What a shock to Alice when Johnnie Mae had learned to walk and suddenly was moving away from her mother. It was as if a part of Alice's body had suddenly had the power to detach itself from her torso. And Clara had done so, too. Clara had moved away and learned to walk and run. And now she was moved away for good, coming back in waves of feeling and thought.

The first time Alice drifted into sleep after the drowning, her head lolled on her right shoulder as she sat in a chair in their bedroom. Willie walked the floor, polishing the wooden floorboards with his heels. He looked at his sleeping wife and saw a child's quiescent face. He pitied her that she would wake and recall that her baby was drowned—snatched to the bottom of a river that seemed to care little about what it had taken from them. The river had flowed on despite its transgressions and continued to do so.

Alice shifted her body slightly in the chair as Willie watched her, and a mewling escaped her lips. She cried in her sleep, and the sight of her and the sound from her wracked him and he sobbed loudly between her whimpers.

The pool of women Willie had known was small—Big Mama, Little Mama, Ma Tibo, and some other Evas and Coras and Maes. None was a dimpled woman. Alice was the first woman he'd seen with dimples in her cheeks. Her dimples were the punctuation to her more generous smiles. They were there when she released her lips and cheeks from tight politeness—when she forgot cares or remembered delight.

Willie liked to place his fingers into the grooves of her dimples. He wore an expression of surprise often. It was his habit to appear to discover and then express wonderment and delight in the manner he had of lifting his brows and brightening his eyes. So many things surprised him—Alice's dimples for one.

When three weeks had passed since Clara died, Willie sat on the side of the bed, stroking Alice's hand. She lay flat, crossways on the mattress, looking at the ceiling. She had been sitting upright on the side of the bed and had finally, simply, laid herself flat. A tear followed, one more and another slowly down her cheeks. She stopped crying as Willie stroked her arm gently, rising higher, going higher up the arm with each downward motion and return. Eventually, he lay down next to her.

Willie thought of how this lying together gazing into the distance was like it had been with him and Merle. When they were out at Big Mama's cabin after she had died, they would pass the long summer evenings gazing up at the sky and remarking on the stars. They counted breezes and tried to identify the sounds of night creatures. Merle would marvel if she were here now, listening to Georgetown in the black dark. If Merle could hear these sounds—like the *ooga, ooga* of passing automobiles or the *clip-clop* of horse hooves on the cobblestone streets—she wouldn't know where she was. As tired as they were, Merle and Willie would lie together and talk on into the night. And he could still remember exactly how Merle's voice sounded and how her breath smelled and how she looked to him. He could remember everything about Merle.

Alice stopped crying. As Willie stroked her, her breathing deepened and the nerves along her spine tingled slowly and gently. Her body remembered a certain pattern of response—his fingers on her arm and her nipples tingling and just beginning to harden. His breathing slipped a notch deeper—a reverberant interior rumbling. The reverberation traveled through him to her—through her flesh. Alice began to move softly against the mattress. Willie became urgent quickly. As soon as she quickened and gasped a little, he climbed over top of her and pushed her down into the mushy mattress. The mattress offered no resistance and swallowed them up in its softness.

When they were done and finished, they lay flat on their backs, eyes turned up to the ceiling. Everyday, ordinary tiredness drained out through their backs and was absorbed by the mattress. Neither was yet sleeping, but Willie knew he would soon be if he continued to lie still. He turned over onto his side and studied Alice's profile. He marveled at how still she was and knew that she was trying not to stir the bed. She was trying to let him know she didn't want any more lovemaking. But a man can always let his wants be known, and a good wife like Alice would let him do it as long as he was kind and gentle. He lifted his hand quietly and rubbed it over her body, more like a doctor checking for infirmity than a husband. He was surprised to realize that his wife did not feel like herself. Her skin seemed to have lost its soft springy cushion of flesh.

Lord knows she'd never be considered a fat woman, but Alice Bynum was no string bean either. She was a gently filled-out woman—pleasingly plump, as they say. But now, the pillow below her waist had disappeared. This was the spot he'd always loved to rest his head on when he'd done it and was glad. This spot was where he'd first felt the baby Clara quickening. This flesh had become tight and cold. His wife's soft, bouncy bottom was lost now, too, and was as flat as a pancake. She'd not been eating much, not resting much, and not sitting down enough. Alice's grief had her in a stir. The flesh on her upper arm—which used to pinch up teasingly when he played with her, coaxing a smile from her busy face—had melted away. Her full, dimpled face appeared to be getting thin, and even the places under her eyes were darkening. He thought that a better man would leave this woman to her grieving. But the touching and stroking had got his nature up again and he knew she wouldn't resist him. He went ahead and did it again, though a better man would have left this woman alone.

8

Losing a loved one, a family member, is like losing a tooth. After a while, those teeth remaining shift and lean and spread out to split the distance between themselves and the other teeth still left, trying to close up spaces. In this way, Johnnie Mae, her mama and papa, and her aunt Ina shifted themselves to close the spaces created by Clara's absence.

Johnnie Mae peered over the lip of the big pot at the back of the stove. A few minutes before, she had filled it with water. The water was still. She looked at it awhile and stepped back. Ever since she'd been helping her mama in the kitchen—which had been since the earliest time she could remember—she had never been allowed to stare at a pot on to boil without hearing the admonition "a watched pot never boils." The women of her family said it so regularly that Johnnie Mae thought it must be a sort of prayer needed to get the pot to boil—an assurance to the pot that no one would peep at it if it would just go ahead and boil. No one she knew had ever been watching at the very moment the water started boiling. One always had to turn away and give the pot its privacy. Often Johnnie Mae had seen her mama lost in reverie over a pot on the stove for rice or corn or bathwater or water for cleaning the face and hands or the hush-hush place between her legs. Mama would turn her head to some other task, and when she turned back, the water would be moving.

The yellow gingham-check curtains at the two windows looking out on the backyard rustled gently. It must have been human breath that stirred them since the late afternoon air was tight and unmoving.

Just back home from her Saturday half day's work, Alice sat wide-legged on a chair with a pan between her knees, catching string beans. A mound of slender, green fingers lay on the table. Alice slit the two sharp ends off with her nail and snapped each crisp bean into three pieces—some long ones into four. The odd one that would not snap was consigned to the waste.

"Cut that piece of fat meat in half, Johnnie. I want to have some for the black-eyes tomorrow." Alice didn't look up from her work; she spoke out of the corner of her consciousness that automatically gave out directives to her daughter. Her eyes remained on the mounting pile of beans in her lap.

Johnnie Mae picked up the thick, long-bladed knife they used for rough slicing, hacking apart chicken, and gutting. It was a heavy knife that had darkened with use and kept a musky odor of metal and blood. The wooden handle was buttery smooth and had been part of the collection of utensils, crockery, pots, and pans that Alice's mama had left when she died.

"Keep your mind on what you're doing. That thing will

take your fingers off," Alice said each time Johnnie Mae picked up the knife.

"Yes, ma'am," she answered. It was an absent answer. Johnnie Mae's ears conveyed her mother's directives to her hands automatically. Anyway, it was not as if she didn't know the steps for cooking string beans. Johnnie Mae knew her mama was just running through a mental checklist.

Alice had the habit of performing each task as if it were, in the time span she was engaged in it, the key to eternal salvation. An essential part of her existence depended on tasks being done well. Each chore was reduced to a series of efficient steps. "Go on and get your work done. Then, you'll have time to sit down" she was fond of saying. To Johnnie Mae there never seemed a time when all the work was done.

When Alice and Ina worked together in the kitchen, their hands crossed and recrossed each other while they chattered. Picking or prodding or slicing, they punctuated their tasks with laughter and tooth sucking and gossip. When she worked with Johnnie Mae, Alice didn't talk or laugh much. Her instructions were gentle commands, but there was no chatting. Part of her idea about work was setting an example for her daughter. Alice was forever saying that a child should keep her mouth closed and her mind on her work.

Clara's voice had been a constant chattering undercurrent in the kitchen. Clara always had questions and comments nobody was interested in. Now, without her, the kitchen was too quiet. Johnnie Mae wondered if her mother was saddened by the quiet, and she wished she could run off at the mouth like Clara used to. But she couldn't find a way to break the silence.

"Go out to the yard and rinse off these beans, Johnnie," Alice said as she rose and flicked bits of beans off her apron.

Out behind the house, Johnnie Mae held down the top of the hydrant and sloshed clear water over the string beans. She emptied the beans from pan to colander and back, rinsing out the grit that settled to the bottom of the pan.

After the third rinsing, the water ran clear. Johnnie Mae dumped the beans back into the pan, rinsed the colander, and held it above her head to see that no grit was left on it. She peered through the star-patterned holes punched into the enamel. Tiny rivulets of water trailed down Johnnie Mae's face and neck and onto her shoulders.

Johnnie Mae came back into the kitchen and leaned again over the lip of the pot on the stove. The water bubbles had grown, were bouncing off each other, and were becoming numerous. Bubbles traveled up a column from the center, then separated at the surface of the water and dispersed to the sides of the pot. The bubbling action of the water hypnotized her. Perhaps the admonition not to watch the pot boil was a way of keeping the boiler from being mesmerized by the water.

"Johnnie Mae, the water boiling?" Alice asked.

"Yes, ma'am," she answered without thinking. Her mind had slipped into a place where it was letting her arms and legs and mouth work for themselves smoothly and efficiently without any direct communication with her wandering mind. Her thoughts turned to Clara and what had happened to her.

The day had been hot—had been pancake-griddle hot. The water of the canal was heavy and stagnant. The water of the Potomac was not cooler, but it was swirling movement. All that day Johnnie Mae had thought about the pool on

Volta Place. It must be cool. Rat said they filled the pool with chunks of ice each day. It must be the coolest place in Georgetown except the icehouse.

Rat used to say that the people who ran the pool must come down to O Street early in the morning and get Mr. Blind John Ransome to cut them off a piece of ice that was a perfect big block. Mr. Blind John Ransome had the job of cutting off a chunk of whatever size piece of ice people asked for when they came to the Imperial Icehouse at 27th and O streets. Even though they could buy ice off the huckster wagon, many folks came themselves to the icehouse. Of course, it was a penny cheaper if you got it yourself and hauled it away. But a lot of people came especially to see Mr. Blind John Ransome do his cutting.

Mr. Blind John was always remarkably accurate and never cut off his own fingers or anyone else's. And no one ever disputed Mr. Blind John's reckoning. He held his chin pitched higher than most people and laughed along with each person who came in saying, "John, you got the coolest job there is!"

Rat said, on that day as they left Aunt Ina's after dinner and napping, that Mr. Blind John Ransome would admit it if the people from the pool bought their ice from him. She said they should go past his stall in the icehouse and ask him. But Johnnie Mae had known that Rat would never ask Mr. Blind John any questions. She'd been scared of him. She'd hardly ever speak up to ask him to cut a nickel's or a dime's worth of ice. Clara only liked to stand around in the crowd of small children Mr. Blind John called "little shavers." The little shavers would gather around him and stare at Mr. Blind John using his ice ax to hack away at the big blocks of ice. Rich people would get Mr. Blind John to carve figures like horseshoes or ribbon bows out of the ice blocks for their parties. It was an added attraction that the ice carvings were done by a blind man. Mama called him a real character and Papa said watching him was better than the vaudeville show.

The string beans Johnnie Mae poured into the boiling water came alive as they touched the water. They wriggled like garter snakes. Her eyes stayed on them as they hit bottom then floated to the top. A foamy substance bubbled on the surface of the water and Johnnie Mae reached for a slotted spoon to skim it from the pot. As she stared down into the pot, something more brown than green seemed to emerge from the steam clouds.

Nervously Johnnie Mae skimmed the foam, afraid that her mother would see the brown stuff continuing to rise to the surface and think she had not rinsed the string beans properly. The fat meat with its thick, tan backside bobbed up and down in the pot. From the center of the cauldron, a mass seemed to form. It appeared to come together in the shape of a heart, disperse like a cloud, and then reformulate into a solid mass. It seemed to come together this time as a heart-shape face with amused eyes. Slender green plaits emanated from its skull and framed the face. It was a laughing Medusa with wriggling green plaits. Through the bubbles rose two small hands. The fingers came toward Johnnie Mae as if to tickle. The expression on the face was a sly menace and the fingers drew back to clamp themselves under the arms of the figure. Giggling, the figure placed string beans inside each of its nostrils. It let out an uproarious snorting laugh. The heart-shape head ducked beneath the surface and boiling water closed over it.

Next, what looked to be a small brown hand with tiny bubbles around the wrist appeared in a cloud in the middle of the pot. Appearing and disappearing, the hand teased Johnnie Mae. She stared at it. There was no sound in the room but the bubbling laughter in the pot.

Johnnie Mae felt a hand suddenly grab at her shoulder and yank her back from the stove. The pot lost its balance and spilled the boiling contents. Johnnie Mae turned to look at her mother. Alice howled when hot droplets sprayed her chest. For a moment their eyes locked. Alice's mouth widened in pain. She grabbed Johnnie Mae's hand and looked at it. There were no burns! Alice's own arm was darkening rapidly and the pain broadsided her. Johnnie Mae's hand and arm felt cool.

Johnnie Mae's jaw dropped as she watched her mother run out back to the yard and put her arm in the rain barrel up to the shoulder. Tears rolled down Mama's face. The water in the barrel absorbed the heat from her arm and drew off some of the pain. But outside the water, the barely stirring air seared her arm. The arm quickly started to wrinkle, go pale, and blisters began to form in two places.

The suddenness of the pain's return brought Alice's mind back to what had happened. Johnnie Mae! She had been about to put her hand into the boiling pot of water! Johnnie Mae had stood there staring down into the water with a look of puzzlement. She had raised her arm and made as if to plunge it into the pot. Alice remembered feeling a jolt run through her. Every muscle in her body had rushed to help her child.

"Mama!" Johnnie Mae ran out to her mother. She still couldn't quite put together what had happened.

"Johnnie Mae! Girl, your hand's not burned, is it?"

"No, Mama."

"Lord, but . . ."

"Mama, your arm . . ."

"It's burning from the water. I reached in to keep you from getting burnt. What were you thinking about, girl?"

Johnnie Mae searched her mind for a plausible explanation. She tried to figure out the sequence of events. She had been looking at the bubbles. Had she meant to put her hand in the pot?

"I wasn't thinking of anything, Mama."

"Go quick and get your aunt Ina. Tell her I need her to see about this."

Johnnie Mae ran all the way. Passersby caught their breath, seeing the Bynum girl running. Before she reached Ina's door, Johnnie Mae started calling out, "Aunt Ina, Aunt Ina! Mama's arm is burnt."

Ina rose from her chair by the window. Still bent over from sitting, she peered out. Seeing Johnnie Mae, she called, "What is it, Johnnie?"

"Mama's hand is burnt. She wants you to come take a look at it."

Ella Bromsen appeared suddenly from behind the box elder tree. "What's happened, girl?" she said and reached out her arms to Johnnie Mae. The girl rushed toward her, but Ella stopped her at arm's length and grasped her wrists. She looked down at Johnnie Mae's hands, turning the palms up to study them.

Ina went back into the house to grab up her long-handled satchel. Johnnie Mae twisted her torso away from Ella and followed Ina with her eyes. Ella and Johnnie Mae looked for a minute like they were dancing. Johnnie Mae broke free when Ina came barreling out of the house and caught up with her, heading down Volta Place. Ella Bromsen called after, "I'll bring a poultice and a salve."

"Alice, girl, what happened?" Ina said, rushing toward her cousin sitting on the top step of the back porch. Alice's eyes were focused off into the distance. Her face wore an expression that Johnnie Mae had never seen before.

Blisters had formed on Alice's right hand, and several spots along the arm were deep red. She cupped the elbow of the burned limb and held it out toward Ina. Her face was tight and her forehead looked like a cloth being wrung out. Staring at Johnnie Mae, who was standing back near the azalea bush, Alice asked Ina, "She tell you what happened?"

"She said you pulled over the pot of boiling water. And your arm got burnt."

"Study this," Alice said, pointing to her arm. "I could have sworn she was getting ready to plunge her hand in that pot. What in the world were you grabbing for, Johnnie?"

Johnnie Mae didn't answer but slunk back into the lap of the bush. The women's stares froze her. Her mother's eyes asked for some bit of explanation. What had she done to her mother? She hadn't meant to cause this. How had she brought this on?

Ella came through the back gate into the Bynums' yard and saw Alice, Ina, and Johnnie Mae frozen in a tableau. Alice's arm was extended toward Ina, but both women's eyes were on Johnnie Mae. Ella carried a parcel containing three smaller bundles wrapped in Sears and Roebuck pages. "Miz Alice, let me tend to your burns now," she said quietly and walked ahead of the others into the house. She unwrapped the packages and laid out various roots and twigs on the kitchen table. "Y'all got a crock of cider?"

"Surely." Alice rose from the porch step and walked back into the kitchen. Ina followed and patted Alice on her back and led her to a chair.

"Johnnie Mae, won't you get your mama a cup of cider?" Miss Ella assumed command with her low-pitched, steady voice.

"Yes, ma'am," the girl answered.

With a small razor, Miss Ella sliced the green skin off both sides of a plant and placed slithery lengths over the blisters and red places on Alice's arm. "This will draw the heat off," she explained.

Alice shook her head like she was trying to rearrange her thoughts. "What you make of that?" she said, her words hissing out from between clamped teeth. Without answering, Ina looked around the room, as if some explanation might be lurking in the corners or behind the cupboards.

When Johnnie Mae returned with the cup of cider, Miss Ella Bromsen was mixing the contents of her packets together. She said, "Miz Alice, you quieten your fears. We'll take care of this." She dipped out a bit of the boiling water that had not spilled and moistened her herbs. "Johnnie Mae, get me some lard the size of an egg," she said, pouring off the water. "Put it there." Her pointing finger was a golden brown color and Johnnie Mae saw that she had a ring of what looked like woven twigs wound around it.

Ella folded the lard into the herb mixture to form a smooth, greenish brown salve. She removed the strips of the plant and spread the salve on Alice's arm with her fingers. Unwrapping the last packet, she drew out a long roll of cheesecloth and a ball of a thin, lacy-looking material.

Ina came up behind Ella and looked over her shoulder. "What all is that, Ella?" she asked. "That looks like a spider's web."

Ella very gently unfolded the web, raised it to the level of her face, and muttered words while gazing through it. She then lay the web over Alice's burns. "Yes, ma'am," she answered. "This is the web of a granny spider. It'll heal a burn before you know it."

Alice and Ina exchanged skeptical looks while Ella worked. Johnnie Mae marveled at Miss Ella. Miss Ella Bromsen was as unusual a person as had ever drawn a breath.

She finished dressing Alice's burns by wrappng her arm with cheesecloth. "Thank you, Ella, it does feel cooler," Alice said politely with a questioning look. "What all was that you put on me?"

"Just a salve made from plants. My daddy taught me."

While Ella collected her herbs and carefully rewrapped them into her satchel, Ina started to drain off the remaining string beans in the pot. "Johnnie Mae, go about gathering up those beans from the floor," she commanded the girl, afraid that her idleness might set something else in motion.

Ella Bromsen stopped Ina as she tipped the pot over a colander. "Let's draw off a cup of that water to take auguries," she said. Ina opened her mouth to question the idea of water reading, but Ella took the pot from her decisively and poured out a cup of water.

Ella took the cup in her left hand and swirled it counterclockwise. Johnnie Mae's eyes followed the swirling cup. Ella reached out and drew Johnnie Mae to her side without taking her eyes from the cup. Johnnie Mae looked down into the cup and then up into Miss Ella Bromsen's face. She saw the yellow flecks that sometimes came into Miss Ella's eyes. Aunt Ina said Miss Ella Bromsen had the cat's eye. Johnnie Mae didn't know what having the cat's eye meant, but it was in the category of things that were talked about in husky whispers—the subjects that had to do with your "pocketbook" or your bosoms or bathtub whiskey or anything to do with men and women.

Miss Ella's right palm was cool when she touched the side of Johnnie Mae's face. She grasped the girl's elbow and slid her palm down to take Johnnie Mae's hand in hers. "What did you see in that water, Johnnie?" Ella's voice was sweetly coaxing. "Did you see something in the water?"

Surely they didn't actually want to hear about what she'd seen. It was Clara—pure and simple. There was a face in the boiling pot and it was Clara's face. Johnnie Mae's mouth got dry, then moisture flooded into it and set her head and stomach whirling. Heat started traveling up her body, and she thought that it was Miss Ella's palm heating her body. Miss Ella's fragrance started to overwhelm her, too—a fragrance or blend of fragrances that was hard to separate out. Miss Ella Bromsen—everyone who ever got close to her said it—didn't smell like other people. She smelled sweeter and stronger and odder, and, in the kitchen, cloying.

"Nothing," Johnnie Mae said. "I didn't see anything." She wanted to sit down. She wanted to say the right thing and sit down. The aroma of Miss Ella and Aunt Ina's nervousness and her mother's fear and annoyance pressed in on Johnnie Mae.

Alice broke into the dizziness. "Why'd you go to put your arm in? You were reaching for something! You lose your sense? Getting ready to put your arm in boiling water? You scared the life out of me!"

"It could've been some evil thing that made her do that," Ina said. She came around behind Johnnie Mae and pushed down on the girl's shoulders. "Sit down, Johnnie Mae. What did you see in that water?"

"Yes, it could have been some evil thing," Ella put in.

"Now wait a minute! I keep a Christian home. I don't believe in hoodoo and other things." Alice roused up in alarm.

"Miss Alice, I meant no harm. I'm a Christian woman myself. But I believe that water still has a grip on her."

Ina cut back in, her eyes as round as dollars. "She's got red Indian blood, Alice. That's the reason Ella knows all the roots and herbs. And as a matter of fact . . ." Aunt Ina drew up her lips and completed the sentence with her eyes.

"Ina Mae, don't run off at the mouth," Alice countered, warning her cousin with her eyes and pursed-up lips. "I don't bring hoodoo in my house. You know that."

"It's not hoodoo. It's common, backcountry wisdom. She don't talk much about it — that's red Indian for you right there. You know how closemouthed they are." Ina sent Alice another knowing glance and Alice rolled her eyes and twisted her mouth.

"It ought not to still have a pull on her, but . . . I say you should keep her away from all water." Ella's face glowed as she spoke.

"What about bathing?" Alice asked.

"Don't put any part of her down in the water. Not until this grip loosens."

The river water did have a grip on Johnnie Mae. It was not grasping fingers around her neck or something holding her in a vise. It was inside her. It was coursing through her veins and her vitals. When she had dived and dived trying to pull Clara up to the surface, large amounts of the river water had got in her lungs and stomach. The water had gushed through her sinuses, leaving a recollection at the back of her throat. A recollection of the banks it flowed past—fertile, self-satisfied, green countryside and troublesome, tangled, brackish banks. Johnnie Mae still tasted the water. At odd times the taste broke through to her consciousness and brought Clara back briefly. The alchemy of smell and taste created a picture of Clara astride a dull green horse. The horse reared up and, laughing, Clara held its reins.

"Is she regular? Has she been regular lately?" Ina piped up, suddenly thinking that there might be a simpler explanation for the girl's behavior. "Johnnie Mae, you regular?"

The former Carolinians believed firmly that most of what bothered folks could be traced to what they'd eaten or drunk. And if they could flush their bodies of the poison that had congealed in their vitals, they could relieve most ailments of the body, mind, or spirit. Thus Alice and Ina had a firm belief in the efficacy of laxatives.

Johnnie Mae felt herself shrinking in this company. For a few moments, she had been a woman—nearly—a grown woman like the others. But Aunt Ina had managed to reduce her to a baby again. Johnnie Mae didn't want to answer the question but her mother's eyes demanded it.

"Yes, ma'am," she whispered.

Satisfied, the three turned back to their conversation. Johnnie Mae listened. Miss Ella talked about elements and putting the grip on a person. How on earth did this apply to Johnnie Mae? She wasn't frightened of water. She hadn't been gripped by anything. In fact, it was she who'd wanted to grip the small brown hand. She had tried to reach for it in the steam and had brought away nothing. Maybe if Mama hadn't grabbed her away, she might have touched the little hand. Maybe the hand still waited for her. She knew she dared not go over and look into the now empty pot on the back of the stove. Besides, though absorbed in their talk of the mysterious goings-on and the elements and juju and trying to top each other claiming Christian piety, Aunt Ina, Mama, and Miss Ella took turns looking over at her.

Miss Ella told Alice and Ina that there weren't any whiteman doctors back up-country where she was raised. All the healing they did was with the plants and trees. Miss Ella's papa, Mr. Butter Bromsen, had been a root doctor up-country. Mr. Butter was nearly ninety now. He'd spent his first twenty years in slavery, and the next ten years before the war was over he was up-country with the People. He learnt all he knew about healing and root doctoring from the People, the Cherokee and Creek and others who lived up-country. Mr. Butter was blind now. Miss Ella said that he probably could cure himself of blindness, but he said he was tired of looking now anyhow. Miss Ella said she was a child of her papa's old age so she was determined to take in all he knew.

Johnnie Mae stood against the wall, listening. Suddenly Ina turned and asked, "Johnnie, have you been dreaming about water?"

"No, ma'am. I haven't," she answered.

Ina asked. "Ella, you have something to take for the irregularity?"

"Yes, ma'am. It's best to drink yarrow tea. You'll be regular as clockwork by the morning."

9

Pearl Miller did not arrive in the sixth-grade classroom on the first day of the school year in September 1928. She didn't arrive until ten days after the first day. By that time, all the seats were assigned and everybody had staked out a clique to gossip with. Before Pearl arrived, there had been only two new faces. One was a boy whose cousin was already in the class and the other was a tiny little girl from across the bridge. This new girl, called Dumpling, lived in the shantytown on the Virginia side of Key Bridge and arrived at school with a strand of sweat beads on her forehead from the long walk.

On school mornings, Georgetown children were pushed out of their front doors when the swarm of other school-bound youngsters appeared in their block. The eight of ten Wardleys who were still school age and lived all the way west near Georgetown University started out for school early. At each block children joined the eastward throng and kept with it until they got to school. Many of the bigger children kept on going east out of Georgetown, on across into Washington city, to go to the Armstrong high school or the prestigious M Street school. Children who lived east of Wisconsin Avenue amassed at each block, too, and proceeded in a throng west to Wormley School. Excited chattering and thundering brogans signaled this throng of children wearing runover, dog-eared leather shoes. Some children's feet pulled out of their shoes with every step. Some children's shoes were so tight that their toes curled under and came to rest on top of neighbor toes. Some of the ill-fitting shoes were stuffed with newspapers. Some had cardboard soles, causing children to leave pieces of cardboard all along the route. Early or persistent or lucky mothers found soft leather lace-up shoes with the smooth soles of the hardly worn—and no scuffs—at the church rummage sales or got them from the white folks they worked for. Lexter Gorson, the shoe-shine man, was swamped just before school started. He rehabilitated the rummage and hand-me-down shoes by putting a high gloss on them. The recently arrived country folk quickly yielded to the decorum of the city: Shoes on the feet of all schoolchildren. All school-age children must go to school.

Because Johnnie Mae was one of the tallest girls in the class, she was assigned a seat in the back of the classroom, near a window. Lula Lavery, who'd been Johnnie Mae's best friend the previous year, was seated nearer the middle of the room. She was mad not to be closer to Johnnie Mae and madder still that Johnnie Mae seemed unconcerned about their seat assignments. Lula turned around in her chair when all were seated and waved to Johnnie Mae. Johnnie Mae only stared back blankly.

Though Pearl Miller was of medium height and actually a

hair shorter than the girl seated in front of her, she was told by the teacher, Miss Elizabeth Boston, to sit across the aisle from Johnnie Mae Bynum.

Sit was all Pearl did the first week. She sat bolt upright in her chair and placed her body directly behind the girl in front of her. She did not speak one word to anyone. She did not even answer when her name was called in the roll by Miss Boston. Johnnie Mae glanced sideways at Pearl on each of these mornings, wondering at the stock-still girl. Pearl reminded her of a field rabbit facing down a dog; hands folded on the desk, legs clamped together, head straight up on her neck, she stared directly in front of her. When the class went into the school yard for recess, Pearl walked behind Mildred Gloe. She stood alone next to a bush and spoke to no one. Johnnie Mae's three friends from the river — Lula Lavery, Hannah Jackson, and Sarey Tyler — clustered around her in a display of compassion. Johnnie Mae, however, had little to say to them and did not smile.

"Pearl Miller," Miss Boston trilled. Pearl shifted in her seat but did not open her mouth. Johnnie Mae looked at her out of the corner of her eye.

"Here," Johnnie Mae said. Miss Boston raised her eyes from the seating plan and wrinkled her forehead.

"Who said that, please?" she asked sharply.

Johnnie Mae raised her hand tentatively and said, "Ma'am?"

"Why are you answering for Pearl Miller, please?"

"She's here, but she won't answer," Johnnie Mae replied. As her voice trailed off, she glanced at Pearl.

"Pearl Miller, stand up please," Miss Boston demanded.

The half a minute or so it took Pearl to stand seemed like half an hour. Each child in the classroom turned completely around to stare. A few boys and girls snickered. Nothing Pearl had done or dreamed of doing had ever drawn so much attention to herself. The scrutiny of the class was sizzlingly painful. Pearl felt her skin broiling under their stares.

Pearl Miller was dark black with smooth, glossy skin and medium brown eyes. She wore her hair cornrowed tightly, and the neat geometric pattern of the cornrows could be traced on the top of her bowed head.

"Miss Miller," said Miss Boston, "when you are in attendance at this school you are to answer when the roll is called. Do you understand?"

The thought hit Johnnie Mae that the girl was a mute at exactly the moment Pearl opened her lips a crack to whisper, "Yes, ma'am."

Miss Boston's patience was fraying rapidly. If there was one thing she couldn't abide, it was a weak, mealymouthed response. "Once again, Miss Miller, with more vigor."

The sound that next came out of Pearl was closer to a shriek. No one would have guessed there was that much wind in the girl. The class guffawed, especially the boys, who started up grunting like pigs.

For Elizabeth Boston, the daughter of a cook and a Pullman porter, the Eleventh Commandment was "Thou shalt maintain decorum." A genuinely intelligent person with a sincere desire to impart knowledge, Miss Boston was also keenly concerned that her students learn the proper way to behave. Their learning to read and to figure were no more important, in her eyes, than their learning to control their urges to laugh, spit, shout, or belch. Pearl's outburst caused the teacher's slim lips to become a straight line. "Next time something above a whisper, something below a bellow, Miss Miller. Please take your seat."

Pearl sat down stiffly and buried her head on her desk. She turned her head once to the left to stare with a cold hatred at Johnnie Mae, then quickly turned her face away when Johnnie Mae looked back. She kept her head down the rest of the morning and slipped a thumb into her mouth after everyone's attention had finally turned toward the lessons.

Besides sucking her thumb the way Clara used to do, Pearl had the same scared-rabbit look that Clara had had. Watching her sent a shower of recollections down on Johnnie Mae. For the rest of the morning her mind raced up and down the streets of Georgetown with the ghost of Clara. The Clara in her mind chattered and bent over to pick up blue glass medicine vials like they used to. Gathering discarded glass on the streets and in underbrush was the Bynum girls' first job. They had made their spending money in this way. Clara had been good at spotting pieces of glass.

This daydream was much like Johnnie Mae's nightly dreams. Strong, fragrant, tactile dreams full of colors and sounds—full of Clara. There was a carefree abandon about the dream Clara that was different from the flesh and blood, used-to-be-earthbound Clara. The dream Clara kicked her feet up nearly to her waist when she skipped along the open field. She threw her head back and giggled with an energy that was rare for the real Clara. But this girl of the dreams was Clara for sure. She had Clara's hair, smelling like sweat and pomade. The back of her neck bore a greasy line at the end of a humid afternoon like Clara's. The girl's left front tooth was missing like Clara's. She imagined the girl's hand was warm and moist, the fingers wiggling like worms in Johnnie Mae's palm, like Clara's.

When Johnnie Mae's mind returned to the classroom, she considered that the recent appearance of Pearl Miller and her resemblance to Clara were not accidental. Maybe Pearl was the ghost of Clara come back to visit. Perhaps this was why Pearl was afraid to draw attention to herself. Perhaps a ghost can't do what it's supposed to do if you pay it too much mind. Johnnie Mae resolved to wait, stand back, and watch this new girl. Maybe, if not agitated by too much notice, the ghost would reveal itself as Clara.

Miss Boston had put Pearl Miller next to Johnnie Mae, of all the people in the classroom. Was there a plan here? Church folks were always fond of speaking about God's plan. Well, it could be that this was a perfect example. But there was a disturbing thought that Johnnie Mae could never quite sort out. Were haints and ghosts and spirits of the dead sent from God, or were they agents of the Devil? And if they were agents of the Devil, wasn't it dangerous to have anything to do with them? Pearl didn't look like an agent of the Devil. But she did have Clara's demeanor and posture of neediness.

Some weeks went by without a word from Pearl but "yes, ma'am" when her name was called. Each day she was neatly dressed and her hair was tightly cornrowed with oil glistening in the parts. She sat in her scared-rabbit posture and slipped her thumb in her mouth from time to time. Johnnie Mae observed her patiently. Content to bide her time, she waited to see what the haint—for she truly believed now that Pearl was a haint, a bona fide haint—would do.

Pearl Miller's reputation as a crybaby was enhanced nearly every day by a fit of weeping during recess. She stubbornly refused to socialize with any of the other students, even after a delegation of girls approached her. They ringed around her, chattering and trying to pull her into a game of hopscotch or Miss Mary Mack, Mack, Mack. Pearl looked down at her toes and tried not to stick her thumb in her mouth. After a few attempts to draw her out, the delegation gave up and started calling her Sugar Tit. Johnnie Mae stood back from all of this, watching and waiting.

Boys like to pinch and pluck a target and draw their victim into full-scale conflict. They lose interest quickly, though, if all the victim does is stand and cry. Girls like to gang up on a victim too, but they enjoy it most if the victim never fights back but just keeps on crying and meekly submitting to torture. So among the girls in the sixth-grade class, it got to be a good game to figure out ways to make Pearl Miller cry.

At the southernmost end of the recess yard, the roots of an aged tree had rearranged a section of the hastily constructed outer stone wall around the school property. The tree's upper branches spread halfway across the yard and provided shade to three quarters of it. At its base, the tree was split into two large sections, with ugly irregular roots running outward above the ground. The strong lower branches had for years, even before the school was built, been used as a sitting place. Smack in the center of the tree's broad trunk was a knothole bigger than a human head. This knothole had been tarred over repeatedly but the tree had simply kept metamorphosing until it was difficult to know what material was tree and what man-made. Growing in the center of the knothole was a toadstool as big as a king-size flapjack, tan-colored and terraced.

Mildred Gloe told everyone that her mother said toadstools were poisonous. So she dared each girl in the class to lick the toadstool at the center of the knothole. Each girl stepped up to the knothole, made an elaborate display of facial contortions, and stuck her tongue out. Most missed the toadstool by a mile but passed muster for at least marching up and aiming their face in its direction. Johnnie Mae, not believing that any toadstool was poisonous, stepped up and raked her tongue across it real good. She didn't see the point in it, though. What could licking a toadstool prove?

After everyone else had had a turn, Pearl Miller still stood back. Mildred and some others decided that they would have to force Pearl to lick the toadstool. With some ceremony two girls grasped Pearl under the arms and led her to the knothole. To the delight of her torturers, Pearl started to cry buckets. She stood in front of the tree looking miserable, tears streaming down her face. A chant of "Lick it, lick it!" started and grew loud.

Johnnie Mae had trouble deciding who was silliest: Mildred and the other tormentors or the worthless crybaby Pearl Miller. Just as Mildred Gloe began to push Pearl's head toward the hole, Johnnie Mae churned her way through the crowd, put her arm around Pearl's shoulder, and pulled the pitiful, crying girl away from the group. For good measure, she socked Mildred Gloe in the middle of her back. Mildred, a garden-variety bully, had no comeback to this.

Like Pearl, Sarey Tyler was regularly teased and taunted too. But she defied her torturers. Though often ridiculed about her unkempt hair, Sarey didn't shed a single tear. She simply rolled her eyes and tossed her shoulders when they said her head looked like a rat's nest.

Sarey's yellow skin would have given her high status among the girls, but her head of hair diminished its value. "That's a whole lot of yellow gone to waste" is what Tiny Sham's mother said about Sarey. And Tiny repeated it to any and everybody in the school yard.

This spiteful comment didn't particularly faze Sarey. She had heard it before—and worse. Folks who knew her mother rarely hid their surprise when they saw Sarey's hair. Sarey, the daughter of a light, bright, damn-near-white woman with straight, silky hair, had a headful of cockleburs and tangles she'd inherited from her father. It was a shame! It was tragic! It was the most unfortunate set of circumstances imaginable!

Looking at the top of Pearl Miller's braided head was a fascinating exercise when Miss Boston was drilling the new spelling words or rhythmically beating out the times tables on the edge of her desk. Some days the braids started around Pearl's head in a spiral that culminated in a neatly twisted topknot. Other days her hair was parted down the exact middle of her head with the cornrows proceeding down the sides, linking up along the circumference and ending in plaits at the back.

One afternoon during spelling lessons, Johnnie Mae noticed that one of the braids at the back of Pearl's head had begun to creep loose. The rubber band, twisted at its end, had fallen onto the collar of Pearl's blouse. All the rest of her hair remained perfectly neat. Pearl's hair reminded Johnnie Mae of Clara's hair: bushy, and brushed and combed and twisted into braids that only eternal vigilance prevented from coming loose all day. The whole afternoon Johnnie Mae stared at the loosened braid on Pearl's head.

When the class rose and gathered their papers at the end of the day, Johnnie Mae felt an impulse to touch the bushy, loosened plait on Pearl's head. Clara's plaits had been Johnnie Mae's obligation. In fact, of all the duties she had helping her mother with "the baby," the plaiting had been the most pleasurable. Having the authority to pull Clara's head back firmly and order her to hold still was part of Johnnie Mae's big-sister prerogative. Brushing the hair back from Clara's hairline, sectioning it, braiding overhand, daubing oil in the parts and along the hairline, massaging it in to shine, attaching a ribbon for Sunday or a rubber band for everyday, gave Johnnie Mae a feeling of being the boss. Clara's mouth would turn down in a pout until Johnnie Mae spun her around and demanded that she look at herself and see what a beautiful, neat job had been done. Days when she was in a magnanimous mood, Johnnie Mae would let Clara climb a box behind her and brush and comb her own hair, which was long and like the bristles on a stiff paintbrush. Mama and Aunt Ina said it was Indian hair— a strong, energetic head of hair that flattened along her head when Indian sage pomade was vigorously brushed into it.

Johnnie Mae put her hand gently on Pearl's collar. "You're losing your rubber band," she said.

Pearl jumped at the touch and snapped her head around. She felt along her collar anxiously.

"Your plait came loose. Let me fix it for you," Johnnie Mae said with gentle authority. The voice she used was one she'd used with Clara. All the other students pushed past Johnnie Mae and Pearl, who stood frozen, staring at each other in the aisle. Pearl finally turned obediently, and Johnnie Mae began plaiting the loose braid by first unraveling it further, then making it back up to match the other. She finished plaiting and reattached the rubber band at the end of the braid. Pearl faced Johnnie Mae and lifted her chin farther than Johnnie Mae had ever seen her do. She said, with a small smile, "Thank you. Thanking you warmly." The girl sounded curiously like an old woman, which made Johnnie Mae chuckle. But the voice Pearl now used was friendly.

10

As Halloween approached, Johnnie Mae was sure her bona fide haint, Pearl Miller, would reveal herself. She made up her mind to keep an eye on Pearl to see how a haint might act on Halloween. Except that she was tiresomely, unnaturally timid, Pearl seemed like anybody else. But on Halloween night, something might happen that would reveal her true nature.

It occurred to Johnnie Mae that a real spirit might not come out on such an obvious night as Halloween. Perhaps she had to lay low with all of the foolishness going on. This didn't seem to jibe, though, with Pearl's timidity, or even Clara's. If Pearl was the spirit of Clara come again she ought to act pretty much like the real Clara. And Clara was not cunning. Clara loved Halloween. Clara had stuck to Johnnie Mae like glue as they roamed with the other children through the streets of Georgetown. And Johnnie Mae had held tight to Clara's hand because, in all the hoopla and confusion, it would have been easy for a little girl like Clara to get lost. Of course, Johnnie Mae didn't know much about the dead—how they behaved, if they "behaved" at all. Were they just gone like a puff of smoke, or did they keep close by, watching, looking, still feeling for the folks left behind?

Pearl had stared blankly at Johnnie Mae when she asked her what costume she'd be wearing. Then Johnnie Mae took a turn at being surprised. Where could this girl be from where they didn't dress up for Halloween? But in all of the laughing and giggling and apples and rock candy of the evening, Pearl was nearly forgotten. Johnnie Mae didn't see her after school let out. She wasn't among any of the groups that gathered at houses or fell in together at the street corners. She didn't come to the community house to bob for apples and hear Reverend Jeter tell ghost stories.

When Johnnie Mae paraded herself dressed in the baby girl's christening gown she'd cajoled Aunt Ina to sew, Mama and Papa caught their breath. It was a short white gown trimmed with eyelet lace around the hem, neck, and sleeves. There was a baby's bonnet trimmed with lace and tied with a satin bow. Johnnie Mae skipped around in front of the stove with her slim, coltish, cinnamon-stick legs and rouge smeared on her cheeks. They were delighted for a brief moment that childlike frolicksomeness had returned to their house.

Alice's Halloween face was drawn and tearful. She slumped with a cup of sugary coffee at the kitchen table after Johnnie Mae left to join a group of schoolmates. Though it was soon clear that trick-or-treaters were avoiding the Bynum house, Willie walked up and down peeping out of the windows, on the lookout in case a costumed child stumbled up the steps to ask for candy. The Bynum house was still too full of Clara to tempt the uneasy sanctity of Halloween. Poking fun at spirits didn't seem safe.

The Bynums were probably the only people in Georgetown not promenading down M Street. Maybe in some other cities or towns Halloween was a holiday for children only, but Georgetowners of every age costumed themselves and walked up and down the M Street thoroughfare. A great many folks, big and little, smeared charcoal or talcum on their faces and stuck their heads through holes in old sheets. Lexter Gorson stood on his regular shoe-shine corner with the battered silk top hat he wore every year. Across his mouth he wore a red bandanna.

The rich people's Halloween was a night of fancy parties and carriages drawn by horses with plumed headdresses. The Chesters up on R Street were throwing their usual big Colonial costume ball and had hired Snow Simpson to wear a white powdered wig, a silk jacket, and knickers of robin's-egg blue. He stood on the portico bowing the guests through the house's grand columns and into the vestibule. Knots of costumed colored children paused on the south side of the street and peeped through the doors and windows to glimpse the guests and the massive gold-and-crystal chandelier in the foyer. Johnnie Mae and the others in her group laughed at Snow from across the street on their way to the cemetery. Duck Dudley lobbed crab apples at Snow's wig. The first crab apple hit the center of the oak door, but the second caught Snow upside his head and knocked the powdered wig sideways. The group ran off laughing at Snow trying to settle the thing back on his coal-black head.

It had been the tradition from as far back as any of the families could remember that on Halloween the costumed children trooped up to the Mount Zion cemetery to tempt fate by running and hollering like banshees among the oldest headstones. Johnnie Mae went along with the group and was fully in the cemetery before she remembered that Clara was now among the ones six feet under—the bone folks—the inhabitants of the boneyard. Clara was one of the very ones the Halloween children were defying and fooling with their oversize old-lady hats. Mabel Dockery had stuffed one of her mama's old housedresses with pillows in the front and was running and dodging behind the bigger headstones. She had put talcum powder on her face in a haphazard fashion and it picked up the scant light from the torches that an earlier group had stuck in the ground.

Press Parker stood with his back against a tree that had been propping people up since before the Flood. He watched as he did on every Halloween to see that none of the headstones got toppled in all the chasing and hoo-rawing. He kept an eye on the torches and the little ones so that no one crawled into a crypt playing hide-and-seek and got suffocated like the little Henderson baby had back in '09.

Press was sure the bones didn't mind some company one day a year. They hadn't heard the sound of children's feet slapping on top of their heads since last Halloween. Most of the children came to the cemetery with their folks on Decoration Day, when the adults came to clean up the graves and slap backs and tip hats. But on Decoration Day, the children were shushed up and made to behave and set to raking and pulling weeds or carrying water. And even if a few children had been here accompanying a new dead person—like Johnnie Mae Bynum—they'd have been walking solemnly with lead in their heels. This would make a heartbreaking, thudding sound on top of the bones' heads. A sound to make the dead sad and make them try to tote up the number of eyes they'd made to cry. No, most of the bones surely welcomed the children's lighthearted steps on Halloween. A happy sound to remember until the next year.

The grounds of the Mount Zion cemetery were snaggled with small, square, granite headstones. Some had winged baby angels growing out of their corners, the bent-headed angels looking lovingly down toward names: MOTHER ANNIE DIGGS; BELOVED WIFE AND MOTHER, BESSIE DINAH TINSDALE; HIRAM HENDERSON. Plenty of the stones had gone lopsided in the mushy earth.

IN MEMORIAM
ELLA
Beloved daughter of
Henry and Mary J. Logan.
DIED JULY 1, 1877
AGED 32 YEARS

She resteth well
No tear is on her cheek
No sighs her bosom swells.

Ornamental iron fences squared off the plots of wealthy bones, white and black. Some folks laid down in the easternmost portion of the cemetery had been there since the Female Union Band collected funds in the last century to purchase plots guaranteeing a resting place for every freed black in Georgetown. Here most of the markers were wormholed wood or a soft, mealy type of stone. Still, the ground around them was neatly swept and weeded every Decoration Day.

In the part still called by some of the oldsters the old

Methodist burying ground, slave owners and their bondspersons lay. They'd been buried so long that they were now jumbled together in the shifting earth.

Jabboe Coleman, dressed like a pirate, popped his head out from behind a granite obelisk that was chiseled with the name of a family whom no one could now recall. The raging carpet of English ivy had not yet died back from its summer onslaught and it tangled the children's legs, adding to the fun of "Look out! The haints have got you!"

Press Parker was startled when he saw Johnnie Mae Bynum cavorting with the rest wearing an outfit done to look like a little baby's. She was not the only one with that type of costume. A few others wore christening gowns and baby bonnets, too, and on them the incongruity caused the expected laughter. But Johnnie Mae's costume looked too much like the gown they'd laid out Clara in. As she lay in her coffin, Clara's small face had recovered somewhat. It was finally warm brown and soft like jelly, with all the swollen, bruised bigness sunk away. Press had studied her as he polished the casket. There was no expression on her face. If, as some believe, the sins of the dead rise to the surface and leave an imprint on the visage documenting travails and opprobrium, then Clara Bynum died without a sin on her soul and no sorrow or its memory. There was neither a horrified expression nor a puzzled one.

The purpose of death changed then in Press's mind. He realized only when he stopped thinking it that he had long considered death to be God's punishment for transgressions. Even the welcome deaths of the grans and granpops were punishments in not coming till they'd suffered just as much as they were due on account. And to the saintly ones who suffered grave, disfiguring illnesses and bravely told God they'd suffer on, death came when it came and cut short their penance. Always, death was God's weapon to say, "That's enough. This much and no more." But Clara's death shook Press's certainty, and he questioned the purpose of death. Because surely it was not Clara's time. This was not on the books. There was no account. This was a false tally. This was cheating. This was Father God caught cheating. And if Father God had cheated Clara—who couldn't have knowingly sinned against him—or if he had just got tired of caring about her, how much more tired would he be of tending to Press? And it's a shaky thing to wonder if Father God has got tired of you. Because who is to know when the time has come when Father God is through with worrying about you and calls you home?

No, Father God had had his thumb on the scale this time. He had not given what was due. He had made Clara's parents believe they were getting a full measure and had shorted them instead. He had shorted the girl because life is a long thing, or ought to be, a billowing thing, a thing more than what Father God had given Clara. Clara! Clara! Clara! Exhorting in threes: one, then one higher, then come back—the wail by threes. He knew it. Had mourned his mama, his pap, sisters, brothers, half-sisters, lover women, little babies, Aunt Clea, Bo Romney, and others. By the threes—one, then one higher, then come back: unh, uh, unh.

Press Parker thought that Johnnie Mae Bynum might not even be thinking that her baby sister was buried here at Mount Zion. Maybe it wasn't at all clear to the youngsters whooping and chasing around in the graveyard that this was where the bones lived all of the year. This was their home.

Johnnie Mae had not been up here since the day they

buried Clara, and she couldn't be expected to remember much about that day. But maybe, Press thought, he ought to caution her. Her dead was too recently here for her to be chancing things by playing about in this place. Why in the world hadn't her people kept her at home tonight? Some people didn't have the sense God gave a rabbit.

Now he was confused. While ago he'd thought it was all right for the children to dance about playing tag among the headstones. Now, seeing Johnnie Mae, he wasn't so sure. What did the bones want? Did they want the playful company or did they want to lie in peace?

"Johnnie Mae, Johnnie Mae Bynum, go home now. Leave the boneyard to the bones. Go home now."

Johnnie Mae broke from the gaggle of costumed boys and girls and stared into Press Parker's face. Surely she had seen him since the day of the drowning, but seeing him now she couldn't recollect a meeting since that day.

> *Dry bones going to gather in the morning*
> *Come together and rise and shine*
> *Dry bones going to gather in the valley*
> *And some of those bones are mine.*
>
> *Some of those bones are my mother's bones*
> *Come together to rise and shine*
> *Some of those bones are my father's bones*
> *And some of those bones are mine.*

Had Press Parker actually spoken to her? Johnnie Mae wasn't sure. He no longer looked at her but at the other groups of children. He shifted a stick around in his mouth and gave no indication that he'd said anything to anyone. Johnnie

Mae left Mount Zion at the tail end of a group that was led by a boy with a hat made of cornstalks.

After a few blocks, she broke away from the group and walked to Pearl Miller's house. She approached the Millers' house on Dent Place warily, as if she expected haints to fly out from under the eaves or jump out from behind a bush. There appeared to be no lamps lit. A big tree on the sidewalk hid Johnnie Mae from the view of anybody in the house, in case Pearl and her mother were in there peeping out. Johnnie Mae craned her neck from behind the tree to see if a sliver of light could be seen beneath the drawn shades. There wasn't even a jack-o'-lantern on the porch to throw a creepy shadow. She stood there a full fifteen minutes staring at the dark house, the nippy night air creeping up her gown.

What about the swimming pool? Aunt Ina had said that the white people's swimming pool was built on hallowed ground. She said that it had been the very site of the old Presbyterian graveyard. She said that men who worked there—who'd turned over the ground—had found pieces of jewelry and gold teeth and such. And one of the men who had sold a gold crown he'd found had perished in a fire. Surely that's where some haints were. Why, Pearl Miller was probably up there dancing with other haints right this minute!

The acorn moon was high and round in the sky and illuminated the streets as Johnnie Mae headed toward the pool. Red cobblestones on Volta Place seemed silver-edged in the moonlight. Johnnie Mae walked past several groups of costumed children without greeting them, making her way briskly to the fence surrounding the pool. The aqua water had been drained and there was only the light blue tiled pit where the beautiful water had been. Leaves and debris lay flattened on the bottom of the pit. The shade trees leaned conspiratorially in toward the playground, blocking a clear view from the sidewalk. Johnnie Mae pressed her face against the diamond-shape holes in the fence, searching the area for the sight of Pearl Miller or perhaps Clara or some other haint cavorting. But the pool and surrounding playground were dead still.

Disappointed that she'd not been able to see any real ghosts roaming the streets, Johnnie Mae decided to walk back to Pearl Miller's house before going home. Maybe Pearl and her ghost confederates had been out when she had stopped by the first time? What about her mama? Was Pearl's mama a haint too? Johnnie Mae swung back toward Dent Place, ruminating on the question of whether ghosts had mamas and papas and whether they needed them and whether Clara now had a ghost family. The moon was still high and bright in the sky.

At the corner of 34th and Dent Johnnie Mae caught sight of a figure moving quickly toward her. The figure was hunched over but didn't seem to have on a costume. As the figure approached, Johnnie Mae's heart almost stopped in her chest. It was Pearl Miller moving furtively down the street! This looked like the certain proof that Pearl was a haint. Here she was skulking down the street like a thief on Halloween night.

As Pearl got closer, Johnnie Mae could hear that she was sniffling and that there was another sound — a mewling — that was coming from her vicinity.

"What you got there?" Johnnie Mae asked, trying to peer at the thing Pearl was hugging to her chest.

Pearl started at the sight of Johnnie Mae and drew her bundle under the thin coat she wore. "A kitty," she said in a voice that had little more gumption to it than the pitiful noises the thing she held next to her was making. The only young person out on Halloween night without a costume, Pearl had a thumb-suck demeanor, seemed to have shrunk from her usual size, and was making small squealing noises like a piglet. As soon as Johnnie Mae saw the crying kitten under Pearl's coat, she also caught a whiff of it. The smell was burned fur and burned flesh.

"What happened to it?"

Pearl Miller had never become entirely certain that Johnnie Mae Bynum meant her no harm. Sure, she had come to her rescue in the school yard. But she seemed motivated more by curiosity than a desire to be friendly. Pearl had a feeling that Johnnie Mae was studying her, trying to gain some knowledge of her. She wasn't sure that Johnnie Mae didn't have some cruel prank up her sleeve and was only waiting for a chance to spring it.

"Some children set it afire in the alley. It's burnt all up," Pearl wailed out loud. Johnnie Mae thought how different this wailing was from the usual sniffling that Pearl did in school.

"Why they do that?"

"They was just being mean." Though she didn't holler out loud, Pearl Miller was mad as a wet hen. Johnnie Mae could tell by the way her face was torn up that anger and indignation were liable to erupt from her like lava.

"Is it gonna die?" Johnnie Mae asked Pearl outright. The wailing intensified and Pearl backed away from Johnnie Mae as if she thought the girl intended to finish the kitten off. "You ought to take it to Miss Ella Bromsen on Volta Place, next door to my aunt Ina. She knows about fixing up burns. She fixed my mama's arm when it got burned."

Pearl weighed Johnnie Mae's advice for a moment, then followed behind her to Miss Ella's. Johnnie Mae led Pearl and the kitten, who continued mewing loudly and desperately, through all of her shortcuts, toward Volta Place. She shaved off some of the distance by cutting through backyards and skirting behind trees. Both girls scratched their ankles on bushes that grew along the footpath behind the Piggly-Wiggly store.

As usual Ina Carson was seated at the front window of her parlor looking out at passersby. Halloween night was particularly interesting and she had been handing out candy treats to every group of children that stopped by. She saw Johnnie Mae and Pearl coming down the block and thought to get up and get them the last of the cookies and two apples. But as they approached, Ina could tell that something was wrong and that they were not heading to her door. The girls walked straight past her door and went up on Miss Ella Bromsen's front porch.

Since Miss Ella Bromsen was generally thought to be a witch or a root woman or at the very least unusual, the front windows of her house had earlier been smeared with soap by roving tricksters. Johnnie Mae shook a bit and thought to call out for Aunt Ina at exactly the moment that both Aunt Ina's and Miss Ella Bromsen's front doors opened.

"What all is the matter, girl?" Aunt Ina asked, looking like an owl peeping out of her door, the size of her eyes magnified by her spectacles. In contrast, Miss Ella seemed calm. And her eyes, shaped more oval than round, had a dreamy quality.

"Pearl found this little cat that somebody set afire," Johnnie Mae answered. "Can you fix him, Miss Ella?"

"Lord have mercy! The things that people will do!" Aunt Ina exclaimed.

"Come to the back," Miss Ella said. She opened her front door wide, turned, and walked away. The house's interior was black dark. Johnnie Mae thought that Miss Ella must have been upstairs in bed because there seemed to be no lamp lit on the first floor. She couldn't remember if she'd seen any lamplight coming through the upstairs windows. Had Miss Ella been in the cellar stirring potions? Miss Ella lit a candle, and as she walked through the house she lit several other candles from the one she carried. Johnnie Mae followed her from candle to candle, pausing as Miss Ella did. As each candle illuminated the foyer, a corner of the parlor, another corner, then the hallway, then the kitchen, an ambiguous series of rooms was revealed. Pearl followed Johnnie Mae with the bundled-up, mewling cat. And Aunt Ina, drawing her wrapper close around her body, came over from next door.

Johnnie Mae wondered if the head cloth that Miss Ella had tied on her head was her Halloween costume, the usual thing she wore to bed, or some necessary uniform for her broom making and root doctoring. The shelves and windowsills in the kitchen were stocked with jars and tin cans, and Miss Ella moved quickly about the kitchen assembling her paraphernalia. She reached her hand in several tins and pulled out a portion of leaves or powder and shook these ingredients together in a bowl. Miss Ella's lips moved as she worked, though neither Pearl, Aunt Ina, nor Johnnie Mae could hear what she was saying. She quickly got a fire stirred up in the stove and put a pot of water on to boil.

In truth, the pitiful animal Pearl held under her wrapper appeared not to have much chance of survival. Miss Ella directed Pearl to uncover the animal and place him in the center of her kitchen table. Large patches of fur were completely burned away from the creature's back and head. The kitten trembled in the center of the table and didn't cease crying. Miss Ella daubed the burned places with wads of cotton dipped in tinctures from several bottles on her shelves. She took a box — one of many of various sizes that were stacked near her back door — filled it with cloths, and placed the animal in it. He continued making noises until she covered his small nose with cotton saturated with some substance from a small blue bottle. Miss Ella then made a poultice from her herbs and swaddled the poor thing in bandages soaked in the mixture.

The two girls and Ina watched Miss Ella work. Johnnie Mae stood at her right elbow and Pearl stood at her left. Aunt Ina, too, drew in close and peered over the woman's shoulder. Miss Ella didn't seem to have any oil lamps in her house so the only light in the room was from the still bright moonlight coming through the windows and the eight or ten candles she had lit and put about in corners. These candles threw up shadows against the walls, and the movement of Miss Ella's arms and the silhouette of her head cloth made her shadow look like a large bird's.

After she wrapped up the cat, Miss Ella put away her medicines. "It goes against common sense to prolong the suffering of a pitiful injured creature," she said. "God's creatures have their job to do and then they pass on. It's against God's plan for us to try to wring more out of them so they can be of service to us." Miss Ella looked sternly at Pearl's tear-streaked face and Johnnie Mae's dry-eyed, inquiring visage. "Howsomever, a cat is a peculiar creature. A cat's got nine lives, and a root doctor has got a special charge to try to save a cat. Because a cat will take up your bond if it should ever come to that. And the old people say that a person would do well to save a cat's life when they're young 'cause a cat won't forget and it'll remember your good deed. Because it's always good for your soul and for your people if a cat walks across your final resting place, and double good luck if that cat stops to paw at the dirt covering you, and triple good luck if the animal makes water over your head." Miss Ella smiled at the two girls.

Pearl smiled wanly back at Miss Ella. And despite its tentativeness, this smile was more than she gave Johnnie Mae. Pearl still looked nervously at her classmate out of the corner of her eye.

Observing the furtive expression on Pearl's face, Johnnie Mae got to thinking that maybe Miss Ella would know whether Pearl was a haint. That was it! Miss Ella would certainly know about a thing like that, being that she was a witch. She'd know if Pearl was a ghost or a haint or a spirit walker or some such.

Miss Ella turned her funny-colored eyes on the kitten and smiled. Johnnie Mae thought that since Pearl had been the one to rescue the cat, she would no doubt be lucky enough to have this cat or some of his descendants peeing on her final resting place. Perhaps Johnnie Mae would be able to join in this good luck. After all, she'd had a part in helping the animal. Perhaps some cat or other would walk across her grave or paw the ground covering her. Maybe when Miss Ella's potions and poultices had worked on him, she and Pearl should take this cat up to Mount Zion and coax him across Clara's grave.

Papa stood in the doorway when she got back home.

"Where you been, girl? Don't you know your mama is worrying? What make you walk off from the other children? What make you wear them doll-baby clothes? What happening to us, I want to know." He stood in the middle of the parlor floor with his hands on his hips. Questioning was his way of conversing since Clara'd been gone; all his words seemed to be asking. Johnnie Mae chafed under his nagging questions. She never had an answer, but he never seemed to actually want one. He just kept asking.

Johnnie Mae stood before Papa with her eyes down at her shoes, yet she flickered her lids upward to glimpse him. She wanted to laugh at the way he was flapping like a rooster, but she kept herself still.

Her mama had always been the disciplinarian, and it was her method to use her voice to cudgel obedience from Clara and Johnnie Mae. Her papa now tried to fill the void in this difficult time, but he was unused to demanding obedience.

—

Johnnie Mae cornered Pearl in the recess yard during the midmorning break on a razor-cold day in November.

"Clara," she called to the sadly composed face of Pearl. "Clara, when nobody's around you can speak up. Clara, answer me back, girl," she said, looking directly into Pearl's eyes.

Drawing her brows together and spoiling the blank expanse of her forehead, Pearl asked softly, "Why you callin' me Clara? My name's not Clara."

"Clara."

"Who's Clara?"

"You're Clara. You're just like her except for looks. You're Clara really, you know. Except you won't speak up. Clara's my sister that drowned, but I know you're her come again. Why don't you speak up?"

Pearl's facial expressions changed so quickly from incredulity to shock to something approaching horror that Johnnie Mae stepped back and took the measure of her own words.

"Don't be scared of me. I know who you are. I mean to tell you that I want you to come back. It's all right. I won't tell anybody about you."

Pearl slapped her hands up to her face to cover her eyes and stood there like a stump. She said nothing. Why was this girl torturing her so? After a moment Pearl started to sniffle and rub away tears with her fists. Johnnie Mae's train of talk ran out of steam. There was nothing to say—she could only mumble comforting words begging Pearl to stop crying. When the recess bell rang, Johnnie Mae reached down to the shorter girl's shoulders and led her, with her face still covered, into the girls' line.

Miss Boston noticed Pearl's state as they filed past her into the classroom. "Pearl Miller, what is the matter with you now?" There was a tiresome quality to Pearl Miller's demeanor. The solemn, often tearful eyes and the well-behaved, butter-wouldn't-melt-in-her-mouth manner were truly exasperating after a while. Even Miss Boston, who thought all children should be quiet and deferential to adults, was puzzled by Pearl.

Mildred Gloe chimed in with Lula Lavery to say in unison, "She's a crybaby, Miss Boston."

Nervous about maintaining order, Elizabeth Boston was ever prepared to rein in her students. "Young ladies, I want no name-calling and I did not direct my question to you, Mildred, or you, Lula. Pearl, why are you crying now?"

Fearing that Miss Boston's tone would further frighten

Pearl and possibly push the timid spirit of Clara deeper down inside, Johnnie Mae spoke up. "She hit her head outside, Miss Boston. She hurt herself."

"Johnnie Mae, are you speaking for Pearl again? You better go to your desk and attend to your own business."

Johnnie Mae reluctantly released Pearl's shoulders, afraid the girl would collapse to the floor or dissolve into a wisp of smoke. But Pearl was secure on her feet; in fact, she seemed to have turned to stone beside Miss Boston's desk.

"Are you hurt? Are you bleeding?" The girl did not answer. "Well, then, go back to your seat and try to compose yourself."

Finally removing her hands from her face, Pearl walked down the aisle. Miss Boston's eyelids fluttered toward the ceiling as she looked at Pearl Miller's back. The students knew this expression well. It was a softly pitying look that expressed Miss Boston's inability, despite fervent desire, to tackle the overwhelming problems of their economic, intellectual, or behavioral shortcomings.

Elizabeth Boston decided that afternoon that she would pay a call. Come Sunday after church, she would seek out Mrs. Miller and ask to discuss Pearl's troublesome behavior. It wasn't healthy for the girl to be so reticent—so fearful of her teacher and classmates that she hardly spoke. Perhaps the mother could help her draw the girl out and perhaps she'd learn whether Pearl knew anything at all of her schoolwork.

Pearl slid into her seat, folded her arms on the desktop, and lay her head down. She turned her face to the left and stuck out her tongue at Johnnie Mae with the angry expression of a terrier.

Johnnie Mae was startled that her attempt to draw Pearl

out had failed so miserably. What to do next? All she wanted was to be friendly—to put the girl at ease. Then maybe the haint would come out.

A person like Clara certainly ought to be allowed back. Her life had been so short and uneventful. It was as if all the events of her life were reduced to the one or two moments it took for her head to go under the water and not bob up again. Clara's whole life fit so neatly inside the boundaries of Johnnie Mae's memory now. And except for the first few moments, she had witnessed the whole of it. Now the whole of it seemed so small it fit in the palm of her hand, which she closed tight until tiny drops of sweat leached out of the skin and her palm smelled like Clara.

Her first sight of Clara—a little brown nut in white swaddles—had been from between the hips of Aunt Ina and Ma Dear. Aunt Ina pushed Johnnie Mae forward and she pulled back into Aunt Ina's stomach and was pushed forward again to kiss Clara's little hand, a hand her weary-looking mother uncovered and presented to her lips. Her mama was a mound of white sheets and Ma Dear's blankets, with only her head and arms visible. The mystery of how Clara had come out of her stomach remained shrouded beneath the layers of cloths. Her mama didn't stir from the shoulders down. Johnnie Mae had a pinprick of worry about whether her mama would ever walk again. Johnnie Mae's face came down toward the hand and brushed her mama's cheek. Her mama held Johnnie Mae close for a moment, then gently eased her back to Aunt Ina. Clara's hand was so soft it felt like cotton on her lips.

Smelling her palm and recalling Clara, Johnnie Mae thought about sitting in the dark in the Blue Mouse Theater all the whole of Saturday afternoon. They loved the Blue Mouse Theater. Johnnie Mae generally paid Clara's way into the matinee because, though Clara had her own pennies, she did not have many.

On Saturday afternoon in Georgetown, few children were anywhere but at the Blue Mouse Theater watching the moving pictures. Most of the children raced through their morning chores and odd jobs, and the pennies and nickels and dimes they earned poured into the Blue Mouse's coffers. Chewing on whatever they had gotten in paper bags—penny candies and hard things to suck on—was a pleasure for the Bynum sisters. Each ate a hot dog in the theater. Johnnie Mae helped Clara handle her slopped-with-mustard dog, taking it up to her mouth to lick the sliding mustard off the sides. Responsible for keeping Clara clean, Johnnie Mae was all the afternoon chiding Clara and often resorted to licking sticky messes off her baby sister's fingers.

Clara sat forward in her seat with her short legs dangling above the gooey messes on the theater floor. Her eyes were glued to the screen. Halfway through the first picture, Clara would slump back in her seat, asleep. Her hands would fall away from her bag of candy. Her hands and the bag would be moist with spittle and sugar.

It had been in the Blue Mouse Theater that Johnnie Mae and Clara saw newsreels of the great swimmer Gertrude Ederle doing the Australian crawl all the way across the English Channel. Slathered with grease to coat her in the freezing water, she looked like no other woman Johnnie Mae had ever seen. She was a marvel! Johnnie Mae told Clara that she was going to swim the English Channel just like Gertrude Ederle. Clara laughed. She said Johnnie Mae was silly.

11

Every Sunday since coming to Georgetown, Hattie Miller had waited for a delegation of church ladies to call on her. "Surely it's the custom here to welcome decent Christian families to the church?" she remarked to her daughter, Pearl. All these eight weeks, she held on to the hope that the women of Georgetown would judge her and Pearl worthy of their churches and send someone to call on them. In the meantime, she and Pearl prayed in the parlor.

In preparation for the call, each Sunday morning Hattie Miller dressed in her finest, most Christian dress and shoes. Her face was prunelike and very dark, with small gold hoop earrings adding the only glint of color around her face. She sat rigidly with her Bible in her lap in the tiny front room of her house on Dent Place. The high-necked silk crepe dress she wore was well made but past the fashion, and her ankles were completely covered by the dress's full skirt. The high-topped shoes that peeked from beneath her hem were soft with wear but held a lustrous shine.

After services at Mount Zion, Miss Elizabeth Boston

asked Mrs. Alice Bynum and Johnnie Mae if they wouldn't accompany her around to the narrow house on Dent Place where Hattie Miller and her daughter lived. She took it as her duty to become acquainted with her students' families and she was curious to know more about the unusually quiet and retiring Miller girl.

When they reached the Miller house, Elizabeth Boston rapped on the door. Hattie pulled open the door before Miss Boston's hand had returned to her side and smiled broadly, but not easily. The ladies were surprised. Mrs. Miller seemed to be expecting someone; she acted as though she were waiting for them.

"How do you do," Miss Boston chirped.

"How do," Hattie Miller replied.

"Mrs. Miller?"

"Yes, ma'am."

"I'm Elizabeth Boston, your daughter's teacher."

"How do."

Miss Boston gestured toward Mrs. Bynum and said, "This is Mrs. Alice Bynum and her daughter, Johnnie Mae. Johnnie Mae sits next to your Pearl in class."

Pearl's hand pushed aside a panel of the beige filet-crochet curtains on the front-facing window and peered out at Miss Boston standing on the stoop with a woman she didn't know and Johnnie Mae Bynum. Pearl's mind ticked through a list of possible reasons for Miss Boston's visit. She'd been ever so quiet in class. There couldn't be a complaint. Maybe Johnnie Mae had made a complaint against her? What on earth could the teacher want on a Sunday? Maybe Miss Boston was making the long-awaited formal church call? Pearl's chest got to pounding with emotion that traveled off her mama and settled on everything in the room. At long last Pearl and her mama were going to be welcomed—would be taken in—by one of the churches.

"Oh, how do you do. Please step in." Pearl's mother could barely contain her excitement. "Pearl, your school friend is here to call," she sang out. "How do you do, little lady."

"I hope we haven't come at a bad time, Mrs. Miller." Johnnie Mae's mother spoke in a formal but very friendly voice.

"No, ma'am. Please step in and take a seat, won't you?" Hattie Miller opened the door wide and directed the visitors into a room filled with very large, carved furniture of the same dark brown color as she. The path through the chifforobe, vanity, several chairs, end table, and oval dining table was narrow and winding.

Pearl hopped to her feet and arranged her dress when the visitors entered the room. As on every school day, her hair was neatly done and her skin glossy with oil. Her mama had told her to smile when company came and this she tried to do when Johnnie Mae, her mother, and Miss Boston entered the parlor. But the expression that passed for smiling with the Millers was so bland a thing as would cause a stranger to call them both dour.

Johnnie Mae's smile too was tight with politeness and nothing else. She hadn't wanted to come along, but Mama had made her. Mama said they had a duty to welcome folks and make them feel at home. It was especially important for newcomers to feel that the church welcomed them. And Miss Boston thought it was a good idea for Pearl and Johnnie Mae to get to know each other. Johnnie Mae thought Pearl was a bump on a log and as dull as dust.

Hattie had baked, brewed strong, flavorful coffee, and

washed the four matching china cups and saucers in anticipation of this visit as she had done each Sunday morning since they'd arrived in Georgetown. Her only fear had been that more than four ladies would come.

"Miss Boston, Miz Bynum, won't you take a cup of coffee?" Hattie Miller trilled in her most proper, company-come-to-call voice. Short of stature, she moved about the room like a spinning top. Pearl sat back into a chair by the front window and resumed reading her Bible, peering intermittently over the book at Johnnie Mae, who sat on a chair next to her mother. Neither girl spoke to the other.

"Yes, thank you, Mrs. Miller. I'd love a cup of coffee if it won't be too much trouble," Miss Boston said.

"Oh, no. I keep a pot on every Sunday the Lord sends. I been expecting a call from the church," she said and spun off to the kitchen.

Elizabeth Boston's face got warm suddenly. "Let's see, how long have they been in town? Several months at least. And no one from the church has called on them? Some of the old customs are surely fading. It's unforgivable." She muttered to herself and clucked her tongue at this lapse in Christian custom.

Hattie Miller carried in a large silver tray, on top of which were three cups of coffee and three matching plates holding large, moist wedges of cake. The lemon cake sat high on the plates, topped with lemon icing. It was the kind of cake, with perfect layers and perfectly blended flavors, that does its own boasting, speaking eloquently for the woman who made it.

"Pearl, take Johnnie Mae out to the kitchen. There's cake

in there for you girls and buttermilk if you want it," Mrs. Miller practically sang out to Pearl. She was pleased to be exercising her hospitality.

Pearl was taken aback by her mother's directive. She should have known that she and Johnnie Mae were going to be sent to the kitchen. Of course her mother was going to want these ladies all to herself. Of course she was expected to take care of hospitality toward Johnnie Mae. She sprang up out of her chair, shot a glance at Johnnie Mae, and looked away before Johnnie Mae's eyes locked with hers. She wound her way through the furniture to the kitchen. At a nod and a brief wrinkling of the brows from her mother, Johnnie Mae followed Pearl to the kitchen. She'd known, too, that banishment was likely.

The kitchen was a neat, well-furnished room. A large table dominated the center of the room and chairs enough for six people were placed around it. Mrs. Miller had set out two glasses of buttermilk with the lemon cake proudly in the middle of the table. Johnnie Mae stood next to one of the chairs that had a plate and utensils in front of it and looked about the room. She wondered if Pearl and her mother had boarders. There seemed to be so many places at the table. Waiting for a signal to sit and eat, Johnnie Mae turned to Pearl, who stood next to the other place setting with her head bowed. Pearl was the hostess and she knew she was supposed to make her company feel at home. But she was still ill at ease around Johnnie Mae and she wasn't quite sure what to do. Finally she said, "Take a seat, please," and Johnnie Mae sat down.

Pearl took up the cake knife and cut pieces for her guest and herself. The girls ate in silence. The door from the kitchen to the front room was left open and the two strained their ears toward the talk in the parlor.

Miss Boston first pecked at her slice, then returned for a healthy bite. "Mrs. Miller, this is a fine cake."

"Quite nice of you to say so, miss. You are from Mount Zion Church?" In the past weeks, Hattie had promenaded past each of the Georgetown churches that appeared to have Negro congregations. Their denominations mattered less to her than good preaching and a fine, upstanding, well-dressed congregation.

"Yes, we do attend there." Miss Boston meant to eat the cake more delicately than eagerly, as she'd been taught, but couldn't resist its lemony taste. She stared at the silver tray and the delicate porcelain cups, saucers, and plates. Why, her own mama served proudly on mismatched pieces of crockery pilfered from the Pullman cars on which her papa had worked. Miss Boston had never seen a set like this in any colored person's home. She was in grave danger of forgetting her manners in looking from Hattie Miller's dark, lined face to the smooth bone china and the fine, tasteful furnishings.

"It's a mighty fine edifice." Hattie parroted a phrase her papa had found so useful. The stone buildings in their hometown of Tecumseh, Oklahoma, were always "mighty fine edifices" to her papa.

"Oh, yes, it is a handsome church. We are very proud. Every brick laid by a member of the congregation," Miss Boston said, eager to crow about the church.

"You've got every right to be proud. You Georgetown folks are prideful people." The women smiled graciously, each proud of her own demeanor.

Elizabeth Boston placed her plate carefully on the oval table at her elbow, picked up her coffee cup, and placed two small spoonfuls of sugar in it. The coffee, too, was uncommonly satisfying. It had the robust flavor of strong country brew, and Miss Boston longed to slurp it down. After a few demure sips, she took a healthy slug of it, put down the cup, and came around to the subject of her visit.

"Mrs. Miller, I've actually come to speak to you about your daughter, Pearl."

Hattie's pleased smile faded and lines bored deeper into her forehead. "Is she the cause of some trouble?" Hattie asked.

"Oh, no, no. Pearl is a lovely, sweet, well-mannered girl, Mrs. Miller," Miss Boston maintained.

"It's very nice of you to say so, miss."

"We're very happy to have her in class."

"Thank you."

Pearl figured that all that had been said up to now was merely polite preamble. At any moment, Miss Boston's true purpose in coming would be revealed. And further, Mrs. Bynum and Johnnie Mae had something to do with it.

"You have just recently moved to Georgetown?" Miss Boston asked.

"Yes, ma'am," Hattie Miller answered.

"May I ask where you have come from, Mrs. Miller?" Alice Bynum asked.

"We come from the territory. We come from the Oklahoma territory, Miz Bynum."

"Oh, my, that's very intriguing." Elizabeth Boston prided herself on the words in her vocabulary that added the scalloped edges of adventure and passion to mundane thoughts.

Intriguing was one of these. Though Mr. Ernest Boston, her father, was always on the road with the railroad, her own traveling had been limited. All of it had been done in the pages of books and by the tales told by her father and the people she met. In all her years she'd left Georgetown only once, to visit some of her people in Philadelphia.

"My nearest people are buried in the state of Oklahoma," Hattie Miller said.

"How come you all to be out that way, Mrs. Miller?" Alice Bynum asked.

"That's way out west, isn't it? There are a great many Indians out there, Mrs. Miller?" Miss Boston blurted out.

"Yes, ma'am, a great many. We number some of our people among them. Our folks have been out on the frontier since Emancipation."

"I declare," Miss Boston said.

"My papa's papa's papa brought himself and a wagonload of folks out there as soon as they said he was free to go. He swore he wanted to strike out for where things were new to him. The woman who birthed my papa was a full-blooded Creek, miss."

"I declare," Alice Bynum exclaimed.

"I declare," Elizabeth Boston chimed in. "And do you consider yourself to be one of the Creeks?" Miss Boston asked.

"I don't do much considering on that, miss. We had our entitlements, though, same as the rest of the Creeks."

"Entitlements?"

"Our parcel of land from the government. All of the Creeks got title to a plot of land and we did, too, on account of my papa's mama was a Creek. My nearest people are buried beneath that land, though it doesn't belong to me anymore."

Hattie rubbed the head of a fat cherub carved on the arm of the chair she sat in. The cherub had identical brothers on each of the arms and finials of the room's dark furniture. She looked into Elizabeth Boston's face, whose smooth tan skin was alight with interest above the eyebrows and along the tops of her cheeks. Hattie wondered at the frank show of curiosity by a young woman so determinedly proper and corseted. "Pearl's papa and my papa were shot trying to face off a mob of grafters. That was after 'twenty-one—after the big rioting and burning in Tulsa in 1921. These grafters were bent on taking the entitlement and showing us a lesson, too. I buried Papa and my husband. They're out there laying right now in the state of Oklahoma."

Alice Bynum, too, hung on Hattie Miller's words. She had heard plenty about the burning of Tulsa in '21. "My husband and my cousin and her husband were planning to go out to Oklahoma. But we came here instead."

"Oh, my!" Miss Boston could barely conceal her eagerness for more of the tale. Elizabeth Boston had a wandering, inquiring mind. Mostly it was reading that gave her the chance to roam vicariously, but a fondness for combing the backgrounds of people newly met supplied excitement too.

"Before James Miller, my husband and my Pearl's papa, had got cool in the ground, a gentleman I thought was right nice came to call on me. I was scared, being a woman alone with a young girl. I took up with him for protection. We went to the justice of the peace and got a marriage ceremony. Shortly after, he ran off from us and I was turned off the place. I tell you I cried a bucketful that day!"

Not wanting to take her eyes from Hattie Miller's face, the schoolteacher nevertheless flicked her eyes toward the kitchen, concerned that Pearl and Johnnie Mae were listening. Hattie Miller seemed not the least inhibited in telling her sad story.

"See, he—that man I married with—he had been put up to marry me and get the claim to my entitlement to give up to the grafters. Little Pearl and I had to leave there with just the things you see here and our clothes. My people had a mighty lot of things my papa made. He was a carpenter. He made all his own things. Most of it were farming things and we just left them behind."

Alice Bynum asked, "Did your father make all of this furniture here, Mrs. Miller?"

"Yes, ma'am, he was a master carpenter."

"The frontier—Oklahoma—it sounds so colorful—so exciting—so free!" said Miss Boston.

"I don't know about that, miss. There was a sense that we owned—that we belonged there."

"We heard that colored owned lots of land there—that colored had their own towns, their own sheriffs and all?" Alice questioned eagerly.

"Yes, indeed! You want to see some towns, you just look at Tecumseh and Boley and some others. These towns were full of our folk. Our folk ran those towns and plenty others. And you ought to've seen Tulsa! There was plenty of colored there—big Negroes. I met my husband there. A couple of times a year, Papa hauled a dresser or a chifforobe or a table to sell to the big Negroes that lived up there."

"We were going to settle out there—me and Willie, my husband, and my cousin Ina, and her husband, Cap. But we heard about the trouble and changed our mind," said Alice.

"I met my husband in Tulsa. He was shining shoes for the oil people and hanging out in the joints drinking Choctaw beer. That stuff used to turn folks crazy. It was worse than moonshine liquor. Papa convinced him to come out to our place and work it. James Miller was kind of a city boy at that time, but he wasn't too smart. He got so that he did the farm work as well as Papa and he got to like it real well. Pearl was born and raised on that place and I put two other little ones in the ground down there, then my husband and Papa. Pearl and I left there and went up to Tulsa when we got turned out. I kind of wanted to stay, but the reverend said Tulsa was no kind of town for a young widow with a girl child, especially a widow who had already been fooled. Tulsa is a wide-open town. He told us Washington city was a better place for us. I didn't really want to leave Tulsa. But I went along with the reverend's say-so. You ought to have heard the bands that played in Tulsa! They had the brass bands, bands that played at the dances and the carnivals and all. They had great lines of men walking and playing their horns!"

Brass bands on the frontier! Brawling, brash, braying— Oklahoma brass bands! Elizabeth Boston played with the sound of the words in her head. She had the habit of storing up words and descriptions of things and places to use later in pictures of her own. Adding them to the words in all the books she'd read, she put her own pictures to Hattie's words and felt the passion of the towns Hattie spoke about. She could see folks lining the dirt tracks that passed for thoroughfares on the frontier and felt the tremble in her bowels at the thought of tubas, kettledrums, and trombones. Her father boasted that he did all the traveling in the family so his women could stay put and nest, like hens are supposed to. He always said it as if he'd done them a big favor by eating up the world and leaving them at home on their duffs.

Elizabeth Boston was fast becoming the thing she'd been heading toward all her life. She was becoming a fluttering, mercurial person inside a well-mannered, predictable, chilly shell. A great conflict was going on inside her at this moment. Lord, how much she'd love to grasp Hattie Miller's hands and beg her to continue with the story. She didn't want her to stop until she'd recounted every detail. How she'd love to draw her feet up into the wing chair. And how much she'd love to cross her palms behind her head and just listen to the sound of Hattie Miller's voice!

In the kitchen, the girls were gripped by Hattie Miller's narrative too. Pearl, familiar with it, was nevertheless riveted by her mother's telling. It sounded exciting and she marveled that these events had concerned her. Her life sounded like a story out of an adventure novel, yet she had known it to be sad and frightening and in the final analysis mundane. Listening to the tale brought Johnnie Mae to a new way of thinking about old namby-pamby Pearl Miller. Why, she could have the school yard gang eating out of her hand if she had the gumption to tell them about Oklahoma—about the Indians and the grafters.

"Mrs. Miller, we're so happy to have your Pearl in our school. We see to it that the colored students get a fine education here. We have a long tradition." Johnnie Mae listened to Miss Boston going on as if making a speech. "Mrs. Miller, your Pearl is a lovely girl. However, I do worry about her. She is so abnormally quiet and retiring. I mean, she never speaks up even when I call on her for the lesson. I thought there might be something troubling her."

At this, Pearl raised her eyes and looked toward the front room, then across the table at Johnnie Mae.

Miss Boston felt her face trembling, became unsure of her voice. Why in the world couldn't she just admit to people that she was curious about them—that she wanted to hear their stories—that she really did care about their children and wanted fervently for them to learn. Why couldn't she just plainly say that she was confounded by this girl's mealy-mouthed demeanor?

"I s'pose it's because of the trouble we've seen. Since the trouble, she's been real scary." Hattie Miller looked toward the kitchen with a pitying expression.

"Well, perhaps with time she'll feel at home here. The situation for our people is a little more fortunate in Georgetown than in some other locales. We have our share of troubles in this municipality, but we also have a great many educated and upstanding Negro citizens here." Miss Boston declared all this as she drew herself up to the proud posture with which she'd entered the house.

"That's what the reverend said. I declare, I hope so. Pearl and I saw a fair amount of trouble in the territory."

"Perhaps she will develop a friendship with Johnnie Mae. I wouldn't be surprised if they became fast friends," Miss Boston said.

Pearl again looked up sharply and caught the ambiguous look that Johnnie Mae gave her. Johnnie Mae had taken an interest in her, but Pearl was sure there was a cruel prank in the offing. And there were those who said Johnnie Mae'd been acting strange since her little sister drowned. Funny that Miss Boston wasn't mentioning this fact to her mother!

Elizabeth Boston collected all the remaining cake crumbs onto the tines of her fork and slipped them demurely into her mouth during the lull in conversation. Hattie urged, "Won't you have another piece, Miss Boston?"

"Oh, no, Mrs. Miller, I must not. However, this is about the finest cake I have ever had."

"Thanking you warmly. Baking is a thing I've always had a good hand at." The women sat quietly looking into one another's faces, smiling.

After a few moments, Alice Bynum and Elizabeth Boston chirped and clucked about having enjoyed their visit. Johnnie Mae sighed with relief and left the kitchen table to return to the living room. Mrs. Miller's lemon cake was, as Miss Boston said, most delicious. But Johnnie Mae had been bored silly and pretty salty at being forced to endure Pearl Miller's company in the kitchen. Johnnie Mae heard Miss Boston and her mother urge Mrs. Miller to come to Mount Zion Church and to the community center.

Miss Boston stood first and extended a small hand at exactly waist level toward Hattie Miller. She shook Hattie's hand. Alice Bynum also shook Hattie Miller's hand, and Johnnie Mae, standing next to her mother, curtsied briefly. Turning to Pearl, Mrs. Miller pressed her amiably to bid Miss Boston and Mrs. Bynum and Johnnie Mae good-bye and to thank them for their visit. Pearl obediently gave a short curtsy and, with her eyes boring into the parlor rug, said, "Thank you, Miss Boston. Thank you, Miz Bynum." In the instant that none of the women was looking at her, she glanced upward and licked her tongue out at Johnnie Mae.

Hattie stood in the doorway and watched her visitors' straight backs as they walked away. Miss Boston and Mrs. Bynum turned at the sidewalk and gently inclined their heads before moving along down the street. Hattie Miller attempted a sweet smile at her visitors. She was enormously pleased. The ladies' visit had been satisfying and well worth the wait.

12

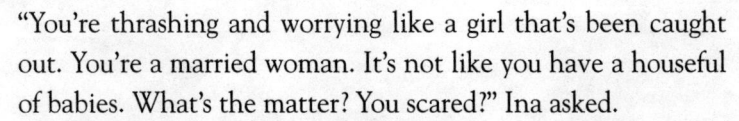

"You're thrashing and worrying like a girl that's been caught out. You're a married woman. It's not like you have a houseful of babies. What's the matter? You scared?" Ina asked.

"You know my mama died bringing me. It makes me a little scared," Alice explained.

The women's voices had the tone of clarity that talks between two women out of earshot of husbands and fathers and children have. But, anxious about being overheard, Alice kept her voice low. Johnnie Mae would be getting up and coming into the kitchen soon. The two women wouldn't have much time alone together to sort this thing out. And it would have to be sorted out soon. Too much longer and the decision would be made for them.

The women had risen early to get a good start on the Thanksgiving Day cooking. Ina had come over to her cousin's kitchen several hours before sunrise—around the time that late became early—and the women had divided up the many tasks. For most of the past two weeks, Alice and Ina had shopped and planned out the cooking and baking for the two Thanksgiving dinners: the Bynums' family dinner and Alexis St. Pierre's.

Ina looked up from cleaning the collard and mustard greens. She said, "It's better here. Colored can go to the hospital. You can get better help than your mama did. They've got colored doctors here. You know that ol' bastard doctor they had down home didn't care about colored."

"Ina! Shh! What kind of thing are you saying?" Alice was surprised at the vehemence of her cousin's words.

"Well, we're not no children. You know who I'm talking about." Ina's normally placid face became tangled with anger. "That old drunk man that was the doctor for colored down there didn't give a damn about helping colored women to bring babies. They called him when my time came because I was having trouble. He said the reason the baby wasn't coming was 'cause he was strangulatin' on his own cord. Then he sent all the women out of the room and he reached in and brought the baby out with pincers. I've always believed that he strangled my baby himself. That old bastard hated colored people and wouldn't come to help any of the colored women bring a baby unless she was close to dead. I think he fixed me, too. I think he fixed me so Cap and I couldn't make any more babies." Ina swabbed at her eyes.

"That was a sad time, Ina Mae," Alice said, patting her cousin on the shoulder. "I'm just not sure this is the right time for me to have another child. You know, with Clara so recently gone."

"Alice, girl, that's not your business," Ina said, recovering herself. "That's God's business. My mama said it's the Lord who decides what is the right time to bring a baby."

"The Lord. The Lord's the one who decides when to take them, too."

"Yes. It's the Lord's decision no matter what we think about it. You thinking about going up Number Ten to that woman up there? It's a big risk. She could ruin you for good."

"I thought about it."

"Does Willie know yet?"

"I don't think so—yet."

"Go into it with a light heart, girl. It'll be a joy for all of us—you, Willie, Johnnie Mae. It'll be good for her. It'll ease you over the loss of Clara."

"No. It won't. That's the thing it won't do."

"Do it for him, then. Do it to hold him. Do it to make a home."

"There's something to be said for having one chick and putting all your energy in that one chick."

"There's something to be said for a yardful of chicks with some as a fallback in case adversity wipe some out."

"I want to put my heart through it? You know that lady down home that had thirteen children and lost twelve? How'd she do it? How'd she keep bringing them and putting them in the ground—bringing them and putting them down? How'd she do that? And still keep getting up herself?"

"Some women are like brood sows. They keep bringing 'em," Ina said flatly.

"I don't believe that. I don't believe she could keep bringing 'em and putting 'em in the ground and not think a thing about it. I don't believe it."

What would Johnnie Mae think? Her feelings ought to be considered too. It was hard for Alice to escape the thought that putting too much responsibility on her for Clara was what had caused the accident. But girls back home took care of their mama's babies. That was the way it was. The older girl was always her mother's helpmate. And here in town, the young girls cared for the younger ones while their people worked.

Had she put too much on Johnnie Mae—stealing her childhood? Well, a colored child couldn't waste too much time on childhood, no matter what her circumstance. How was Johnnie Mae going to feel about a new baby? Maybe she'd be mad or scared about it.

Alice recalled with a pinging in the middle of her chest how Ina Mae had boo-hooed into her apron when they'd sat around the kitchen table at Papa's house talking about Sam Logan's baby in Alice's womb. They'd cried together, then smiled. At last, Ina had said she was happy for Alice. She'd wiped Alice's cheeks and stood up to Alice's papa, taking most of his angry slaps. He crowed and cawed like a double-crossed rooster. He shouted about Alice being a whore and Ina being a whore, too, for defending Alice. All women were whores and fools! He squared off and raised his fists at little Ina, who stood a good foot shorter than him. Ina put her arms across her chest, not striking Old Man Walker and not fending off his wallops, only yelling at him to stop his raging—shaming him with saying that he had no right to harm Alice's coming child nor nobody else. He finished by calling Ina's mother a whore and Alice's mother a slattern. The women who had scrubbed and tended to his every need. Them he called whores!

"Don't let that man keep you from your life," Ina had said to Alice after Old Man Walker had finally stopped spouting off. "He's got no right to do it. Don't let him ruin your life."

After meeting the stone wall of the two women's implacability, Old Man Walker had turned his anger on Sam Logan instead. The bad-mouthing had spread like molasses—slowly but surely miring everything in its path. Old Man Walker talked to Cal Jackson for the first time in ten years. Soon Sam Logan wasn't able to get a day's work on anybody's place within ten or twenty miles. Finally, Sam had cut his losses and taken off. He left for Indian country, folks said, and had never seen his daughter. He'd never seen Alice again either.

Johnnie Mae came into the kitchen, greeted her mother and aunt, and noted the conspiratorial looks on their faces. Clearly, they'd been discussing something before she entered the room that they considered too adult for her to hear. She passed through and out to the toilet.

When she returned, Johnnie Mae saw her mother thrust her arm into the turkey's cavity. Alice scraped her hand around inside and pulled out the entrails that were still attached to the bird. It was an indelicate procedure and her face changed from the determined neutrality of busy to disgust. When she brought out her hand, it was holding a round, amber, gelatinous glob.

"Mercy," Mama said. "He told me this was a tom. I called myself buying a tom. This thing is a hen. Ina, this bird's got an egg in it."

"What say?"

"I say, this bird has got an egg in it. There's an egg with no shell up inside it," Alice exclaimed. It was still too early for sunlight and the coal oil lamps threw shadows up on the walls. With her hair tied back in a scarf, Alice looked like a sorceress, holding the incompletely formed egg in her hand.

"Something about that takes away my taste for turkey,"

Ina said as she deftly used the nail of her right thumb to slit the collard leaves from their tough veins. She screwed up her face. "I always prefer a tom turkey."

"Oh, Ina, don't be foolish," Alice said. "The bird is for eating. There's nothing to an egg being inside it."

"Well, you were the one going on about the egg. Could be a funny kind of omen or something."

"For a churchgoing Christian woman, you pay plenty of attention to heathen spells and signs."

"I'm talking about the power of nature. Better wash that thing out good with vinegar. Who'd you get that bird from?"

"I always wash my turkey good. As long as it's tender, I'll have no quarrel."

"In my experience, toms are the most tender."

Though Alexis St. Pierre had promised to hire out for parties, she had worked on Alice in her sweetly charming way to get her to agree to cook and serve the holiday dinner. She'd pleaded, "Douglas's old school chum and his wife are coming and I dare not trust the dinner to some slacker." Appearance being so important, it was politic for Douglas St. Pierre to seem prosperous for his guests. Alexis wanted ham and turkey and yeast rolls and sparkling crystal and pumpkin pies and a maid.

To bribe Alice, Alexis St. Pierre had offered to pay for the Bynums' turkey, too. Because of the steep prices of the birds, the Bynums and Ina Carson had not had a turkey for Thanksgiving since Cap died. The very enterprising Cap Carson could always manage a bird. One year, he'd even gone all the way back home to Marabel for one and brought it back on the train in a wooden crate. He'd come through Union Station like Moses down from the mountain with the turkey's ugly head sticking through the slats of the crate.

Because of the agreement between Alice and Mrs. St. Pierre, Johnnie Mae and her mother had gone down to the market stalls on M Street for two fresh-killed turkeys. The fat things, some with white feathers, some with gray, had been crammed in large pens. Alice had moved between the pens, examining the general condition of the birds. Every now and then, one turkey would hop up and flap its wings. After she'd skirted the outside of the pens, scrutinizing the birds, Alice had raised her hand to catch the eye of the man selling. She pointed to one white-feathered bird that looked to be the right size and then another one that looked the same size. The man, who had a thick head and neck—a true bullet head— had waded into the pen and grabbed up Alice's choices by their wings. There'd been a faint snapping sound as the wing joints were broken. Grinning, the man held the birds up for Alice to examine closely. Johnnie Mae had watched her mother place her palms across the breasts of the birds and spread her fingers in order to measure the width of them. She'd pinched and prodded them a bit too, feeling for ample flesh.

"Are they toms?" Alice had asked the man pointedly.

"These is all toms—lots of breast meat—big drums— sweet meat," the bullet-headed man said. His hairless face had two tiny eyes out of all proportion to his head.

"I'll have them," Alice'd said.

He laughed. "Yes, ma'am. These is good ones, too."

He'd put the neck of one of Alice's turkeys in a vise and the bird flapped futilely as the man brought his ax down on its neck. Then he killed the next. Blood ran from a sluice carved into the chopping block down into a pan near his feet. A dog that had watched the man's every move skulked forward on its belly and waited near his ankle to grab each turkey's severed head when it fell.

Johnnie Mae and her mother arrived at the St. Pierres' at about eight o'clock and met Alexis's frantic face at the kitchen door. Both were wearing long black skirts and long white starched bib aprons.

"Well, at last. I thought you'd never arrive," Alexis said.

Knowing there was plenty enough time for the job and not wanting to waste any of it, Mama brushed past Alexis into the kitchen. "Good morning, Miz St. Pierre," she said.

"Good morning, Miz St. Pierre." Johnnie Mae echoed her mother and followed her inside.

Alexis wrapped her peach-colored dressing gown tighter about her and sighed audibly. "Good morning."

No one person could do all this—she knew that. It was barely going to get done by the three of them. Alexis felt suddenly easier about it now that Alice and company were here and suddenly peeved at herself for sinking into this dependency. She couldn't do all the housekeeping and hostessing by herself. Nobody could. But she didn't feel comfortable having the colored woman—and now her daughter—into everything. Still, Alice's presence in the house meant there was going to be little to worry about that day. Alice hadn't turned her face toward Alexis when she entered the kitchen. A blind man could see she wasn't happy to be there today. But she had come. That was important. She had come.

Alice knew that Alexis would be the dancing dog today. Though she always talked about "my Douglas" in honeyed, adoring tones, Alice knew that Alexis was uncomfortable when her husband was in the house. She was jittery around him. She found it difficult to sit a chair with him in the room and constantly popped up to fetch one thing and another or check on things that needed no checking.

Douglas St. Pierre was taller and slimmer than the white men Alice had seen around Marabel. Those men were all broader, less sinewy than Douglas, and more florid. They were mostly men who worked outside and ranged in color from swarthy to lobster-red. She remembered none as milk-white as Douglas, who had an office job in the government and didn't get out much into the sun.

※

Douglas St. Pierre's school chum was tall, like him, and slender. The two men embraced at the front door with a lot of helloing and harumphing while they shook hands, a secretive gesture that looked like they were rummaging in each other's pockets. The school chum's wife stood behind him in the doorway and looked at the men sweetly, not seeming to mind that they ignored her completely.

Suddenly recollecting her duties—she, too, was watching the men's ritual handshake—Alexis crossed toward the wife, grasped her elbow, and relieved her of her coat. It had been arranged that Johnnie Mae would follow Alexis unobtrusively and take the guests' coats as Alexis handed them to her.

Johnnie Mae managed to haul the two guests' coats into the anteroom, where she'd been directed to place them on the chaise. The wife's was a full-length mink coat as dark as coffee and more silky than anything Johnnie Mae had ever felt. Hearing a gentle clacking of pans in the kitchen and the excited tittering of Alexis in the parlor, Johnnie Mae knew she had at least a split second to leap onto the coat and burrow her face down into it.

"Better leave that alone and see if your mother needs help," he said gently, quietly. The words stung Johnnie Mae like a slap. Her cheeks became warm with shame as if she actually had been slapped. How could she have let herself get caught by Douglas St. Pierre doing such a babyish thing? He stood in the doorway betraying no amusement as Johnnie Mae smoothed the rumpled coat and her own clothes, then slipped past him out the door. If she had known the language of Douglas St. Pierre's moods and expressions, she would have known he was amused at her antic, as he was often amused at the foibles of women. Johnnie Mae was little different, in his eyes, from Alexis. To him, females could hardly help the silliness of their nature—little matter their age or color.

By three P.M., Douglas St. Pierre had poured so many glasses of wine that Alexis's head was light. At five after three, Johnnie Mae was sent into the parlor to whisper to Alexis discreetly that the rolls would be compromised if dinner was delayed much longer.

At three forty-five, dinner was served. The dining table was anchored at one end by a large ham that was scored, stuck with cloves, and drizzled with syrup. At the other end was the large roast turkey with stuffing. Alexis wanted the table to be groaning. Douglas's school chum must see how well things were for him, so there was enough food on the table for ten people. The two slim men and the two slender women were dwarfed by the array of dishes: candied sweets, mashed white potatoes, tiny green peas, corn pudding, stewed tomatoes, cranberry sauce, and yeast rolls.

In the kitchen, Mama fixed two biscuits with sausages and put two cups of coffee at the edge of the kitchen table. She pushed a sandwich toward Johnnie Mae. "Don't spoil your dinner," she commanded her, knowing she was surely hungry with the working and the smells of the food.

Alice was anxious not to spoil the Thanksgiving dinner with Willie and Ina and all of them around the table. The big holidays — the feasting holidays, Thanksgiving, Christmas, Easter — these were the times when she missed her papa's house in Carolina. Alexis St. Pierre thought she had a table groaning! That woman had never seen the table of a man who loves to hunt, who has three sons and three daughters and a wife younger than himself and a few milk cows and hogs and chickens and bursting sacks of cornmeal and a cupboard full of preserves and pickles and headcheese.

Johnnie Mae and her mother left Alexis's house when all the dishes except for the dessert things were washed and put away. Alexis St. Pierre left her guests still eating the Martha Washington cake and came into the kitchen. She insisted that Alice take the ham, as well as the leftover rolls and cakes and pies. Why, there was still more than half of a Virginia ham!

As they headed down Wisconsin Avenue, Johnnie Mae trailed her mother, pulling the loaded wagon. At P Street, Mama stopped in the middle of the cobblestoned street for a moment and looked down into Johnnie Mae's face. She took the girl's hands, put her fingertips against her lips lightly, and kissed them. Alice stood a moment and enjoyed the smell of food and bleach on her daughter's soft fingers. Johnnie Mae's fingers were still soft despite doing grown-ups' work. They were still a child's hands. But not a baby's — no longer a baby's hands — Lord, no! She stood a moment, mourning for the baby child who was fast going away, and then thinking herself a silly woman to moon about a child who won't stay a baby.

The only way for a baby to stay a baby is to die, and each day of a child's life marks the death of the day before—a day the mother mourns.

Releasing Johnnie Mae's hand and falling into step beside her, Alice continued down to O Street. She felt an oddness down in her vitals—some kind of a fluttering feeling. She was thinking about the coming child and she felt ashamed of herself in Johnnie Mae's presence. She felt a little ashamed that having Johnnie Mae might not be enough.

Alice paused for a moment on the top step of their house. Exhausted, she reached down to catch a second wind. She called out to Willie and Ina as she and Johnnie Mae came through the door.

Ina's intentions were as pure as daylight. Alice knew that and Alice knew that she couldn't possibly have managed to have a Thanksgiving dinner for her own family and cook and serve for the St. Pierres if it hadn't been for Ina. But coming into her kitchen and seeing Ina bustling about, basting the turkey and turning out biscuits onto a pan for baking, gave her a small, unhappy feeling. This feeling was so small and spiteful that it didn't have a name, and in a good person's soul it wouldn't last very long or do much damage. It was the small feeling that had to do with not quite knowing who she was in her own kitchen. Ina moved aside quickly, handed Alice an apron, and exclaimed over the extras Alice and Johnnie Mae had brought from the St. Pierres'.

This act—this giving-back to the wife and mother control of her own domain—was thought by Ina, and not disputed by any of the other southern women, to be her due. If the colored woman couldn't claim much of her own in the world abroad, at least her kitchen was her legally sanctioned bailiwick. Here she was the boss. And no other person—no daughter or sister or cousin or man—could cut her hair in this precinct. She determined the measures and the portions. She was the chooser. She gave the most succulent piece of chicken to the husband or the child, determining which piece of the meat which person got.

Willie, because he liked the leg and thigh, got the fat plump pieces rather than the other ones ever so slightly drier because they had stayed in the pan too long. The driest pieces Alice put aside for herself out of the widely held notion that the cook accepted responsibility for all mistakes. She was the one who gave Johnnie Mae the breast that was the size she could eat, rather than the one slightly larger that would turn off her appetite. Cracking the wing pieces apart and separating them for Clara because Clara hated to rip them apart but loved—loved only—the tender, sweet wing meat. She carried the portions and preferences in her head and as strict as it sometimes was, it was also thrilling control. She said which and how much for them and for herself and always retained the power to give herself less. She, the loving, dutiful mother, could account for every meal her two children had eaten and every meal her husband had had since he married her. And the limits of her energy and the skill and resourcefulness and cleverness of her buying and cooking for them—and for Alexis and Douglas St. Pierre—determined how they would be fed.

"Take those clothes off and lie down a few minutes. I'll call you when dinner's ready," Mama said, for she could see that Johnnie Mae was more worn out than hungry. A little nap would give her a second wind.

Papa sat listening to the radio with his ear up close and his face turned away from the women as they crisscrossed the room putting dishes on the table. He'd done his part by setting up the table in the front room, and now he was sulking about the late dinner. The last few days he'd argued that their working for the St. Pierres on Thanksgiving Day made a comment about him that he didn't like. People would think he didn't give a thing to keep his family, that his wife and daughter had to work on Thanksgiving Day — cooking in someone else's kitchen. A family woman, a woman with a husband and children, should be able to pass up a day's work on Thanksgiving Day. On a day like that a woman ought to be in her own kitchen.

Alice had answered him again and again that she was doing it as much as a favor as anything else. Douglas St. Pierre was having his important friend from Harvard College and Miz St. Pierre couldn't take a chance on hiring out a stranger. Alexis had appealed to her like a friend or neighbor.

That part galled Willie. Alice was letting Alexis St. Pierre put a claim on her for friendship.

A whiff of Clara's fragrance — a sweet yeastiness — struck Alice like a glimpse of the girl as she walked the candied sweets to the table. Their color was the color Clara's stomach had been early on when Alice had wrapped her.

All the day's smells had been so bounteous. Since early — since just at sunrise — Johnnie Mae had been inhaling the odors of cooking food. The richness and the complex mingling of sweets and sours and pungents had been absorbed under her skin. Now the food heaped on her plate made her feel like gagging.

"You eatin' your dinner, Johnnie?" her father said in his plaintive inquisitiveness. "All this food and nobody got an appetite."

"What're you talkin' about, Willie? We eatin' as hard as we can," Ina said.

"Johnnie Mae is just peckin'. She must've ate up at Miz St. Pierre."

"We didn't eat up at Miz St. Pierre," Mama said, rolling a swallow of water in her mouth. "We saved ourselves to eat dinner at home."

"Couldn't work all day and not eat. Sittin' on the side in the white folks' kitchen like a backyard chile. This girl ain't no backyard chile. This chile ain't no backyard chile. I'm raisin' her. I'm feedin' her, ain't I?"

"I wanted us all to eat together," Mama said quietly, trying to deflect a fuss.

"Now what you hollerin' about, man? This is Thanksgiving. We all sittin' here together eatin' our dinner. What you hollerin' about?" Ina said.

"Alice, you raisin' this chile like you doin' it alone. I got somethin' to say about workin' in the woman's kitchen on a holiday. If she care about her husband's friend, why can't she cook her own dinner?"

"Now, Willie, you know Miz St. Pierre can't manage a big dinner for people." Alice answered him sweetly, hoping to edge him away from his annoyance.

"Why she can't? Why she can't do it?"

"Oh, don't talk silly. You know they don't know a thing about working hard enough to do all that," Ina countered.

"All she knows is to wring as much out of a colored woman as she can."

"Aw, don't let it worry you and spoil your dinner. She'll pay for her easy life. There'll be less heaven for her, that's all. And she'll be sorry she spent this short lifetime without toiling when she sees the half measure she's gonna get in heaven. I intend to be there with my feet up and my head on a downy pillow, much work as I've done in this life, and you, too." Ina averted the strife handily, and all of them finished the dinner laughing and easy.

13

Still somewhat reticent with adults, Pearl was not in January the scared rabbit she had been in September. She walked briskly out of the classroom and threaded her way into the crowded hall before Johnnie Mae could catch up to her. For the first time that Johnnie Mae could recall, Pearl Miller was walking purposefully ahead instead of measling along behind her or standing still. What kind of bug did she have in her drawers? Johnnie Mae noticed that Pearl's eyes were now on level with hers. She was holding her chin up and not ducking her head. Pearl Miller seemed to have developed a new, curvy body. The knobs on Pearl's chest had blossomed and she now wore a brassiere. Pearl Miller was becoming a new person!

Johnnie Mae's breasts were still little more than nubbins, but they had become more noticeable. Neither her mother nor her aunt Ina had discussed it with her, but they'd decided between them that Ina must now get to work on a brassiere for Johnnie Mae. It was no longer appropriate for her to be going around wearing undershirts like a boy or a baby child, her nubbins bobbing around for any to see. She was coming on to be a woman.

Mama said that everybody matures at her own pace and every girl gets her monthly and develops a bosom. It's just a matter of time. Mama was brusque in her way of talking about these "woman" things. According to her, some subjects aren't worthy of a whole lot of ruminating. The things that make a woman a woman didn't bear much conversation. Only a slattern would fill her days running off at the mouth about what's up underneath people's clothes. A decent woman had too many other things to do with her time. All she said that morning before school was that Aunt Ina had something for her to try on. So Johnnie Mae must come home right after school let out.

The thing was simply made of white cotton and delicate eyelet lace on the straps and cups. It was small, and even with it on, her breasts made hardly a ripple on her blouse. Aunt Ina saw the bit of disappointment on Johnnie Mae's face when she looked at herself. "Just give it time," Aunt Ina said. "Don't try to hurry up to be a woman. You're going to have to be one for the rest of your life."

To Johnnie Mae, time seemed to be having its own sweet way with her. Here was Pearl Miller, who used to be a sack of potatoes and a scared rabbit to boot, now looking like a grown woman! And her chest still looked like a boy's!

~

Johnnie Mae came straight through to the kitchen. Mama stood at the stove with her back to it. Johnnie Mae stared at her mama's stomach. She saw the rounding and couldn't believe how foolish she'd been not to have seen it sooner. How could she not have noticed something so obvious? Her own mother, someone she saw every day, looked unfamiliar. Mama's face was puffy along the cheeks and her waist was completely gone. Now that Pearl had pointed it out she could see it clearly.

Pearl had said matter-of-factly, "Your mama's having a baby, isn't she?" Johnnie Mae had been struck dumb at the idea. No one had told her a thing. Now she put her hand tentatively on her mother's stomach. The belly was thick and tight. She was shocked, not only at the obvious swelling there but that her mother allowed her to touch it. Johnnie Mae took her hand off, backed to the other side of the table, and looked at her mother's stomach from across the room. Mama seemed to her to be standing way far off on the other side of a valley. She was visible, but removed a distance from Johnnie Mae. Mama's words, too, seemed to be straining across a chasm. "I'm going to have a baby, Johnnie Mae."

Johnnie Mae looked at her mother's face then quickly down at the floor. "Don't act a baby, Johnnie," her mother said. "You're a woman yourself nearly. It's natural for us to bring another child. It'll add to our joy." Mama's words were strange—not unintelligible, just unfamiliar. Yet there was a familiarity. The conversation had gone like so many of their talks. Mama said Johnnie Mae was a woman, but she spoke to her, as always, as if she were a child. Despite her mother's smooth, calm delivery, there was an undercurrent to her words. Was Mama frightened? If it was the state of natural circumstance for a woman to be in the family way then why was she trembling a bit, sucking in her bottom lip?

When Papa came into the kitchen, Johnnie Mae and her

mother were on separate sides of the room. Again there was a shift, a realignment of the tectonic plates of the family ground. The earth beneath them was shifting and they would be moved by it as they'd been moved by the death of Clara. They would be a different grouping with a new baby. Would it be a boy? They always say a man wants a boy. How would Papa feel about her after he'd gotten his boy?

Johnnie Mae wanted desperately to be grown-up. She wanted to have a glorious bosom and the calm, smug womanliness that everybody said would come to her one day. But she was scared that even though she wanted to move away from these people, this new baby might knock her completely out of their lives.

14

"Never take advice; can't keep still all day, and not being a pussy-cat, I don't like to doze by the fire. I like adventures, and I am going to find some." Johnnie Mae began chapter five of *Little Women* with her elbows flat, her shoulders hunched, and her chin resting on the kitchen table. Dinner and dishes were over and the family—Mama, Papa, Aunt Ina, and Johnnie Mae—were sharing each other's breaths in the kitchen before bedtime. The women passed the time sewing up holes in socks. Papa sat back in his chair, working a toothpick in his teeth.

Wormley School had few books other than the hand-me-down texts given to the colored schools by the school board. Miss Clementine Chichester, the librarian at the Mount Zion Church community center, had highly recommended *Little Women* to Johnnie Mae. Miss Chichester, a college-educated woman who did laundry work for very rich families, took it as her mission to disabuse colored people of the notion that the only fit book for them and their children to read was the Bible. Georgetown's alley residents were her biggest constituency and she considered it her calling to promote health, hygiene, and education in those precincts. A cadger and an irrepressible social reformer, Miss Chichester visited the homes of wealthy Georgetowners on her laundry rounds and hauled off any unwanted books to build up the center's lending library.

Miss Chichester was impressed with Johnnie Mae's reading ability and urged her to borrow a copy of *Little Women*, with the caveat that the book must not be put down in a pan of gravy, that her hands must be washed before opening it, and that Towser must not be allowed to chew on it. She praised it, promised Johnnie Mae that she would enjoy it, and that, upon her signature in the record book, it could be kept for a full two weeks.

Alice's and Ina's talk around the stove was full of the doings and goings-on of Miz St. Pierre and Miz Mary Ann Clarke. Johnnie Mae drew down into the book and let their voices play above her head. She fancied herself like Jo, a girl with too much moxie to sit around chattering about other people's business.

When folks talk about a person talking up a blue streak they usually mean somebody like Miss Mary Ann Clarke. Ina's best customer, she was a tall, angular woman who talked constantly while having her fittings in the front parlor. Miss Mary Ann Clarke talked so hard and fast that she hardly seemed to be breathing. The stream of words flowed endlessly outward. Never mind if someone thought to answer her. Answering wasn't at all necessary when Miss Mary Ann Clarke talked.

Ina told Alice what Miss Mary Ann Clarke had said about the St. Pierres being in financial trouble. Earlier that afternoon, Ina had cleared her throat and drawn her lips tighter around the row of straight pins in her mouth as she pinned the hem of Miss Mary Ann Clarke's new black serge skirt. Seated on a small hassock, she'd removed each pin from her lips, slid it into the fabric, and leaned back to get perspective on the work. Miss Mary Ann Clarke stood on a slightly taller hassock. Ina's front parlor floor was an obstacle course of hassocks. The four square wooden stools with legs at graduated heights and plush upholstered centers like nougats were used for measuring and pinning customers' hems. Cap had made the stools and Ina had fitted them with cushions at around the time she decided to put a SEAMSTRESS sign in her front window on Volta Place.

"My sister said that woman, Alexis St. Pierre, has been taking her family silver service down to the Jews on M Street," Miss Mary Ann Clarke said. "They say her husband is tied up in some bad business about money down at the agency where he works. My sister says he has run through all their money. How come you don't take in laundry, Ina Mae? You could make a pretty penny if you did laundry and pressing along with your sewing. As it is, I've got to send my things down to the Chinaman on Water Street."

Ina's mind had wandered and she was sorry she hadn't caught more of what Miss Mary Ann Clarke was saying about the St. Pierres. But a body would lose her mind if she tried to keep up listening to this talkative woman. Removing the last of the straight pins from her mouth, Ina had replied, "Miss Mary Ann Clarke, you know I don't do laundry. I never have. That about the length you want it now?"

Glancing in the mirror, Miss Mary Ann Clarke had answered, "Yes, Ina Mae, that will probably do. If a decent woman like you took in some laundry, we wouldn't have to deal with Chinamen."

Always prepared to sew, Ina now pulled another sock with a hole at the heel from her running bag. She took a needle from the place above her heart where several threaded needles were worked through the dress and set to work on the sock.

According to Alice, Alexis St. Pierre had been acting nervous lately. She seemed especially nervous when her husband was at home. It was as if she were guarding herself against saying something to him. For his part, Douglas St. Pierre appeared to be avoiding his wife. When both were in the house, there was little conversation. And the only time there was lively talk now was when Douglas St. Pierre entertained his acquaintances. Alexis was fluttery and irritable on these occasions and became increasingly so as the talk turned to investments and speculation in the stock market. Douglas became downright giddy then and took a child's delight in tales of wild speculation on the stock market. Alexis would look at him with a dull, puzzled face and refuse to join in the gaiety.

As a senior clerk at the department of the treasury, Douglas St. Pierre afforded a comfortable, though not opulent, lifestyle. The backbone of the St. Pierres' financial position was Alexis's inheritance.

When the women's talk wound down, Willie rose, stretched, and went out to the toilet for his evening constitutional. Johnnie Mae closed her book and hurried to wash up near the kitchen stove before going upstairs to her chilly bedroom.

At the St. Pierres' house the next day, Alice counted

Alexis's silver pieces and found many missing. Miss Mary Ann Clarke was right. They had been selling off their belongings. This was coming at a bad time—with the baby coming. Alice had wanted to work right up until the baby came and then have Ina work in her place until she could take her job back. But if the St. Pierres' money was getting tight, then soon they wouldn't be able to afford to keep her on. Better be asking people if they've heard of anything.

Alice ruminated on the St. Pierres and their financial troubles while she worked. All she was going to learn she'd have to learn at the keyhole. Though they'd had a respectful camaraderie over the years, Alice knew that Alexis wouldn't discuss her troubles. Alexis would consider it unseemly to talk about these troubles straight out and honestly.

Around the time that dinner was ready and Alice prepared to serve it, she heard Alexis and Douglas arguing in the parlor. When they moved into the dining room, she could hear their conversation clearly from the kitchen. She was embarrassed for them at first. Then she got angry that they were not ashamed to air all their business within earshot. She listened quietly, seated at the kitchen table with her hands folded as if praying. Douglas St. Pierre spoke to his wife in a low, sullen, growling voice. Alexis's voice danced above his in a tearful, high-pitched whine. "How can they do that? How can they do it? Douglas, how can this happen?" Alexis's words were clearly intelligible. Alice was unable to discern Douglas's reply. She could only hear his growl.

Alice decided not to go into the room. There wouldn't be any way to pretend that she wasn't aware of their argument. The sound of a door slamming followed. Alice waited impatiently in the kitchen. The argument seemed to have run out with the slamming door. The next noise from the room was Alexis's crying. Alice was in a tangle about what to do. She wanted to get the dinner served and get home. But she was reluctant to go into the room. Her annoyance grew into anger while she waited the dinner. She fussed to herself that she had better be looking for something else if they were going to start acting like this. She didn't want foolishness.

Around eight o'clock, Johnnie Mae came to the back door of the St. Pierres' house and looked through the kitchen window at her mother. Mama was sitting at the table with her arms folded across her chest and her face as tight as Dick's hatband. The family had been waiting for her and Papa had sent Johnnie Mae to see if there was trouble.

At the sight of Johnnie Mae, Alice rose from the table, signaled to the girl to wait, and marched into the dining room. Alexis sat alone at the table, staring at the place settings. Alice quietly informed Alexis that she had put up the food and was going home. Alexis said nothing, but tears ran down her cheeks. She sat at the table looking at the chair her husband was accustomed to sit in and continued crying. He was not there, but she looked as if she were hanging on to every word that came from the empty chair.

Alice left the St. Pierre house feeling angry. When she'd gone a block she thought to be ashamed of herself. She was mad at Alexis—and Douglas—but she hadn't stopped to feel sorry for Alexis crying into her sleeve like that. He'd made her cry. He'd fussed at her and lied to her most likely and done something that caused her to cry and Alice was only feeling sorry now that she'd left their house. Up underneath them in the house, her compassion was squashed by annoyance with them, and this annoyance had crowded out her better feelings.

Wintertime brings a closed-in feeling that creates hazards and annoyances. Households draw in toward their centers for warmth in cold weather, and emotions and conflicts that are dispersed in balmier air keep circulating and threatening to strangle folks when they're inside so long huddled against the cold. In the house with them, Alice hadn't given Alexis as much sympathy as you'd give a dog. But out in the sharp air she could hear the woman sobbing and wished she'd given her some show of feeling.

Alice walked down Wisconsin Avenue feeling grateful that Willie had sent Johnnie Mae to see about her. She had a feeling that she wanted to gather up her loved ones and crush them to her. Then her mind went to Clara—the fact of her being gone. And a twinge passed over her. Alice's thoughts raced ahead to the coming child and she wondered if every joyful thought would now be diminished a jot by longing for Clara.

Johnnie Mae skipped down the street ahead of her mother. When Alice caught up with her at the street corner, Johnnie Mae was staring into the large pit that was the construction site of the new Francis Junior High School swimming pool. Johnnie Mae stood under a streetlight with a dreamy look on her face.

After much agitation on the part of Reverend Jenkins of Mount Zion Church and Reverend Souter from the First Baptist church and Reverend Walker from Jerusalem Baptist and Dr. Tyler and Miss Elizabeth Boston and Miss Clementine Chichester and others, the District of Columbia had finally agreed to build a regulation swimming pool for colored children in Georgetown. The churchmen had organized the most prominent of Georgetown's colored people to press the district government and the Congress to recognize that colored citizens were paying taxes. And being taxpayers, they were entitled to recreational facilities and libraries for their children. The leaders cited business after business in Georgetown owned by colored citizens who paid their taxes as certainly as their white neighbors. Hundreds of signatures were gathered on the petitions, and the pastors made the rounds of countless meetings.

Building the Francis Junior High School swimming pool was a compromise, though. The government was immovable and the white citizens were adamant that the same playgrounds, pools, and libraries not be used by both colored and white. And as long as there was something for everybody, nobody could squawk. Though there was something like progress about the pool, there was something else, too. They had built a pool for the colored children. Colored weren't allowed into the whites-only pool on Volta Place and never would be — that was final.

The swimming pool had become the biggest topic of conversation in Georgetown. People wrote to their people back home about it. Little as it was, the colored folks had got something for themselves.

To Alice Bynum the new swimming pool was tangible proof that their opportunities were better in Georgetown. "As long as we're making progress," she said to herself, "no matter how slow. As long as we're not standing stock-still with our shoes in the mud!"

An odd thought came to her as she stood back a bit watching Johnnie Mae. She tried to think back to when she'd begun thinking of progress and better times and accomplishments as something for Johnnie Mae rather than for herself. After all, she was not an old woman. But comes a time for a woman when she stops thinking of herself as a girl, as a person of possibles. She starts looking at the plain facts of herself. Her body that's become the body that she has and her habits becoming the habits that she's written in stone. Her "haves" being the ones she's got and maybe not getting any more. Alice knew she was still able to work hard, was still a clear thinker, was still pretty enough. But there had recently come about a transference. She had come to a kind of resignation that real progress was not going to come in time for her to really latch on to it. Johnnie Mae would get it. Johnnie Mae would be coming around just in time for the brass ring. And what there was chiefly for Alice and Willie to do was to make sure Johnnie Mae was ready. They would prepare her — be sure she'd be able to reach for it. Johnnie Mae must be able to finish school, must go all the way through. Maybe she'd go on after high school to a college? Maybe she would find work as a teacher or a nurse? Alice's dreams took on an ever-rising spiral.

Johnnie Mae would perhaps be a schoolteacher and a big woman like Miss Nannie Helen Burroughs or Miss Mary Macleod Bethune or some other Negro women. That's why Alice and Willie worked — why they'd come to Georgetown. And now there was the baby to dream for. And they needed to keep their children from being ground down by want so much that they wouldn't be able to dream dreams for themselves. She and Willie could have filled their bellies and shod their feet in Carolina, but for schooling and dreaming their children were better off here. Yes, it had happened. She had ceded the future to her children.

Johnnie Mae's dreams fetched closer to hand. She had been watching and waiting for the swimming pool to be completed. Each day since the work had begun, she'd looked down into the hole that was fast becoming a trench that would eventually be lined with tiles and by June would be filled with water. Nobody was more excited about the new pool than Johnnie Mae and nobody more eager to jump in.

15

"Come on" was what Johnnie Mae said to Pearl that afternoon after classes let out. It was a January day with bright sunshine and soft clouds. The phrase that had always rallied Clara to her cause, whatever it might be, had the same effect on Pearl. At first she'd just stood there. Johnnie Mae walked away a few steps, looked back at Pearl still standing on the steps of Wormley School, raised her eyebrows in a way that questioned the girl's moxie, and walked down Prospect Street. Pearl followed. Johnnie Mae was right to call Pearl a scaredy-cat. She was scared a lot of the time. Since the Millers' troubles out in Oklahoma, Pearl had started to be skittish and to shrink away from people. But she couldn't stop herself from following Johnnie Mae either. Johnnie Mae had said come on and she couldn't disengage herself from the pull of the girl and make any kind of firm decision to stay put. So she followed along.

The blessed freedom of walking in and around the clusters of people buying or selling or toting a load buoyed the girls.

"Step on a crack, break your mother's back!" Johnnie Mae looked like a ballerina or an aerialist walking from cobblestone to cobblestone not stepping on the cracks, placing her feet on one rounded stone then another. She held her arms out away from her sides to balance and Pearl tried vainly to copy her.

Johnnie Mae scuttled away from the crowds of folks on Wisconsin Avenue and wound her way up and around and through alleys. She went past Stevens's fish market in order to see Pearl's eyes pop. She knew that the sight of the huge swordtail hanging in the window would make Pearl gape like Clara used to. They took the alley behind the fish market and down toward Water Street. A group of men with bloody aprons sat on crates gutting fish. "Watch out!" Johnnie Mae called to Pearl, not stopping, only skirting the men. Pails of waste water cascaded out of doorways all along the street, running over the cobblestones and sluicing toward the river. Johnnie Mae followed beside this septic freshet to the nasty tangle of wild growth and human waste at the river's edge.

They followed along a pathway that was merely a ribbon of bare ground pounded out by numerous feet. Pearl got winded and was breathing out of her mouth like Clara used to. Once, Johnnie Mae pulled up and turned around to face her with arms akimbo and chest stuck out. Pearl bumped smack into her because she had had her eyes on the ground. Pearl took the blow and stopped and looked at Johnnie Mae with alarm. Johnnie Mae didn't say anything, only stomped her foot. Pearl wondered if this meant she was to turn around and go back. But when Johnnie Mae resumed walking, she continued, too.

The path was filled with mud puddles and rocks of all sizes. Some of the rocks were sharp-edged and some smooth and slippery. Every kind of stick and board with splinters was calling "Step on me, I dare you!" And some whipsaw shrubs lashed their ankles. Despite the cold and the even chillier breeze blowing in off the water, Johnnie Mae peeled open her coat, perspiring with the exertion of cutting through debris. Pearl, struggling mightily to keep up the pace, was nevertheless chilled to the bone. She held together the place at the waist of her coat where a missing button left her abdomen exposed, and her gloveless right hand developed a white crust. She lubricated her lips with saliva in the face of the river wind lashing them and the wind quickly seized this moisture and dried her lips still more. By the time they reached the end of Water Street and continued down under the Francis Scott Key Bridge, both their faces were tight and ashy.

The brambles became ever wilder as they continued westward. The two, with Johnnie Mae leading, sidled past the Washington Canoe Club, a cozy clapboard structure perched on the riverbank with a fancy dock attached and stacks of canoes on two sides. MEMBERS ONLY and NO TRESPASSING signs sprouted here and there on the periphery of the club's property, and an irascible hound patrolled the fence to keep the hoi polloi to the public side of the path.

"That's the Three Sisters—those rocks out there—that's the top of their castle. That's where Clara is. But you know that 'cause that's where you came up from." Johnnie Mae pronounced all this as if there could be no doubt as to its veracity. People in Georgetown had always spoken of the Three Sisters as if it were both an identifiable trio of female spirits and a place in space and time. It was there and it was them. It was near and yet not at all near to the bank. All that was between the three boulders and the shoreline on either side for a span of perhaps a mile was the mysterious bailiwick of the female spirits who inhabited the Potomac.

Pearl had never been so close to the edge of the river. She could never have imagined herself at a point so close to the boulders. She shook her head briskly as if she meant to dislodge her confusion and struggled to figure out why Johnnie Mae was so convinced that she was a part of her sister's drowning. How in the world had she gotten hold of this idea?

Suddenly, Johnnie Mae ran up the embankment away from the river, turned on her heels, and ran fast back down toward the river's edge. Pearl expected that she would stop at the lip of the river, that this was some version of a game of whirligig. But Johnnie Mae continued into the river up to her waist, soaking her shoes and socks and most of her clothing.

Pearl backed away from this spectacle, afraid that she would be pulled into the frigid water by Johnnie Mae or by some force at work to grab young girls. For the first time she started to believe that some power could be at work around the banks of the Potomac. She wanted to beg Johnnie Mae to come out of the water, to just come out and let them go on home and never come back down here. But she didn't know how to get it said. Often she got plain disgusted with herself for not being able to say out loud what was struggling to get said. It was at these moments—and there were so many of them in a day—that she would shake her head from side to side. So many moments required this head-clearing motion that it was fast becoming a mannerism of the girl. She blurted out, "You pushed your sister in the river! You're mean and you didn't love her and you pushed her down in the river and made her drown."

The words stopped Johnnie Mae's whirling. This was the most she had ever heard Pearl Miller utter. And this string of words was nothing less than a quiver of arrows fired straight at her. This was the test of her theory that Pearl Miller was in some way Clara come again. Because if Pearl Miller knew what actually happened, if she knew things about the events at the riverbank, then it was certain proof that she was some sort of haint.

The trouble was that Johnnie Mae herself hardly knew what had happened. The girls were swimming, cannonading, swimming in circles around each other. Johnnie Mae was pearl-diving. Clara was sitting on the back end of a log and there was a big splash and Johnnie Mae thought it was her own body slicing the water. But it had been Rat. Rat had hit the water with a big splash. Rat and the log—and Rat had never come up again. And she never saw her again—never saw Rat alive again.

She had bobbed up to the surface of the water and didn't see Clara. Clara sitting on the log on the bank was a marker—a place on the shore that placed the swimmers, that showed where they were in the water. Then Clara was gone from the log. Johnnie Mae looked and counted the other heads above the surface of the water. They were all there giggling and laughing, but not Clara. Johnnie Mae dove down below. She opened her eyes to see beneath the water. Everything was green and cloudy. She couldn't see a thing beneath the surface. She came back for air. She sucked in air and dove back down. Her chest was on fire. She couldn't see Clara when she came back to the surface. She saw the white ribbon that was on Clara's plait — that she had tied to Clara's plait. She thought momentarily to be angry that the white ribbon was off the plait and floating and going green in the slimy water when it should have been fastened to Clara's hair. She went down again and forgot to close her mouth. Water came in her throat and through her nose.

She duck-dived to retrieve Rat, but Rat never came back to the surface until she was dragged up by the men from the city. Johnnie Mae hadn't actually seen it, of course. She hadn't even been told about this. Her mama and papa hadn't thought it was appropriate to tell her how Clara's body had come up out of the river and been prepared for burial. Snow Simpson—his skin was dark and glossy like a ripe eggplant—was mad about being always called Snow. One day—for meanness, because Johnnie Mae had not let him have one of her pencils—Snow Simpson had told her all about the men pulling Clara from the Potomac. He sidled up to her ear in the school yard and said that the men from the city had come up and stood around and had dragged lines in the water and had finally snagged Clara like a big old carp and hooked her and reeled her in and started to throw her back for being too small. This last he'd said over his shoulder, gliding past smirking. And Johnnie Mae had hit him in the back so hard the bones in his back stung her hand.

At the river now, the cool water coursed through her legs, sloshing her labia, chilling them and causing a shiver. Warm urine let go and streamed down and warmed the labia. The cool water was less cool, then cooler again. The coolness called her back to herself and the freezing cold water slapped her out of her reverie. She barreled out of the river. Out of the water, the freezing water seemed to burn her skin. Mad at herself for peeing on herself like a baby, she ran up the embankment to Pearl and pushed the girl's chest.

"I didn't. I didn't push nobody. I didn't push Rat."

"You musta pushed her like you're pushing me!" Pearl Miller heard a girl yelling and could feel her heart in her rib cage fluttering. Standing toe to toe with Johnnie Mae she had a sensation of floating. She could hear a lot of angry talking and she could see that Johnnie Mae's lips had ceased to move and so she concluded that the girl yelling into Johnnie Mae's face must be herself. She felt a thing taking hold of her, trapped as she was with the river ahead of her and her feet mired in all kinds of debris on the riverbank. And Georgetown was up the slope and people were walking by on their own business and not many of them even noticed her. And Johnnie Mae, the only person who seemed to take a notice of her, was badgering her about being a haint and seeming to threaten her with drowning. Was Johnnie Mae pulling her out to the Three Sisters, offering her in exchange for Clara? Or maybe she was just working in concert with these mystery forces in the river that wanted to pull down somebody foolish enough to come out here—someone who could never match her curiosity with enough courage to take any daring action.

"I didn't push Rat!" Johnnie Mae said it loud. She said it hard. She was telling herself more than she was telling anybody. Her soul was leaping with happiness that someone had challenged her on the point. Somebody was so mad—so involved with this tangle—that they'd confronted her and asked her if she was responsible. And now she could insist and hear herself say it. "No." She had not pushed her sister. She did not drown her sister. She did not even realize until too late that she had lapsed in her caring for her sister and let the Three Sisters, the Potomac, or whomever take her away.

There was her mother, herself, and her baby sister. And on a day when she had the care of her sister, a day when she chewed down on her mother's responsibilities, she had failed. She'd been trusted as she'd always been trusted—with Clara. She had failed. She had been a little mother countless times. It was her duty.

"Who's Rat?" Pearl asked in a pleading tone.

"My sister," Johnnie Mae answered, exasperated with Pearl's pretending not to know about Rat.

"You call your sister Rat? How your mama let you call her a name like that?"

"She doesn't know it. She doesn't have to know everything. They don't have to know everything."

"Eventually they find it out."

"She don't have to know."

"She's gonna know you've been up to something. Your clothes're all wet."

"Shut up! It's none of your business, scaredy-cat. You're scared of your own shadow—just like Rat. You're scared of everything. Being a scaredy-cat draws trouble like a magnet. Being scared draws a mad dog to you like a magnet."

The angry petulance that had Johnnie Mae in a tangle with Pearl was familiar. Often she had been so angry with Clara. The scaredy-cats were always standing back with their hands folded meekly, hoping to grab fun on the go. They were always hoping to pick up what fun and adventure somebody else would make. They could pick it up like lumps of coal fallen from the back of a coal truck. They got their fun and adventure by accident. Johnnie Mae wanted to make the fun—make the adventure—pull something down into her lap.

The girls stood there on the embankment with arms folded across their chests, mad at each other. Johnnie Mae felt wet and stinky. The river water and her own urine had made her clothes a mess. Pearl was right. Her mother would notice and would demand to know where she'd been and what she'd been doing. They'd better leave right away. She'd better get back to the house and change and rinse out these things and make up some story about it.

"Come on, scaredy-cat," she said, turning her back on Pearl, who was still facing toward the Three Sisters. Over her shoulder she flung a threat. "If you tell, I'll put my foot in your butt."

16

Alice, Ina, Miz Iola Perryman, Miz Hattie Miller, Miss Elizabeth Boston, and Miss Clementine Chichester boarded the streetcar at Wisconsin Avenue and P Street in a fluttery state of excitement to travel to Union Station to meet Miss Gladys Perryman's train. Gladys Perryman, the niece by marriage of Miz Iola Perryman, was arriving from New York to settle with her aunt and uncle in Georgetown. Miz Iola's endless bragging at church about her husband's brother's girl, who was attending Madame C. J. Walker's school for beauty culture in New York City, had whipped up anticipation of her arrival. According to Miz Iola, Georgetown was getting a true artiste of the hot comb. Here was someone who'd surely raise the standards of taste among the tasteful women. Miz Iola gathered up an eager committee of women and girls to meet Gladys's train at Union Station.

Johnnie Mae thought the whole thing was a silly waste of time. Mama insisted upon dressing up in her Sunday things, and Johnnie Mae was made to dress up too. Aunt Ina, who had been going on and on about Miss Gladys Perryman, insisted upon going to the station to meet her. She said she'd invite Miss Perryman to join their penny-savers club and Mama said she thought Miss Perryman might hold herself a bit above such activities.

Riding downtown on the bus and walking through the streets with Mama and Aunt Ina and Miz Iola Perryman and the other ladies, Johnnie Mae slunk back a bit. She tried to lean into a place of shadow created by her mama's body standing against the outside world of Washington. She knew she was too big a girl for this. She knew that this feeling belonged to a time when she was a much younger child and had walked through the streets or ridden on a bus with her parents. When they ventured out into the larger Washington city world, some inexplicable thing, a force or something, was out there that Papa and Mama and Aunt Ina had to buffer against. Their faces and torsos anxiously breasted a tide of strange looks and behaviors. The thing was amorphous, was an ill-defined, unsure feeling that the adults had when they left Georgetown. Mama was always fussy about their clothes and hair when they got aboard a streetcar. Several times on this trip Johnnie Mae brushed off the front of her dress and smoothed her hair.

Mama had insisted that Johnnie Mae ask if Pearl could go along. Upon hearing of the outing, Hattie Miller included herself. Like Johnnie Mae, Pearl was acting sullen on the bus trip to the station.

Perhaps the white people seemed so numerous in Washington city because the colored people were so few on the downtown streets. When Johnnie Mae had gone across town to the Howard theater for a musical show or over to Griffith Stadium for a baseball game, the streets there were thronged with black and brown and yellow people, as well as whites. The U Street thoroughfare was thick with people. But on the streets of downtown, dark faces were scarce.

Gladys Perryman descended from the train and seemed to glide through the station without touching the marble floor. Her tall, willowy frame, outfitted in a chic white wool suit of recent fashion, caused the welcoming committee to sigh and adjust their clothes, smoothing and patting themselves. Miz Iola drew up with pride, pulling in her derriere and hoisting her breasts high with dignity. Asa Perryman's girl was already a sensation and she had not yet set foot in Georgetown!

All eyes went to Gladys's head. On it she wore a jaunty, crescent-shape cloche stuck through with a low-hanging turkey feather. The hair that was visible beneath the hat was arranged in shiny, frothy curls. Touching a white handkerchief to her throat, Gladys said, "How do you do." The committee giggled and answered with a round of "How do." A small, enigmatic smile came to rest on Gladys Perryman's lips. Miz Iola stepped forward and, looking upward into Gladys's pretty face, took her by the shoulders and kissed each of her cheeks. Each woman stepped forward as she was introduced and smiled warmly. Johnnie Mae and Pearl curtsied.

Gladys was pleased with her reception. It had been worth it to drain her savings for the new suit and hat. A stunning appearance was worth every penny it took for a woman in the business of making other women beautiful. As Madame C. J. Walker herself said, "Meticulous grooming is a beautician's best advertisement."

The women allowed Miz Iola to take Gladys's arm while several of them grabbed up her luggage. Johnnie Mae and Pearl tussled over a small train bag and ended with Pearl relinquishing it to Johnnie Mae when her mama chastised her with her eyes. Flanked by her coterie of admirers, Gladys crossed Union Station's waiting room floor with head held high and ambitions soaring.

Gladys had certainly caused a ripple among the women who came to welcome her at the station. She took this to mean that the Negro women of Georgetown were ready to buy the magic she could let loose from jars and combs. She would set the tone! She, Gladys Perryman, graduate of Lelia College in New York City, would lead them out of the backwater of beauty culture and into the promised land!

Gladys Perryman was a marvel to Johnnie Mae. It would be silly to say that the turkey feather was the thing that had done it. But it was the thing that had captured her attention, that made an impression on her. That large turkey feather, sticking through the hat at such an angle, was so lovely and daring. Johnnie Mae had never seen a woman so vibrant. Her own mother was pretty — everyone thought so. And there were other pretty women in Georgetown. But no one of them had the look that Gladys Perryman had when she first appeared at Union Station. She was striking and she looked as if she'd planned it that way. That was it! She wasn't just pretty by accident. Gladys Perryman was beautiful on purpose. And Johnnie Mae could tell that all of the women in the welcoming group were envious of Gladys Perryman's fine clothes and bearing. The whole of the ride home on the streetcar, Gladys could well have been the queen of Georgetown for the fawning attentions she got from the committee. And she sat straight and dignified, wearing white gloves with pearl buttons on the delicate hands that rested one atop the other near her left knee.

～

Dr. Marvin Tyler could have sent his daughter Sarey to Miz Jackson or someone or other to get her hair pressed. Or he certainly could have sent her across town in Washington city to a hairdresser. But there was some feeling akin to shame that washed over him when he considered it, and he reproached himself for feeling shame in connection with so small a thing. He was further ashamed of feeling ashamed of Sarey's hair. He knew that some portion of this feeling sprang from Sarey herself, who seemed so aware of his feelings and stoked the flames of this shame with her eyes and her manner.

The new hairdresser, or "beautician," as she advertised herself, gave the impression of being bound by a professional ethic of secrecy. The neatly lettered sign said simply GLADYS PERRYMAN, BEAUTICIAN, and conveyed a sense of confessional sanctity, a solemn code of confidentiality. She would work her magic and not tell her tricks.

Being used to his wife's light cream color, the doctor was surprised that he was enamored of Gladys Perryman's skin, which was the color of strong pekoe tea, the color of some leaves in autumn. Being used to the delights of his wife's long, straight hair, he was surprised that his eyes fancied Gladys Perryman's glossy black hair.

Gladys ushered Sarey into the kitchen at the back of her aunt and uncle's house. "We'll take our time, Doctor," she said, turning to the doctor, who had started to follow his daughter into the kitchen. He stood looking directly into

Gladys's eyes, wanting to bring his hands up from his sides and touch her face. "She's a big girl, Doctor. I'll send her home when she's done," Gladys said as she accompanied him back to the front door. He paused just inside the parlor doorway and proffered a dollar bill.

"Children are only fifty cents, Doctor. I'll do my best."

"Yes, but please, I have no change."

"Then you won't owe me for the next time," she said, smiling sweetly and taking the bill.

Surprised at himself, Dr. Tyler rubbed the brim of his hat between his fingers like a schoolboy and wondered where the feeling of excitement in Gladys Perryman's presence could be coming from. His voice was scratchy and uncertain when he said, "Thank you, Miss Perryman. I have my calls to make." He turned and left.

Gladys gave Sarey's scalp a vigorous washing over a tub in her aunt's kitchen. However, the brushing and oiling and pressing was done with a gentleness to which Sarey was unaccustomed. Gladys encouraged the girl while she worked, chirping, "You've got a nice suit of hair. It just needs cultivating. We'll work on it." Sarey's hair was as close to a rat's nest as any she'd seen, but Gladys was excited by the challenge of creating beauty out of the mess on top of the girl's head.

Sarey flinched when she felt the heat of the hot comb near her ears. Gladys was careful, though, and no streams of hot grease slid down her neck or seared her ears. Sarey became relaxed after a while, and though she didn't hold out much hope that her head would finally look like Miss Perryman's, she prayed fervently that it would.

Sarey's hair looked perfectly presentable for the first time ever when Gladys Perryman finished with her that day. On subsequent visits—Sarey begged her father to be allowed to go every week—Gladys built upon the cultivation she had begun in the first visit. She pressed and brushed the hair away from the girl's hairline and plaited it tightly in two braids. After several months, Sarey's hair grew and thickened and became lovely. So much had been done with so little that other women and girls were heartened. If Gladys Perryman could work a miracle on Sarey Tyler's head, then she could fix anyone's. It was the best advertising Gladys could have wanted.

Gladys built a clientele so quickly that she had work in her aunt's kitchen every day but Sunday. Within weeks she began to dream of having her own shop. Wednesday evening and all day Thursday, the kitchen mechanics' day off, were busiest. The muscles in Gladys's upper arms would be cramping on her by the time the last of Thursday's heads was done. But this schedule gave her the luxury of resting late in the morning, especially on Fridays. She relished this time when she could take a long, perfumed bath while her aunt and uncle were out working. She could spend time oiling her skin and pressing and curling her own hair. She could loll around and dream about having her own storefront on the avenue. She could put on a pretty dress and take a parasol and walk down Wisconsin Avenue in the late afternoon, coyly shopping for vegetables and fruit.

17

The breeze that was stirring was foul smelling and blew up from the Hopfenmeier rendering plant near the Potomac River's edge. The air was noxious. Alice felt like a rag doll as she walked up Wisconsin Avenue to the St. Pierres' house. When she reached the crest of the hill at Wisconsin and R streets, she paused to huff and blow and dab at her forehead.

A harsh truth had to be faced: the St. Pierres' household accounts were going unpaid. This was the pitfall of working for one family. When their fortunes turned sour, your bread was likely to go unbuttered.

Alice entered the house by the back kitchen door as usual. And as usual, she listened for Alexis's footsteps coming toward the kitchen. In happier times, Alexis was accustomed to coming into the kitchen as soon as Alice arrived. She would begin their day together with a cheery greeting. Alice had liked her for that. Throughout the day, Alexis kept company with Alice when she was not engaged in her club meetings and social obligations.

The house was quiet and dark when Alice arrived. The

drapes in the front room were closed against the noxious air outside, and no lamps were lit. Though it was nearly an hour before she heard Alexis descend the stairs, Alice knew she was in the house. When Alexis came into the kitchen, she was wearing a dull pink wrapper. Her hair was gathered messily into a ponytail, and dried material was caked at the corners of her eyes. The sight of her shocked Alice. Alexis had always comported herself with circumspection about her clothes and hygiene. And though she had always been friendly and easy-going, she was never anything less than properly dressed and ladylike. Alexis had never been one for suffering vapors or lolling about in her nightclothes. She was energetic and she enjoyed her activities, her gardening and her knitting and her club meetings.

"Miz St. Pierre, you feeling all right?" Alice asked with genuine concern. If she was sick it had come on suddenly. Yesterday she had been quiet and threatening tearful, but not ill.

Alexis didn't reply. She pulled her wrapper tightly about her neck and sat in one of the kitchen chairs.

"You'll feel better if you have a cup of tea." Alice put a pot of water on to boil, dunked and wrung a facecloth in warm water, and bathed Alexis's face. She must be coming down with a croup. That could explain her disheveled appearance.

After Alice had swabbed the corners of Alexis's eyes and rubbed the facecloth over her face and down her neck and at her nape and across the exposed area of her chest, Alexis still sat unmoving in the chair. Suddenly she began to shake and sweat. Alice tried to mop her dry. The shaking and sweating continued and tears flowed. Tears broke over her breast like beads from a broken strand. She could not be calmed.

Alice propped Alexis against the back of the chair and

went out through the back screen door. As she moved between the bushes lining the walkway from the back of the house to the front, her hard, businesslike thighs broke twigs along the way. At the street, she saw Mr. Pud Allen going by in his wagon and hailed him and asked him to get the white people's doctor, Dr. Mason.

Alice was unable to move Alexis from the chair and take her to her bedroom. When the doctor arrived, the two managed together to take her upstairs to the large front bedroom. The doctor said that it was most likely an inability to sleep that had caused Alexis's nervous attack. He sent Alice to the pharmacy for a medicinal draft to be mixed in water. Instructions were given that Alexis must rest. He told Alice to assure the woman's husband that she would certainly feel better soon.

When Alice returned with the draft and began to mix it with water, Alexis stopped her. She handed her a letter. "Read. Read what he has written," she said.

> *I am gone. I have taken nothing except all that you had and all that others had. I have lost everything. You may say that I deserted you and get a divorce. The house in Philadelphia is still yours. All else is gone. Douglas.*

Alexis was grief-stricken and tearful, but she was not incapacitated. The circumstances of Douglas's financial ruin were hazy. He had lost all his money. He had lost most of hers. He had looted her inheritance, though he'd not been able to sell her father's house in Philadelphia. He had borrowed from his friends and lost that money, too. He had not been able to borrow against her house in Philadelphia because he could not bring himself to ask her to sign the papers. He had taken money in his position at the treasury department and had lost that money, too. He had simply left.

Alexis had only the house in Philadelphia now and she made arrangements to return there. Alice did the packing though there was less to do than she would have thought. There was mostly clothes and small personal mementos. The jewelry of any value and the furniture had been sold to satisfy Douglas's debts. Alexis had dispassionately handed over her diamond engagement ring and other items Douglas had given her to the lawyer who was settling the accounts. There had been the suspicion that she had joined in Douglas's embezzlement and was possibly hiding some money. She had had to submit to a search of her belongings by the police and representatives of the treasury department.

As she left the house for the train station, Alexis put a brooch in Alice's hand. The brooch was as round as a silver dollar and studded with tiny garnets. Alexis said they were garnets with a touch of apology in her voice. They were not diamonds. They were only garnets. The lawyers had taken all of the diamonds. As she got in the cab for the train station, she urged Alice to remember her.

"That woman didn't deserve that! She didn't deserve it!" Alice said with heat and pity. In her kitchen, she unwrapped four teacups with a floral pattern and the saucers that matched them. Alexis had pressed these on her, too. Alice turned them over in her hands one at a time. These cups and saucers, pretty and fragile, would remind her of Alexis.

"God doesn't think about what you deserve. He's got a plan," Ina answered, sucking a strand of cotton thread. She bent toward the lamp and drew the thread through a needle.

"Oh, hush up, Ina!" Alice snapped.

"What am I doing but telling the truth?" Ina countered with wounded sensibilities.

"I don't want to hear about God's plan now, Ina. I'm talking about that man walking out on his wife like she was a common whore. That's what I'm talking about. He left her with only the clothes on her back practically."

"She's got a big house in Philadelphia to sit up in."

"Ina Mae, what plans has God got for you, I wonder." Alice laughed wryly at her funny, contrary little cousin. She always thought of Ina Mae as younger, though she was fully eight years older than Alice. Ina was the plump little girl who'd stood back on her heels and extended her arms to Alice when she'd toddled her first steps. Ina was the one who'd stayed behind gladly watching the smaller children when others went to dances. Ina had been the one who'd always dreamed of a houseful of children and had never had a single one.

"Well, the Lord made me colored. And on account of that, I'm not sitting up in a house in Philadelphia licking myself like a cat. I got to work for a living whether my husband is alive or dead or playing possum — and you the same," Ina countered.

"Ina, you're being kind of coldhearted. Don't you have any sympathy for that poor woman?" Alice said, only half teasingly.

"I save my sympathy for you. What you gonna do about your job? Instead of worrying about her, you ought to be worrying about yourself. What're you gonna do with those cups and saucers and that brooch? You can sell 'em and when the money's gone, it'll be gone."

~

Electricity came through Georgetown like a wave the same spring that the swimming pool was finished. Block by block, every house — big or small, palatial or pitiful — was wired to accommodate the incandescent bulbs. The gas street lamps were changed to the new electric lightbulbs and everybody in Georgetown, except the big-thighed Fontarellis, was glad about it.

Electric light came through the same year that Georgetown got a swimming pool for colored and a colored lifeguard. The water in the pool and the lifeguard who was studying to be a doctor and the thrill of little round glowing globes of light to cut on and off gave Georgetown many things to look forward to.

That same spring, the District of Columbia recreation department announced it was assembling teams of young swimmers to compete with teams from Baltimore, Philadelphia, and New York. Neighborhood groups throughout town were grooming their best swimmers to compete to be on the city-wide team.

Charles Edward Hughes, a medical student at Howard University and the head lifeguard at the Francis pool, organized swimming classes for the Georgetown children who came to the pool as soon as it opened. With a view to putting together a team, he gave each youngster a test to gauge his or her swimming abilities. Nobody was surprised that Johnnie Mae Bynum emerged as the best of the girls. Charles Hughes —

Charlie, they called him—praised her and made her the captain of the girls' team.

Johnnie Mae was, without doubt, the best female swimmer that Charlie Hughes had at the Francis pool. In fact, she was the best swimmer, male *or* female, at the Francis pool. Her mastery of the strokes was uniformly competent. He was surprised that she'd never had formal lessons. She was as close to a natural swimmer as Charlie had ever seen.

Pearl Miller, Mabel Dockery, Sarey Tyler, Dumpling Mason, Tiny Sham, Lula Lavery, and Johnnie Mae Bynum came to the pool each day for lessons with Charlie Hughes. They all wanted to be as close to Charlie as possible. They had all been swept up in the newness and the adventure and the beauty of Charlie Edward Hughes and the swimming pool.

Pearl was especially determined to learn the rudiments of swimming. But it was more as a means of preserving her friendship with Johnnie Mae than from a passion for water. The water itself exerted no pull on her. It was the pull of the other girls—especially Johnnie Mae. Sarey Tyler, afraid of spoiling her pressed hair, spent most of the swimming lesson shielding her hair from the water. But she, too, basked in the glow of Charlie Hughes.

Johnnie Mae's swimming was fluid, graceful, all that it should be. Why, she could likely win against any but the absolute best swimmers. But it was in the diving that you saw the best of the girl. It was her absolute, flawless ascent to the top of the diving tower full of confidence that made Charlie know she could compete and win. Only occasionally did she not connect well and falter enough to throw off the dive. These times were rare, and with practice were becoming even more so.

Johnnie Mae's innate moxie was what took her off the board and sent her swirling gracefully through the air and into the water. She handled all the dives competently, but it was her utter willingness to jump that was so thrilling. Some who eventually jumped off the diving board would hesitate, sometimes for long moments, before deciding to take the plunge. But Johnnie Mae was never unsure if she would jump. She would always jump. She would jump and descend to the surface of the water with a speed and force that belied the delicacy with which the water's surface parted to let her in. She seemed to break the surface with no more effort than the will to do it—breaking downward, then upward again, passing like a knife through butter.

The first time Pearl saw Johnnie Mae on the diving board, her form was silhouetted against a late afternoon sun slipping down into Rock Creek. Pearl climbed toward the playground up the hill from Rock Creek, coming to the pool for her lesson and for the camaraderie. Johnnie Mae stood on the diving board at the Francis pool with an energy in her limbs that appeared to Pearl to emanate from the sun. She was struck by the sight of Johnnie Mae. She didn't recognize her friend at first, but saw a tall, slim form standing higher than she'd ever seen a body stand. From where Pearl stood watching, trees obscured the platform on which the figure stood. Before the figure raised her arms, Pearl thought that it must be a statue she was seeing. When the figure left the end of the board in a perfect dive, Pearl drew in her breath and ran toward where she thought the figure must land, not realizing that there was water below her.

Pearl stood back and watched Johnnie Mae for a full hour that day. At times she squinted and threw her head back.

Johnnie Mae, completely absorbed in Charlie's assessment of each dive, didn't notice Pearl standing watching her from the fence. Pearl thought to herself that Johnnie Mae didn't look like a graceful little swan when you saw her up close, but atop that diving board it seemed as if she could jump off into the clouds.

She became a part of the water when she entered it, and so her moving through it was effortless and completely without fear. Charlie knew about fear in the water. A river swimmer will know about fear because a river is not a captive. It moves and changes. It can fool you and take you down in a minute if you are not always paying it mind. And it is fear that seals the swimmer's fate. Flailing about to stay afloat is what sinks the swimmer. The not knowing how far to the land again and how far to the bottom. Fear of it makes water fathomless.

Johnnie Mae hopped on one leg to let the water run out of her ear. She changed legs and hopped, letting water run out of the other ear. There was a feeling like ants running up her back. She slapped at her shoulders and scratched her neck. It was like when you disturb an anthill and all the ants come running out. They think it's a fire. That's what Rat said. Rat said they looked like they were running away from a house on fire. And that afternoon—some summer afternoon that was like so many she and Clara had shared—Johnnie Mae told Clara that they could really give the ants a taste of fire if they lit a match and stuck it down the anthill. The two girls looked all over the yard until they found an anthill. Johnnie Mae struck a match that she scraped on the bottom of her shoe. It flared up. Rat got so excited that she bumped Johnnie Mae's elbow. Johnnie Mae told her she'd swat her upside the head if she didn't keep still. And Johnnie Mae held the match steady and watched the flame eat up the matchstick, inching down toward her fingers. Then she jabbed the lighted match down the hole in the top of the anthill. Ants came running out like their house was on fire. Rat yelled because one or two climbed up her silly arm, and she jumped around to knock them off when she could just have slapped them off.

Johnnie Mae wanted to scratch and pull her swimming suit away from her skin, but Charlie had said she must stand still and think only about the water and how wonderful it would be to glide through it. He said to think about how proud everybody would be—especially him. He didn't say *especially him*. He only said that everybody would be proud. She figured he meant to say he'd be especially proud of her too. If she won. She wanted Charlie to be proud of her—and Mama—and Daddy and Aunt Ina and Pearl and Rat—Rat too. Rat must be proud, but Rat must be jealous as well. She wanted Rat to be a little jealous. She wanted Rat to look down on her from wherever she was and wish she herself was getting ready to swim.

Rat couldn't swim. Johnnie Mae didn't want to think about Rat now. But Rat couldn't swim, didn't ever really swim. Rat was scared of the water, but always pretended that she wasn't. Rat never wanted to be left behind. She knew that Johnnie Mae would leave her to go swimming. And Johnnie Mae knew that Rat was truly scared of water and she hadn't cared, that day, about her whiny little sister.

She wouldn't think about Rat right now! Charlie said she didn't have to think about a thing at the time it flashed across her brain. Charlie said not to look at the girls next to her, either. She was not to think about them and what they were going to do. Just listen for the starter's whistle. But don't look! Think about the swimming—think about the swimming—the water. Just tell her arms and legs to wait for the whistle, then go. Tell her arms and legs to be relaxed but ready and bend down and stay loose and let her body go and glide and be strong and glide into the water and don't look back or to the side. Look down at the markers on the bottom and follow them in a straight line and glide and push and breathe and glide and push and breathe and look up and Charlie's face will be there and—maybe Rat's face, too.

When the starting pistol popped in the air above her head, Johnnie Mae launched herself from the side of the pool with her toes. Her body unfurled above the surface of the water like a banner snapping in a sudden wind then relaxing to float on ripples of air. She plunged into the water. The others must have also. She could neither see them nor hear them. It was her lane only, her water before her, and she plowed through it with all the energy she had.

Afterward Charlie said she'd lost it on the turn. She had been ever so slightly slower and wider in the turn than the other girl had been. And her fingers had touched home only a few seconds after the other girl's. But it had been after the girl. There had been a relieved sigh at the judges' table.

The swimmers milled about while the judges had their heads together. They were bumblebeeing furiously. After a bit, one of the judges came forward and said that they were canceling the diving competition. He said they'd agreed that they had seen enough to make a pick. They didn't need to look at any diving.

Charlie snatched the cap off his head and threw it to the

ground in disgust. They'd got scared. They were scared because they knew. Those judges knew Johnnie Mae could ace the diving competition. They'd seen how close she came to beating the other girl and they were scared.

If none of her competitors had been any good then it would clearly have been a case of race prejudice. But they'd all been good. And the girl they chose to represent Washington was a nearly flawless swimmer. Her performance had been flawless in the swimming. But Johnnie Mae would have beaten her in the diving. And the judges didn't want to see that. The deciders were not big people or risk-takers. They were not bold enough in their prejudice to ban Johnnie Mae outright. They had simply been grateful that their white swimmer was good enough. In fact, she was a little more than good enough. So they chose her and did not feel guilty.

18

In the past several months, all the energy in the Bynum household had been absorbed in getting ready for the coming baby. Johnnie Mae was alternately happy at the progress her mother's stomach was making and repulsed by its mushrooming. Additional household duties had been pushed onto her and she'd accepted them without complaint. Mama and Aunt Ina had planned it out that Mama would work at Miz St. Pierre's as long as she could. Then Aunt Ina would work in her place until Mama was ready to take back her job. Johnnie Mae was to help out with Aunt Ina's work and the household chores. All of this changed with the St. Pierres' financial troubles.

Papa picked up extra work running the elevator at the Alban Towers Hotel in the evening. He was lighthearted, however, and unable to hide the pleasure this coming baby was giving him. As soon as the frost had passed and the ground was warm, he put in his vegetable garden. By the time the boy, Calvin William Bynum, was born, on the sixth of June, the tomato plants were beginning to twine around their stakes.

Aunt Ina took charge of the household as soon as Mama's labor began in earnest, around four o'clock in the afternoon. She sent Johnnie Mae up to Georgetown University to say to her papa, "Her time has come." Aunt Ina said it over and over with a solemn, no-nonsense demeanor, not allowing her excitement to change the pitch of her voice. Johnnie Mae knew she was holding her voice steady by dint of great courage because Aunt Ina's voice rose on the slightest provocation. "Her time has come. Go tell your papa. Her time has come."

Johnnie Mae was instructed to get her papa first, then go to Dr. Tyler's office and give him the same message. Willie got Peanut Walter, a tall, slow-moving boy who did pick-up work for anybody, to work in his place at Alban Towers. The boy's name was actually Walter Peanut, and he was the oldest of Horace and Lila Peanut's thirteen children. But he had always been called Peanut Walter around town.

Johnnie Mae was told not to dillydally but to return as soon as she could. She was told to brew the pain-go-away tea that Ella Bromsen had given to them tied in a cheesecloth pouch. And she was told to fix a supper for her papa.

Dr. Marvin Tyler delivered Calvin at the house in the early morning hours of Thursday. Aunt Ina had assisted him throughout the night while Johnnie Mae sat at the top of the stairs outside her parents' bedroom door listening and trying to figure out what was actually going on inside. Mama didn't cry out, only grunted and exclaimed. When Johnnie Mae was awakened by Calvin's first cries at four o'clock in the morning, she sprang to the door and tapped. Roused by Calvin's robust voice, Willie jumped up from his chair in the kitchen, took the stairs two at a time, and crowded in the bedroom doorway. Aunt Ina came and blocked the line of vision into the room.

She sent Johnnie Mae to fix her mother a bowl of cornmeal mush and a cup of coffee half filled with cream and lots of sugar. She pulled Willie into the room while clapping him hard on the back. "You got you a boy, Willie! You got a son!"

Willie, the fifth wheel in the proceedings, had sat by himself in the kitchen the whole long night. He sat thinking about Clara and Big Mama and Merle. And he wondered who this coming baby was. If Clara had been his sister, Merle, come again, then who was this baby come again? If it was a girl it would likely be Big Mama come this time, or his mama. But if it was a boy, he'd be somebody none of them had known. Unless it was his daddy that he hardly could remember. Willie nursed many cups of coffee and pondered. With these coming children we never relinquish the past. We keep seeing somebody gone in each new one.

Willie couldn't say what part of Johnnie Mae was the part she got from someone gone. He didn't know who that could be. He'd never known Alice's mama. He couldn't say if that damnable streak of independence was something she got honestly from her mother's mother or not. Now, Alice was pretty headstrong. But increasingly there was something more intractable in Johnnie Mae. She was daily getting more troublesome.

He didn't know Sam Logan's people at all, except to know they were redskins. Folks in Carolina always said that colored people with Indian blood were sullen and headstrong and clever. Johnnie Mae was, he thought. That was what was in her. Even from a little girl, switching her bottom or the backs of her legs had been pretty much useless as a deterrent. The problem of her disobedience had never been in those places. It was her head—hardheaded, headstrong.

As expected, Miz Fanny Moreen called just after ten o'clock. Miz Fanny, as she was affectionately known by any and all among colored who'd had a new baby or a child with cholera or influenza or rickets, was the licensed baby nurse assigned by the city health department to call on colored families in Georgetown. A fixture at church socials, Miz Fanny always appeared neatly dressed in a sharply tailored black uniform and nurse's cap. Georgetowners admired her, especially for the courage with which she'd assisted Dr. Marshall and Dr. Tyler in the influenza epidemics in '09 and '12.

Upon arriving at the Bynums' home, Miz Fanny drew off her black uniform jacket, undid her white cuffs, and put on the long white apron she pulled from her bag. She handed the jacket to Johnnie Mae and instructed the girl to hang it neatly. Her loud, authoritative voice called Ina from the upstairs bedroom and brought her swiftly down the steps.

"Good morning, Miz Fanny," Ina called out cheerfully but in a tone that gave Miz Fanny absolute jurisdiction in the house.

"Good morning, Miz Carson. We have a healthy big boy I hear." Miz Fanny had by this time marched into the kitchen. Ina was hard on her heels and Johnnie Mae followed. Miz Fanny perused the sink and swept her eyes over all surfaces on the stove, the table, and the cupboards. She judged the diligence of the household's women in stanching the tide of dirt and disease. Her eyes caught on the bundle of herbs that Ella Bromsen had brought to be given to the new mother as tea.

"Miz Carson, we do not need backwoods remedies." She pronounced her disdain for Ella Bromsen's herbs with her nose and lips drawn up.

Ina answered, "Yes, ma'am, I'm sure you know the best."

Miz Fanny then reached in her medical bag and pulled out health department pamphlets on baby care and hygiene and instructed Ina to follow the recommendations to the letter. With her breasts high, she proclaimed the motto with which she concluded all her talks at the church programs: "The health of our people is dependent upon the health of our children!"

Johnnie Mae was tickled by Miz Fanny's crusading fervor but knew she'd better not titter. Nobody dared laugh at Miz Fanny Moreen, for fear of being turned in to the health department for keeping a household that was a menace to public health. Though Miz Fanny had been known to turn in only the worst cases of neglect and slovenliness in the twenty years she'd been working in Georgetown, it was widely known that she had the authority of the health department.

"Have mother and baby been bathed this morning?" Miz Fanny asked as she put on her stethoscope.

"Oh, yes, ma'am," Ina said. She led Miz Fanny upstairs to the bedroom.

"The most important thing, Miz Carson, is to keep mother and baby clean and dry and well fed."

"Oh, yes, ma'am."

19

"Her hair's always wet or nappy. It's a good grade of hair and it's going to be ruined from all that swimming in the pool. She smells funny. She's acting womanish and hardheaded but behaving like a child too. She's not carrying herself like a growing-up young lady. But still and all she's over at that pool in a swimming suit instead of in her clothes. Maybe she's liking it too much." In the kitchen after Johnnie Mae had gone to bed and Ina had gone home, Willie cudgeled Alice with his words.

He was dancin' up to a subject that he'd been trying to set to music for some time now. Alice heard the undercurrent of Willie's comments as clearly as if he'd said it out loud. He was trying to get it said that Johnnie Mae—her daughter—was about to step out of line. He was trying to get it up to say that her daughter was being willful, like she had been. Alice seethed.

Johnnie Mae was completely absorbed with the pool and the competition. Yes, this was getting beyond the two of them. But Willie's intention wasn't pure. He wasn't talking about

Johnnie Mae's swimming. He was trying to get something said about her behavior. And Alice dared him with her eyes. He was a good man. But she wasn't going to allow him to oppress her with his goodness. Because there was a meekness in his goodness that she had always thought unseemly. He loved her, but he had been too meek about it. He had waited for Alice and had got her with his meekness. She had wanted another man but had settled for Willie. Now he was going to raise up on his hind legs at her? He was going to try to talk about her now? And her daughter?

Alice dug in her heels. Willie could see Alice's determination to take her daughter's part, and he backed off.

"We can shinny that fence in no time. And you can stand lookout while I swim. We can do it any old time. If we pick a night in the dark of the moon, nobody can see us." Johnnie Mae spoke with confidence, convincing Pearl that she was perfectly sure of herself.

Pearl didn't see how the pool on Volta Place could still have a pull on Johnnie Mae. The Francis pool was so much better. And she and anybody's colored child could swim in it whenever they wanted. Why was Johnnie Mae so determined to swim in the pool on Volta Place? Johnnie Mae loved the Francis pool. In fact, nobody could have loved it more than she. But there was a principle in this fever about the pool on Volta Place. There was something about the fact that the colored children were barred from it that inflamed her.

Pearl didn't like the idea of scaling the fence in the dead of night, though. She started right away to run over all the dangerous possibilities in the plan, though she knew from the outset that she would go along if Johnnie Mae kept insisting. And what kind of story would she make up to get out of the house past dark? Johnnie Mae said the best plan was not to make up anything but steal out after everyone had gone to sleep.

On the chosen night, Johnnie Mae lay in her bed and listened for her parents' snores. When finally the two began cadenced, sonorous snoring, Johnnie Mae tiptoed out the back door and hightailed it to Volta Place.

They'd chosen a night when Johnnie Mae said there would be no moonlight. The darkness made it difficult to find a path through the trees to the fence that surrounded the pool, and they had to be careful not to step on and squash any of the stinkballs that had fallen from the trees and littered the ground outside the pool. They hid their clothes a few yards from the fence.

The fence provided excellent toeholds for scaling. Johnnie Mae led the way as they climbed monkey fashion up the fence, hooking their hands and feet into the mesh. She left her shoes outside at the base of a tree, but Pearl kept hers on. Johnnie Mae thought Pearl was a pampered sort of girl, but she proved herself full of stuffing in the way she scrambled up and over the top of the fence. As soon as they were over the top, Johnnie Mae leapt to the ground. Pearl eased herself down a bit on the other side, then leapt off the fence, skinning her elbow as she landed. Though it stung, she didn't whimper.

The water appeared black in front of them. In the darkness there was no blue to it. Both jumped into the water and splashed great amounts of it onto the sides. The water had lost the warmth of the day's sun and was, as Clara had imagined it, cool. Maybe Rat was right after all. Maybe they did get blocks of ice to cool down the water.

All the eyes in all the heads on all the pillows in Georgetown were closed, they thought. The only sounds were theirs. The trees overhanging the playground created a sylvan glade and all sound from the street was muffled. There was no breeze to rustle leaves or ripple the surface of the water. It was only them and the pool. The sensation of slipping into water so dark that the blue bottom could not be seen was exhilarating to Johnnie Mae.

Pearl was frightened, though she was determined not to say so. She got out of the pool after a very few minutes and sat dangling her legs from the side. She was scared mostly because she couldn't see where the bottom was. She was nowhere near as confident of her swimming as Johnnie Mae.

Johnnie Mae swam as easily in the dark as in daylight. She glided the length back and forth, and only the triangular trail her body made with her head forming the apex could be seen.

Pearl watched her friend admiringly. Johnnie Mae pulled herself to the side and raised herself out of the pool to the elbows, then dunked herself again and swam off.

"You look like a shark," Pearl said as Johnnie Mae barreled through the water. Johnnie Mae put her head up at the far end of the pool and called back, "You don't know what a shark looks like."

"You better go back home, little girl. You better go get in your bed before your papa finds you gone," Pearl countered, sensing that, despite Johnnie Mae's bravado, she was nervous about being in the pool.

Johnnie Mae shot up out of the water, ran back from the edge, then frog jumped back in. Her body made a roaring splash and sent water out along the sides. Pearl said, "Shh! Don't be splashing around making noise!" She sat on the side of the pool anxiously.

Toby Davis rapped his nightstick along the fence at the same time he yelled, "What's going on in there?"

Pearl jumped in her skin at the *rat-a-tat* sound and the booming voice. Johnnie Mae, instantly alert, whispered, "Get down. Get down in the water so he can't see you!" Pearl slid down into the water quickly, then raised her head slowly, peeping up to see who was yelling. She saw a big, round, red face pushed up against the link fence. The policeman's left eye was framed by a fence link. He shone his flashlight into the dark area around the pool to catch sight of whoever was swimming around in there. He'd heard splashing and was investigating. Wasn't nobody supposed to be cavorting around in there at night!

"Niggers! What you niggers doing in that pool?" Toby Davis yelled out. The face left the fence and Johnnie Mae knew that Officer Davis was going to find a way in. They'd better scramble if they were going to avoid getting caught. There was no funnin' and gamin' in Toby Davis's mind. Johnnie Mae swam toward Pearl. "Go! Run! Get to the fence! He's going to find a way in. Run! Get outta here!" Her voice came out strangled, but the force of it lit a fire under Pearl.

Johnnie Mae swam the width of the pool in nothing flat and jumped out. Pearl ran to the fence and climbed onto it. It bucked and threatened to throw her off, but she scrambled up and then down the other side. She heard Johnnie Mae yell, "Run! Don't turn back. Just run!"

Johnnie Mae put her foot into the links halfway up and tried to mount the fence. She managed to get one foot secure, but Toby Davis, who'd squeezed through the gate at the back of the playground where it was held closed by a chain and a padlock, crossed the ground speedily and grabbed her right foot. The police officer bellowed, "Nigger! Git down here! Git down or I'll shoot you off that fence!"

Pearl's legs, which were readying to run, stopped cold. She turned and looked back, hidden by shrubs. Davis had Johnnie Mae by one leg and was yanking and pulling her, trying to dislodge her from the fence.

"You want to swim, nigger? You know niggers can't swim 'cause niggers don't float." Officer Davis kept tugging on Johnnie Mae's ankle, and she stubbornly held to the fence. The fence wobbled back and forth with the frantic tussling.

Pearl's body went into that place of involuntary action that makes the body act because it cannot not act. She knew that Johnnie Mae wouldn't be able to hold on to the fence much longer. She could see that Toby Davis was serious about holding on. Johnnie Mae and Officer Davis were locked in the situation. Neither one of them was giving in, but Johnnie Mae was likely to come out the loser.

A few yards from the place the two girls had hidden their clothes, the ground was covered with stinkballs—the fruit of the Japanese ginkgo tree. Most every block in Georgetown had some of the decorative ginkgo trees with their horribly stinking fruit. Stinkballs lay all over the ground waiting for somebody to step on them and release the putrid odor. Pearl grabbed up an armload of them and shinnied back up the fence. Despite the wobbling, Pearl gained the top and straddled it. From her perch, she lobbed a stinkball at Toby

Davis, hitting him upside his head. The stinkball glanced off and smashed on the ground at his feet. It released a stinking smell and Davis cursed. Pearl got tickled at his grimaces and threw more of the stinky things onto the ground at the policeman's feet. He stumbled around, stepping on the missiles and releasing their smell. Pearl leapt down, got more stinkballs, mashed them between her palms to release their odor, and lobbed them over the fence on top of Toby Davis.

Distracted by the stinkballs, Davis loosened his hold on Johnnie Mae's ankle. She hoisted herself up over the fence and down on the outside. Pearl, arms full of the stinking missiles, continued to hurl them onto Officer Toby Davis's head and shoulders.

"This ain't no game! I'ma get you, niggers! You ain't got no business to be in this swimming pool!" Toby Davis sputtered with rage as Johnnie Mae and Pearl grabbed up their clothes and ran down the street.

When they got to the corner of Wisconsin Avenue and Volta Place, separating to go their different ways, Johnnie Mae stopped to take a good look at Pearl's face. The girl was laughing, full-out laughing — at what they'd done, at what she'd done. She had pelted Toby Davis all over his head with stinkballs and she was howling like a banshee about it. Johnnie Mae grabbed at Pearl's shoulders and shook her, saying, "Shush! You better stop hollering and laughing. You better hightail it home and get in the bed, little girl!" Pearl kept laughing. She ran off toward home with her head thrown back, laughing.

The distance from Wisconsin Avenue to Johnnie Mae's house seemed great — out of all proportion to the usual distance. She'd run up and down these streets so often that she could recognize each cobblestone by its feel beneath her foot. But tonight, her feet were nearly numb. When she crossed Wisconsin Avenue, she started to run, and the feeling did not come back to her limbs even then. She felt instead that she was flying over the cobblestones and around the tree boxes.

All of the windows in all of the houses were dark. She went down O Street and into the alley behind her house. The only house with a light on was her house. With the curtains drawn, the window looked like a square sun. She ran through the yard and up the porch steps, opened the door with a swift, desperate pull on the knob, and plunged headlong into the room.

Her papa and mama stood when she entered. They stood and looked at her without saying a thing. Their faces indicted her for many and monstrous transgressions. But they wouldn't have thought of it — could not have imagined what really happened.

"You been swimming in the middle of the night? Your clothes is all wet through. You been walking the streets like this at night? Johnnie Mae? You hear me?" Papa broke the silence.

"Johnnie Mae, has something happened to you?" Mama asked. Her face was all torn up. "My Lord, what's going on?" Mama exclaimed and Calvin, who'd awakened at the sound of the loud voices, joined his strident voice to the others'.

"Has somebody done something to you, girl?" Papa asked, his voice climbing higher in volume and pitch. "I'm callin' the law!"

"No! Something happened, but not what you think," Johnnie Mae answered.

"What happened, Johnnie Mae? Where have you been?" Mama asked.

"A girl gets up in the middle of the night and goes tramping through the town. Anything is bound to happen. What is it?" She bowed her head in the face of her papa's voice.

"Where your shoes at, girl?" Mama asked. "What happened to your shoes?" Johnnie Mae had not thought about the shoes since she took them off before climbing the fence. Where were they? Still on the grass by the fence? They were still where she'd left them and she'd come all the way home without them—without even noticing that she'd forgotten them. She looked down at herself—bare feet, dress wet. What a shameful sight!

Her papa said, "Has something been done to her? I'll kill the man that's done it. I'll call the law! Alice, I depend on you to tell me if this child has been taken advantage of."

Fearing the direction their fears were taking them, Johnnie Mae blurted out, "No! We were swimming in the pool on Volta Place."

Papa asked, his anger rising higher, "Who are you sneaking out to see and keeping time with? A young girl like you, keeping time with boys already. I declare! That's what I been talking about, woman!"

"Hush a minute and give her time to tell it. Let her tell it," Mama said. "Go on and tell it, Johnnie," she said firmly.

Papa and Mama sat at the kitchen table and went silent as stones, watching her mouth as if they didn't trust their ears and would have to read her lips. It took her some moments to gather up the story and tell it coherently.

She spoke evenly and included all the details of her and Pearl going to the pool, climbing the fence, swimming in the water, and being caught.

"The police! The police caught you in there!" Papa broke

in and the fear in his voice was considerable. Johnnie Mae collapsed into a chair. Mama sat down, too, and pulled her chair up close to Johnnie Mae. "Go on," she said.

"We scrambled up out of the pool," she continued, "and he caught my foot and held on to me. Officer Davis—"

"It was Toby Davis saw ya'll?" Papa barked at her. He looked at his wife solemnly.

"Yes, sir," she said and continued the tale, telling them all about Pearl throwing stinkballs on top of Toby Davis's head.

Papa banged the kitchen table with his fist and stood up. "God! This is a bad situation!" He sat back down and rubbed his forehead with his palm.

The coffee that Willie had drunk started to worry his stomach. The bottom of his belly felt like a smoldering fire. He wanted to belch and clear it or put something soft in it to sop up the acidy coffee. Alice took bacon and eggs from the icebox and started to assemble a breakfast.

Willie's nerves were calmed some by the fried eggs and bread. Alice tried to eat something, but her stomach turned at the sight of the eggs. She warmed a glass of milk and after Johnnie Mae had drunk half of it, she ushered her up the stairs to bed.

⁓

Nobody wanted to make much of the incident except Toby Davis. He was good and sore about being pelted with stinkballs. But after he told his story to the desk sergeant at Number 7, there was little interest in rounding up the perpetrators. Sergeant Michael Cronin told him to forget it, especially since he couldn't say exactly who the two nigger gals were. He was told to pay closer attention to the swimming pool on his rounds. "Keep the little niggers from gettin' in the pool in the first place!" Cronin bellowed.

Cronin, who considered himself sympathetic toward colored, followed a policy of seeking out a reliable representative when there was a potential problem. And if pickaninnies continued to sneak into the whites-only pool, there was going to be a problem. So he sent Peanut Walter with a note to Reverend Buford Jenkins telling him to come down to Number 7 to discuss a "situation."

When Peanut Walter arrived, Buford Jenkins came out of the small anteroom off to the side of his parlor, where he'd been working on his record books. He'd been noting down the names of those married and baptized and laid to rest since the last time he'd gotten around to working on the church records. The pastors of Mount Zion Church had been keeping records of the whereabouts and circumstances of their members since the church was founded. In the times before Emancipation, the pastors had cryptically recorded the fate of members who'd disappeared due to tragic or mysterious circumstances as "lost." People who were captured by patrollers or bounty hunters and returned to the Deep South were listed as "taken away." The lucky or brave ones who were sent farther along the Underground Railroad to Harper's Ferry and on north to Canada were noted as "gone away."

After reading the note Peanut Walter handed him, Reverend Jenkins closed the record books and put on his suit coat. Jenkins paused in front of a mirror and vigorously brushed his hair. Many a man is sorry to see gray hairs pop up around his temples, but Buford Jenkins was happy to see them. With a bulbous nose that was occasionally decorated with a blackheaded pustule, he was not considered a good-looking man.

Gray hairs helped him look dignified rather than comical. This was all to the good around white folks, especially the official ones. They liked to have someone they could talk to who could speak up for the Negro race with a suit and tie on. And in relations with whites, a colored person always needed an introduction or a tell. A colored man needed some subtlety of appearance, like gray temples or a limp, that proclaimed a mild intention.

Bethel Jenkins, his mama, had raised no fool. Jenkins had sense enough not to wear his best suit or his best shoes down to the police station to see Michael Cronin. Clean and slightly threadbare—that was the best way to dress for talking to the white folks.

When Jenkins arrived, Sergeant Michael Cronin told him plainly that folks weren't going to tolerate colored children getting in their swimming pool at night. He advised Reverend Jenkins to find out who they were and warn them to stay out of there. He described the perpetrators as two young girls. And the police wouldn't be responsible if something untoward happened to half-naked colored children running the streets at night.

The general description of each of the two girls and the direction in which they'd run sounded like one of them must be Johnnie Mae Bynum. Reverend Jenkins knew he'd have to go speak to the Bynums about this matter.

Sunday morning, the Bynum household lingered long over their breakfast. Johnnie Mae waited for her mama to give her permission to leave the table to dress for Sunday services. But Mama kept her eyes to herself and said nothing. She sipped coffee and pushed her food around on her plate without speaking. Aunt Ina, too, was silent, and Papa surrendered his coffee cup after a long while and went out back to his garden. Nobody acted like he or she meant to go to church that day. Was it such a monstrous thing she'd done that they couldn't even go to church?

Reverend Jenkins had called the previous evening and had spoken to Mama and Papa in the parlor. His voice had been sympathetic. He had said more than once that he understood it from the girl's point of view. He felt that having places like that pool where colored children couldn't go was shameful and plain wrong. But there wasn't anything they could do about it now. And for her own sake, she had better stay out of that pool.

The two women sat with their Bibles in the parlor after breakfast and read silently. This time they blamed her. What she had done at the pool had caused the shame they were feeling. And her mama and papa and aunt Ina were not inclined to relieve her misery with exculpatory pats and murmurings. Their glances at her were hard. And though they didn't require her to, she felt that she must sit in the parlor with them and their Bibles and her own Bible.

Johnnie Mae could never remember Miss Ella Bromsen coming up to the front door of their house. She always came through the backyard and scratched at the screen door like somebody they'd always known. It was the country in her, Aunt Ina said, and the fact of her Indian blood. And in the late afternoon after church services, Miss Ella Bromsen came through the backyard, exchanged courtesies with Papa, and came into the house and through to the parlor. Mama and Aunt Ina looked up, startled. Miss Ella Bromsen came into the parlor carrying a brand-new broom with a handle nearly as tall as she was.

"Sister Alice, Sister Ina Mae, we missed you at services today."

Johnnie Mae detected a wash of shame over her mother and her aunt. They knew they'd been wallowing in their shamefacedness, and this mild rebuke caused more.

Aunt Ina closed her Bible, popped up from her chair, and moved to offer Miss Ella a seat. "Ella, take a seat. And won't you have a cup of coffee and a piece of cake?"

"No, ma'am, thank you. I've come to do a thing and have a word with you and Sister Alice."

Johnnie Mae rose at the pointed look her mother gave her and went out to the kitchen.

"Johnnie Mae, take your mother's sweeping broom and put it on the back porch," Ella called after her. Mama and Aunt Ina looked at her in surprise.

Ella Bromsen's reputation as an odd bird was well earned. She proceeded to use the new broom she'd brought to sweep around the periphery of the parlor rug, starting in the farthest corner from where she'd come into the room. She continued around the room, swirling what little dust there was in the room and collecting it back at the spot she'd started from. She swept the few dustballs into her palm and gave them to Alice. "Sister Alice, take your troubles outside and throw them away."

Alice looked Ella Bromsen full in the eyes. She was surely a madwoman, but she'd come with her hands open and her eyes clear. Alice closed her hands over the dust motes and went and released them over the back porch rail.

When she came back to the parlor, Ella was sitting in a

chair as ordinary as any Sunday caller. The tall broom leaned against the inside of the front door. When Ella left by the back door, she took the Bynums' used broom and carried it under her left armpit like a lance. She passed Johnnie Mae on the back porch and said to the girl as she passed, "Don't you give your mama no more trouble, girl."

20

Alice and Ina packed Johnnie Mae's things and set out the clothes she would wear without consulting her on choices. Alice figured this would be the last time she would decide things for Johnnie Mae. She wasn't much more than a child, but she was going away like a woman. She was taking a grown person's concerns with her. Clara was gone and now Johnnie Mae was going. Would she ever come back to them as a girl?

Alice had finally lost the argument with Willie. They had thrashed and tussled verbally in the kitchen, in the bedroom, in the parlor. Willie'd insisted that Johnnie Mae had got wild, and there was nothing Alice could say to persuade him that the girl should stay. He went on and on about Johnnie Mae getting out of hand and insisted that they couldn't control her. Why, they couldn't even keep her in her bed at night! What kind of shame was she going to bring on them next? At least down home, there wouldn't be any swimming pools or bad influences. Old Man Walker would see to that!

Willie held firm to the idea that Johnnie Mae couldn't stay in Georgetown with people knowing she'd been involved in the event at the pool. If she could go away for the rest of the summer, maybe this thing would be forgotten. They would tell folks that she was going south to visit her aunts. Alice countered that it wouldn't matter whether she went away or not; if people knew about the pool, they knew about the pool.

Alice dictated a terse message to Old Man Walker at the Western Union office: WILL ARRIVE RUTHERFORDTON TOMORROW. YOUR GRANDDAUGHTER, JOHNNIE MAE BYNUM.

Johnnie Mae had said very little in the days since the pool incident. Not only her ears but her face was burning with their fussing and fuming. She knew she'd done wrong in going out at night and breaking into the pool. She knew she'd done wrong to drag Pearl Miller into the scheme. And she was wrong to swim in the white people's pool. But nobody would be able to convince her that swimming was wrong. And even Reverend Jenkins himself said that it was wrong for them to keep colored children from swimming in that pool. But Papa and Mama were still talking about her and all the shame she had brought down onto their heads. Mrs. Miller had even said that Johnnie Mae was a bad influence on Pearl and she forbade Pearl to have anything to do with her. The past few days, the two girls had had to sneak around to get a chance to talk to each other.

The plans were set: Papa and Mama were going to send her by train to her grandpa's farm in North Carolina at least for the rest of the summer—maybe for the rest of her life.

She marshaled all her reserves of pluck just to keep straight the things she must do on the train trip—hand in her ticket, look after her bag and her lunch—and the things she must not do—talk to strangers, forget her purse or her bag or lunch or where she was to change trains or where she was to get off the train. She was quiet, calm, in control of herself as she rode across town on the streetcar with her parents and aunt and baby Calvin to Union Station.

The group walked solemnly into the waiting room at Union Station. Mr. Ernest Boston hailed them at once, in a voice that was well modulated but resonant in the cavernous room. He hurried across the room in short quick steps. Whenever Georgetown children traveled by train, Mr. Ernest Boston was sought out and asked to keep an eye on the young traveler. And Mr. Ernest Boston considered it his particular responsibility to assure the colored families that no harm would come to any child traveling on his train. Willie, Alice, and Ina were quite comfortable with delivering Johnnie Mae into his care.

"Miss Johnnie Mae, you look so grown I wouldn't have known you if your mama wasn't with you." Mr. Ernest Boston bent toward her and smiled as if she were a tiny child needing to be comforted.

"You all don't need to worry. I'll look after her till we get to Raleigh and then I'll hand her over to Mr. Sam Gray and he'll get her to your folks in Rutherfordton. We'll drink a glass of milk in Richmond after we change trains and we'll ride in style all the way. Many a child younger than you rides the train by themselves. You're looking glum, Johnnie Mae. Cheer up. When this train leaves the station, it's going to eat up the tracks. We'll be there before you know it."

It was expected that she would smile appreciatively toward Mr. Ernest Boston. And she did so, though her face felt as if it would dissolve into mush. She did not want to cry. Though how on earth was she going to help herself when it was time to board the train and leave them all? She wanted to grab hold of baby Calvin and bury her head in his warm, fat stomach. She knew if she did this he would giggle uncontrollably and this would make her feel better. Mama was carrying a large cardboard box tied up with string that contained Johnnie Mae's lunch. Papa was carrying the suitcase that had her clothes, and Aunt Ina was huffing and puffing under the burden of Calvin's solid bulk. Nobody had said anything all the whole way across town on the streetcar.

Truth to tell, Alice had a feeling that Willie was regretting this decision but was too much a rooster to admit it. She had been thinking about how she might maneuver him into being able to change his mind. But time was running out. Sending Johnnie Mae back home seemed to her like walking backward. What had they come to Washington for if not to get better for Johnnie Mae and Clara? But Clara was gone. And there was Calvin now. What good was it going to do to send Johnnie Mae away from them when they especially needed her now to care for Calvin?

After Mr. Ernest Boston had left them to their good-byes and had pointed out where to get on the train, the Bynum family stood in silence. The Roman soldiers standing at attention around the periphery of the lobby's vaulted ceiling respected their silence, their heads slightly bowed and their bodies still. All around the group, people hurried past to reach their trains. If the angel Gabriel had blown the last great blast on his trumpet, the Bynums and Ina Carson would not have moved. Only Calvin wiggled and twisted in Aunt Ina's arms. They were stopped in the middle of Union Station, considering how to proceed.

Alice plunked the lunchbox down on the floor at her feet, set her jaw, and wrenched and tugged at her hat, changing its placement and then resettling it in its original place. "You can't send my baby off down south," she blurted at her husband. He looked up and saw a furious determination on her face and rocked back on his heels. "You can't separate my babies and my heart. You're a man, but you're only one man. I've got a say in what happens to the child out of my body and I say that she stays or I go with her. I'll take this boy, too. I'll raise them out of my pocket if I have to, but I won't be separated from them!"

Ina Carson drew herself up at her cousin's words. And though she didn't mix in, you could tell what side of the stream she was on. She thrust Calvin's fat, wiggling body into Alice's arms.

"What the matter with you women? You crazy or something? What kind of thing are you talking now?" Willie sputtered and his eyes bulged in alarm. And though he was not entirely ready to give up his pique, he was relieved that things had begun to take a turn. Johnnie Mae had to be controlled somehow. And if they couldn't do it, maybe it would be better to send her back south before something bad happened. But maybe they shouldn't go off half-cocked. They did need her for taking care of the baby. And if the women were going to act this way . . . "What kind of example you setting for this girl? You raisin' your voice at me in this public place!"

Alice stood straight and stared at him without reply. She had provoked him and was letting him carry on in the full knowledge that the storm had, in fact, passed. They were going to be able to go back home together.

Willie snorted and harumphed at his wife and rolled his eyes, but gradually calmed. Alice had given him a way out of this tangle, but he was still not content with things. This swimming! This was the thing that seemed to be the cause of the trouble. It seemed like with this swimming Johnnie Mae had got to feeling that she could do whatever she liked. That wasn't no way for a young girl to behave. Willie stood for a time with his hat in his hands. He stared at the marble floor of the station. Looking at him, one would have thought he was reading auguries in the highly buffed stone.

Johnnie Mae, who'd had her eyes averted to the floor, looked up to see a short, dark figure standing off a ways, looking intently at her. She thought it must be Pearl Miller and got ashamed that she'd not said a proper good-bye to Pearl. It was Pearl standing there. Pearl had come to beg her not to go. Pearl was her best friend and she had come down to beg Johnnie Mae's parents to let her stay.

The sun that streamed in from the east-facing windows made it difficult for Johnnie Mae to read the features of the figure. Was she smiling? Was she mad at Johnnie Mae for not saying a proper good-bye? In fact, all that could be discerned was that it was the figure of a girl. Yet there was something askew. The girl was not standing so far distant that her features should have appeared so muddy. But they were muddy. There was no other girl it could have been. Yet she actually looked too childlike to be Pearl. Johnnie Mae puzzled: it had to be Pearl, but it couldn't be. Pearl would not have worn the ribbon in her hair attached to the very end of her plait. Pearl would not have had the little white ankle socks. Pearl would have called out or smiled or come closer.

Johnnie Mae broke the spell of silence that had the Bynums and Ina Carson frozen in a tableau. She called out "Hey!" and started toward the girl, who turned and ran toward the revolving brass doors leading out of Union Station.

21

In the earliest hours of daylight, the breeze off the Potomac carries the fragrances of wild places upriver and the flora that inhabit them. Air comes down from these places, stoops low over Rock Creek, and blows back across Georgetown, bringing along a scent that has no name other than morning.

Johnnie Mae sat before a pile of onions blowing short breaths between her lips. She wanted to sigh, to expel a long, slow chestful of air. But sighing annoyed her mother so. Mama disapproved of it as a behavior for young girls. She never sighed herself and she never let one of Johnnie Mae's sighs go unnoticed. "Sighing will age you," she said now, going back into a closet of aphorisms and mother-wit mumbo jumbo. *Now isn't that the silliest thing*, Johnnie Mae thought, hoping her mother wouldn't be able to read these impudent thoughts on her forehead. Mama continued, "You see, you turn that sigh into a yawn and it'll clear you out. A yawn will give you strength to get started again. A sigh leaves you down with nowhere to go. Then you have to wait for your second wind." Johnnie Mae cultivated her puff-puffing.

The work of fixing extra-large portions of potato salad, bean salad, fried chicken, and all the required summer picnic foods was boring. Johnnie Mae handled the mountain of onions assigned to her competently, pulling their skins off quickly. She dabbed her eyes and blinked, but skinned and cut the onions deftly. Mama peeled from a pile of hot white potatoes and supervised Johnnie Mae. The two worked along quietly. Johnnie Mae shifted her hips to settle herself on the chair. The unaccustomed cloths between her legs were chafing her. Alice glanced up without moving her head to study the girl slyly. She hadn't said much. Didn't ask any questions about starting her monthly.

For many years, the last Thursday before Labor Day had been the traditional day for the Mount Zion Church picnic under the P Street bridge. Spread out along the P Street beach, it was the biggest social event of the summer. Women who cooked for a living five or six days a week had been up much of the night preparing the picnic and were up again at sunrise. Cakes were made the day before, chicken fried early in the morning, and potato salad mixed and cooled. Daughters had strict instructions for assembling and cleaning and being ready.

A full two days before the picnic, Ina Carson had buried a skinless young pig in a brick-lined pit in her backyard, covered it with basil and sage, and built a slow-burning wood fire atop it, just like Cap used to do. Carolina-slippin'-and-hidin'-buried-in-the-ground roasted shoat had been one of his favorite dishes. Cap used to say that the fact that his daddy had risked the road gang or even his life in stealing the shoat from Cal Jackson when stores were low made it taste extra good. His daddy did this when he and all the kids and Cap's mam had got tired of the wild taste of game. Daddy Carson roasted the shoat really slow for five days or so. He tended it all by himself, guarding the fire and stoking it. Not wanting to risk anybody else's life but his own, he wouldn't even hint as to where he had it stashed. When it was done he'd haul it to their table. And when they were done eating it, Daddy Carson buried the bones in an iron chest under the cabin to foil Cal Jackson's dogs, which people liked to say had the power of augury and could find a missing bone before it was lost.

Ina's shoat had come honestly, with a pretty, soft skin that she rubbed down with salt and pepper. It came up out of the ground that Thursday morning with its flesh crisp brown and barely clinging to the bone and smelling like backwoods Carolina.

Johnnie Mae saved the biggest onion in the pile for last. It was the size of a softball, with a thick, brown-striped skin. Under the shiny skin were two halves joined with a line between the two halves and the hint of another skin. Mama noticed Johnnie Mae's change of rhythm and looked down at the girl's hands to see what she was looking at.

"That onion you're peeling — let me see it," she demanded. Johnnie Mae looked up, puzzled, and held out the onion for her mother to see. Mama's nose turned up into a hard wrinkle. "Put it down. Put it in the garbage. That's no good."

For the life of her, Johnnie Mae couldn't see what was wrong with the thing. She'd been careful to root out any soft-spotted ones. This one was firm and certainly had a sweet pungent sting. "What's the matter, Mama?"

"That's a double-sided onion," Alice continued. "That's bad luck. Throw it out. Don't ever use a double-sided onion,

Johnnie. It's bad luck. Don't even finish peeling it. They say a double-sided onion will divide your house against itself."

Johnnie Mae snickered as she let the onion fall into the pan of garbage scraps. It never ceased to amaze her how many odd things a person had to remember simply to get through the day. Things that had to be remembered because they weren't set down in any book she'd ever seen and certainly weren't taught in school. If you spilled salt you had to quickly throw some over your left shoulder to ward off bad luck. Never sweep dirt in a circle, but out toward the door—and never from the doorstep in. Don't touch the milk pitcher when you've got your monthly, or the milk will curdle.

The list of things not to do when you had your monthly was so long and arcane that Johnnie Mae began to think that most were made up to keep a woman from doing anything at all. And all the grown women—she was one now, though except for this one messy, stinking, achy thing, she didn't feel like it—spent their time figuring if it was coming soon or late or not coming at all. And for all the figuring and wondering, they were all reluctant to speak out plainly about it. When they talked about their monthly, it was in croaking whispers through dissimulating lips.

The annual Mount Zion Church picnic was the largest social gathering of black Georgetowners. All kinds of public and private plans were being made. Some men were running over in their minds which big rock they'd tie a watermelon to so that the cool creek water would bathe it and chill it for after the heavy food was eaten. Ca'line Brown's parlor was busy with folks slipping in for a bottle of home brew.

At sunrise on the morning of the picnic, members of the Elks Club gathered at the P Street beach to stake out the spot where they would set up a huge pot of coffee over an open fire. Members came hauling firewood from all over Georgetown. Mr. Pud Allen even went up Conduit Road to get hickory wood because he so loved the smell of hickory burning under boiling coffee.

By noon most of the family groups had found a good spot to spread out their baskets, and teams had been chosen for baseball and horseshoes. Johnnie Mae's favorite picnic game was the three-legged race, but she'd made herself scarce and hadn't been chosen for a team.

After she helped her mama get settled in a good picnic spot, Pearl left her exchanging pleasantries with Dr. Hiawatha Parmalee and his wife. "Your Pearl is coming up to be a nice-looking young lady, Sister Hattie," Mrs. Parmalee said, once "hello" and "how do" had passed back and forth among the three. "Praise God, she's got all my looks now. And some of her papa's, too," Pearl heard her mother say as she walked off. Hattie Miller had, by dint of conscientious attendance at church services and women's auxiliary meetings, become well thought of at Mount Zion Church.

Pearl wove in and out of clumps of people, looking for Johnnie Mae. She found her finally, off by herself at the edge of the creek, sitting on a boulder. Pearl dropped down beside Johnnie Mae and waited for her to acknowledge her presence. Behind them was the laughing and shouting of the picnickers and in front of them was a merry splashing and sloshing of water over rocks.

The creek was gently conversational—a gaggle of happy voices. The words were indistinct, but the sound was of a group happily talking and enjoying their exchange. The people at the picnic behind them on the grassy knoll of the

P Street beach were also happily enjoying one another's company. Johnnie Mae imagined them talking among themselves and not including her. All were part of a confederacy of adults talking about grown people's things and not including her or any of the babies. And Pearl was now part of them. Pearl, who used to be a scared rabbit who wouldn't make a sound, was now up among them talking about things in a code of womanly dissembling.

That day Pearl's mood had been bright until she came upon Johnnie Mae. She was now more successful socially, having won the friendship of a few more of the girls at school. It was through Johnnie Mae that she'd acquired these friends and Pearl felt she owed her a special loyalty. But today, a day when all of Georgetown was lighthearted and playful, Johnnie Mae was moping and shying away from the activities. Pearl was afraid that sitting on rocks with water all around was having a saddening effect on her. Perhaps that was what was making her sulky.

"What's wrong, Johnnie Mae?" Pearl, tired of the silence on a day when all else and whosoever was laughing and giggling, asked tentatively.

"Nothin'," she said. The kind of "nothing" that begs "Ask me and ask me again till I tell you."

"Somethin' 's the matter. I can tell."

"Nothin'."

"Somethin' 's the matter. What's the matter?"

It took a couple of sputtery tries before Johnnie Mae managed to tell Pearl that she'd finally got her monthly.

"Is that all? Johnnie Mae, you're crazy," she said in the exasperating way she had recently acquired. Pearl was suddenly so womanly that every comment she made sounded like smug pity. She was smug because she'd got her monthly a few months ago and was now quite used to it.

After an hour or so on the boulder in the sun, the two girls succumbed to the lure of fried chicken and potato salad. Like the other young people, they circulated the picnic grounds and took plates of food at every family grouping they passed. At the bake-sale table, each bought a piece of cake for a penny and relished choosing a slice of cake other than her mama's. Pearl's mother's lemon cake was completely gone anyway and Alice Bynum's chocolate layer cake was down to the last crumpling slice. Mabel Dockery's mother was the cake slicer and was installed in a chair at one end of the long table on which the cakes were placed. Her fat arms didn't rise from her sides as she cut the cakes, and between each slice, they came to rest across her wide middle.

Talk around the cake stand was all about whether it was proper for Dr. Tyler to be so openly enamored of Miss Gladys Perryman with his wife dead only three months. Johnnie Mae was surprised at the way Pearl had got all the salient facts of the big scandal and expressed the opinion that Miss Gladys Perryman was the prettiest woman in Georgetown. Gladys Perryman was not the only woman at the picnic with a parasol, but she was the only one whose parasol exactly matched the soft, bright yellow of her dress. The dress hugged her slim figure more closely than some of the talkers thought was proper, but all agreed that she cut a lovely swath while promenading on the arm of Dr. Tyler. Sarey Tyler, wearing a close-cropped head of shiny curls just like Gladys Perryman's, followed behind the couple, absorbing what was left of the admiring glances bestowed on the two. Gladys Perryman had established herself quite firmly in Georgetown. She was a fixture at cultural functions sponsored by the Heliotrope Circle and at the numerous social club functions held at Monticello House. And now there was talk that she would soon open a proper beauty shop in a storefront on P Street.

Pearl Miller, never much for running and jumping, had of late become a real stick-in-the-mud. She shook her head at Johnnie Mae's urgings to cavort. Racing headlong up the hill toward P Street and calling out over her shoulder for Pearl to follow, Johnnie Mae looked back to see an expression of polite indulgence about the girl's eyes. The kind of look any grown-up would turn on a too-playful child. Pearl's steps were measured and suddenly graceful. And she strove mightily to imitate the elegant swoop-and-dip gait that Gladys Perryman accomplished so effortlessly. Johnnie Mae was puzzled at the change and couldn't suppress the feeling that she and Pearl had parted company and were now on different sides of a divide. When Pearl reached the top of the hill breathing hard, Johnnie Mae smiled.

Johnnie Mae got tired of feeling like a baby around Pearl and walked off from her. Pearl had fallen in with a group of girls from their class and was jabbering and trading tales. The conversation got most animated when Charlie Edward Hughes was brought up.

Everybody and his brother was at the picnic and all seemed intimately involved with someone. Johnnie Mae felt excluded. Why, her mother had even said that Johnnie Mae need not bother to look after little Calvin today. And right now her mother was holding court with Calvin on the grass, surrounded by cooing women and a particularly talkative Aunt Ina. They were all acting like they'd never even seen a baby before. Miss Ruby Tilson, amiable but as plain as a muddy-brown wren, was babbling nonsense words to Calvin. For his part, the baby was sitting up on Mama's lap as if he were the king of England. Everybody was having a bright time.

As soon as she let loose in her mind her annoyance at the baby and her mother and all the other cackling women, Johnnie Mae felt ashamed. Maybe it was a good idea for her to stay away from Calvin. Maybe he was safer if she wasn't responsible for him. Over the few months since Calvin had come, she had questioned herself and considered that her parents and Aunt Ina and maybe some of the neighbor folks might think she wasn't responsible enough to look out for a baby. She had been trusted with Clara and Clara had drowned. Was Calvin going to be safe with her? She made up her mind that she was going to look out for Calvin. Be a stalwart guardian, but at a distance. She was going to let her mother have her baby to herself. She loved him—truly did. He was soft and helpless now, and sweet-smelling. He was a happy, gurgling baby. And when all of them were sitting around the stove in the kitchen and wiggling their fingers at him and baby-talking him, Johnnie Mae was happy and comfortable, too. But Calvin was precious to them. He was Papa's precious dream child and Mama's consolation baby. And Aunt Ina shared him. He meant so much to all of them that Johnnie Mae was leery of being too close to him and maybe putting him in jeopardy. It was on account of them. It was because she didn't want them to lose Calvin the way Clara had been lost—lost because of her.

Johnnie Mae meandered back down to a boulder at the edge of Rock Creek. She sat down and pulled at weeds that were holding on like forty, taking pleasure in yanking them up brutally. Her hand closed over the tops of the blossoms and crushed them and tugged them out.

"You thinking about swimming, Johnnie Mae?" The voice was friendly and slightly joking. He was gently pulling her leg, like he always did. Charlie Hughes had the pleasantest manner of any man she'd ever known.

For the children who came to his swimming classes at the Francis pool, Charlie Hughes was the first adult that they didn't have a prescribed code of behavior toward. He wasn't one of them. He was older and more worldly, a student at Howard University. But though he was an adult, there wasn't a stiff distance between him and the children. When he came upon Johnnie Mae, Charlie had been circulating through the picnic crowd. A big picnic like this reminded him of big church picnics they had in his hometown, Valdosta, Georgia. It was a welcome change from his meals at the university. He had eaten, by this time, four heaping plates of food, one piece of cake, and one piece of pie. The muscles in his stomach were worn out from digesting and he simply wanted to sit and give his stomach some rest. He was looking for a quiet sitting place when he came upon Johnnie Mae with her face looking like a mud fence.

"Oh," she said, turning her head with a snap.

He climbed onto the rock she was sitting on and lowered himself down beside her. "You had enough of the picnic? I ate so much my stomach is worn out. Did you have some of the watermelon? They're cutting it up back there."

"No, I'm just sitting here." She disliked the babyish sound of her own voice. But he had surprised her and she hadn't had time to plan out a conversation or pitch her voice to a more mature tone. And looking at Charlie was distracting. All of the girls agreed that he was the best-looking man ever born.

"You look like you've got a lot on your mind, Johnnie Mae," he said. He leaned back on his elbows and stretched out next to her on the boulder like a snake sunning itself after dinner.

"No. I don't know. No." She stumbled over her words. She could have told him volumes because she did have a lot on her mind. But it was impossible to summon up the words. She wanted to say something, though. She would certainly lose his attention if she didn't hold up her end of the conversation. He'd have to be thinking she was a dolt by now.

But she could tell Charlie wasn't thinking she was addled. Maybe he should have been, but he wasn't. He was reclining there, just taking it easy, being companionable. She thought how lucky she was to be sitting next to him. Pearl was going to be jealous. His placid face had no smirks. It was a wide expanse of amiability.

"You know, you're a good swimmer, Johnnie Mae. You've got a lot of native ability. You like swimming?"

Well, he must be asking this just to be polite. Everybody that knew her knew she loved to swim. Her papa said she'd have webbed feet if she kept up swimming every chance she got. And Aunt Ina had said that maybe this wild swimming behavior should stop, now that she was becoming a grown woman. She answered him with a "yes" that was so tentative it made him laugh at her. And she had wanted so much to act mature and hold his interest.

"Oh, I think you like it more than that. I've seen you in the water and I think you like it a lot."

Johnnie Mae and Charlie Hughes sat on their rock for the longest time without talking. The sun, though it was not yet ready to set, had begun creeping its way behind clouds. The sky was light, but the bright yellow had turned pearlescent. The picnickers' voices had begun to soften and lethargy descended on the crowd. Groups of people sat around on the grass, resting themselves and picking food out of their teeth. Johnnie Mae stretched and looked back toward the P Street beach. The bright sun had wearied her eyes and they were now, in the lower light, only hazily focused. Out of this haze, she caught sight of her mother threading through the crowd. Mama walked alone among the people and appeared to be looking for someone. Seen from a distance, woven in among the others, she stood out like a fancy button on a drab coat. Johnnie Mae studied her mother and was fascinated with the knowledge that her mother had not seen her. Who was she looking for? Maybe somebody had walked off with her precious Calvin. The thought struck Johnnie Mae like a hammer. Suppose somebody had walked off with Calvin and her mother was desperately trying to find him? She didn't look frantic, though, only concerned. But Johnnie Mae thought that perhaps at this distance she couldn't see the worry lines in her mother's face. From where she sat, her mother's forehead was like her cheeks and the skin on her arms. It was soft like pudding. But she knew this was just an illusion—a trick of the distance and the waning light and the heat. Her mother's brow was always slightly furrowed. With her there was always a concern. She saw her mother stop and chat amiably with a person here and there. But she soon broke away and strained to see around the milling groups. Though observing her mother unobserved was thrilling, a stinging feeling in her guts spoiled the pleasure. What if something had happened? She sprang up from the rock and said, "'Bye" to Charlie. He chuckled as she leapt onto the bank and ran off toward her mother. A feeling of being small, being nearly helpless and liking it, came over her. On the bank, she lost sight of her mother as she tried to see over the heads of the crowd. The crowd had absorbed her fully and Johnnie Mae's eye followed every yellow dress—there were a great many that day. At last, she saw the nape of her mother's neck above the white collar of her flowered yellow dress. She jostled her way through small clumps of people that stood between them and came up behind her. She tapped her mama's shoulder and said, "Hey!" Mama swirled around and her frown turned to a smile and back to a frown when she saw Johnnie Mae. "Where've you been so long? We've been looking for you." So it wasn't Calvin they were worried about. They'd been wondering where she was. They were looking for her. It had not occurred to her until that moment that her mother might be looking for her.

She had thought that as long as she could see her mother—feel her mother—scent her mother—she was within the sphere of her mother's influence. Her mother would know where she was. And she had not known until now that she could take herself out of this sphere of mother's love and control. She could take herself away from her mother and her mother would be puzzled and would not know where she was. It takes a child who is well loved a long time to figure out that she can leave her mother's house just by walking away.

22

Alice looked at her daughter standing on the diving tower at the Francis pool. The girl looked so teeny up there. This change of thinking was odd. Johnnie Mae had seemed all grown and nearly gone for months. And now, up on the tower, she seemed a tiny little chick. The fear Alice had of water came over her. She had never been tested by river or stream or swimming pool. She had always had a little fear of water, even of her papa's stream back home.

Alice had a dull stomach full of worry all that morning. She'd wanted to change her mind and not come to the swimming meet. But she had said she would. Also, Willie was so determinedly disapproving of Johnnie Mae's swimming that she felt she must go to save face. But she did not want Johnnie Mae to see how disturbed she was at the prospect of watching her in the water.

And yet seeing her daughter from a distance was proving something. Her child was there—there—gone off away from her. Clara had done that and Johnnie Mae was doing it. They had been doing it since the day after they were born. Little Calvin would do it. Little Calvin, whose head was shaped like a perfect honeydew melon, was doing it even now. Johnnie Mae was all of a piece over there. Alice didn't have to worry. A person of so fine a form and grace was her daughter, and she was fine over there. She had moxie and she was smart and there was nothing else to want for her. She'd be taking care of the wants for herself. Her mother would hold on to her still, but she could let her go at any time and the girl would be stalwart.

Ever since the incident at the train station, Willie had been admonishing Alice about her daughter. Saying it that way: "your daughter." "Mind your daughter, woman. See that she does right. It's on you to see that she does right," he'd said over and over. Peace of mind and family peace were at stake since the train station. Willie had made her responsible for keeping Johnnie Mae "in line." She had said that the girl would mind and that it was best for her to stay. She had set herself up to be the one who would be blamed if the girl made a mistake. How dare he box her into a corner like that! There was something between them now that wouldn't be right henceforth. Things were changing, in that deadly quiet way things change between two people. There would be brooding and resentment, and if it never flared up to burn them, it would come close to singeing them surely.

The morning was bright and warm and the crowd of on-lookers was large. The team from Baltimore had brought along lots of supporters, who were thought to be a bit too rowdy by Georgetown standards. Also competing in the swimming meet and the diving competition were boys and girls from Barry's Farm in Anacostia. Plenty of folks had made the long trip across town to see their team compete in Georgetown.

The swimming competition was scheduled to follow the diving exhibition and word got around the milling crowd that Francis Junior High had a powerful swimmer on its team. Press Parker, who'd become Johnnie Mae's most vocal champion, laid down a bet with a man from Anacostia that she would leave the other swimmers in the dust.

All the swimmers were poised at the edge of the pool, ready to launch themselves into the water. Johnnie Mae did as Charlie Edward Hughes had told her: she thought of all the lessons and then she put all the instructions out of her head and simply made up her mind to swim. His voice had been soft and compelling as he'd said it: "Just swim, Johnnie Mae. Forget about the techniques and just swim. Girl, just go with all you've got and it'll be more than enough." Charlie had said that all the coaching she could retain was in her by now and she'd just have to trust herself and swim.

Johnnie Mae dove into the water. Her whole body followed the perfect hole her arms made, slipping effortlessly through the seam. She made no splash. The water in the pool was achingly blue and she swam underwater as straight as a bullet, following the lines on the bottom of the pool.

Opening her eyes underwater, she saw a figure in front of her in her lane. The sight startled her, but did not break the rhythm of her strokes. The figure was like a giant tadpole. Bubbles of water sat on the figure's very large head and reflected sunshine like glass shards. The figure shimmied through the water and began to look like another girl. Johnnie Mae swam toward her, this girl keeping just ahead. Straight onward they swam and Johnnie Mae was puzzled that they hadn't reached the far wall of the pool. The temperature of the water became cooler and its color turned browner. The fragrance changed from the chlorine smell to something nearly putrid.

She became frightened at not having reached the far wall and feared she would lose the race if she brought herself out of the water. But the color of the water and the fragrance and the mysterious girl swimming ahead of her caused alarm. She put her head up and broke the surface of the water. She was no longer in the swimming pool. Somehow she had swum out of the Francis pool. She had swum out of the pool—out of the race—and was following an enigmatic, big-headed tadpole into the middle of Rock Creek. Ahead of her she saw the figure. Its huge head with wriggling green plaits was above the surface of the water too. The big-headed figure laughed and grinned and beckoned her onward. It dove below the surface and she followed. The water closed over her again and she swam in the silent, cool world beneath the surface.

Rock Creek, a snaky waterway through a forest, will take you far out of the district if you follow it. Many a frightened fugitive has waded it and skirted its banks and forded Piney Branch to reach a Quaker in Silver Spring. The water of the pool flowed out into the creek. She swam, following the current, briskly moving past boulders and downed logs and following the big-headed, grinning figure. She swam into the Potomac and knew it as soon as she felt its particular waters against her skin.

She pumped her arms to try to reach the figure swimming in front of her and tag it and say she'd won—she'd beaten it. But the figure stayed ahead of her and kept laughing. The figure continued under the Key Bridge and she followed. Up ahead of them the mossy towers of the Three Sisters' castle appeared. The figure gained the castle ahead of her and took a seat on the rocks. When Johnnie Mae'd got within inches of the rocks, the water turned tide and pushed her away. She plowed the water and struggled to get closer and tag the figure and tag the rocks, but the water would not let her come close. The figure sat on the rocks and laughed.

Her fingers touched the wall perfectly together and her head lifted. A roar went up when she climbed from the pool. A hand reached down to her and she grasped it. It was Charlie's hand and his face was happy. He must have been roaring because his mouth was wide and round. She couldn't hear anything but felt a rumbling, thunderous reverberation. Charlie indicated the crowd of onlookers and she turned to see wide-open faces and clapping hands and some caps flinging in the air. Papa Willie was waving his cap like a flag. Her mama danced up and down and Aunt Ina was jiggling and wiggling and bouncing baby Calvin. Not just the Georgetowners but the whole crowd was cheering. When she turned back to see the other swimmers climbing out of the water, she knew then she'd won it. She'd beaten them all. The other girls ringed her, clapping her on the back.